G000151452

KEEP HER SAFE

JEN FAULKNER

BLOODHOUND
— BOOKS —

www.bloodhoundbooks.com

Print ISBN 978-1-5040-7270-0

For Molly x

1

DAPHNE

I fell asleep, and now she'll die.

Her chest rises and falls beneath the sky-blue blanket, but her hand is cold to touch.

The energy beneath her pale skin is missing, as though her soul has flown away and her body hasn't caught up. The opposite of earlier today, when life radiated from her smiling face and the freckles on her cheeks darkened in the dappled sunlight. When her curly hair bounced as she weaved through the woodland trees ahead of me, pushing the overgrowth out of her way and shouting, 'Hurry up, Mum.' The smell of wild garlic propelled her forward. The chirps of the birds cheered her on. But my heavy legs could go no faster.

'Slow down,' I'd called. 'You're too quick.'

Too full of life, I'd thought. I regret that now.

Branches on the tree outside the window brush against the glass as if trying to caress me and take away my pain.

But they can't.

Because I fell asleep, and now she'll die.

2

CATHERINE

TUESDAY 4TH JUNE 2019

The shadows of the trees shake on the ceiling. My pillow is wet. The duvet sticks to my legs. After visiting one of my more-challenging clients earlier, I suspected I might struggle with sleep, and I was right.

The clock by my bed reads 3am. Sweat drips down the base of my spine, my heart races. But no loud noise has woken me, nor is anyone snoring – there is no dip in the other half of the bed beside me, there hasn't been for years. Fear has jolted me awake. Fear that for some unknown reason, Anya isn't breathing.

My eyes blink and strange shadows at the edges of the room evaporate. Inhaling deeply, I grasp at the nightmare that forced me awake. Fragments ebb and flow in my mind, then vanish. Then a smell I can't place tickles my nose, before a heavy sensation settles on my chest. Pulling the duvet up to my chin I sit huddled in the middle of the bed.

She's breathing, I tell myself, *she's okay.* Words that should soothe me back to sleep don't work. This random new fear is intense.

'She's breathing,' I say to my reflection in the mirror

opposite my bed. My hollow eyes from lack of sleep stare back at me. My heart misses a beat. A lump forms in my throat when I swallow. I reach for the glass of water beside my bed and gulp it down in one.

The meeting earlier has unsettled me more than I thought. I'd come home, showered, cooked a nutritious meal and watched trashy TV. When I'd gone to bed I'd felt cleansed of the whole thing. But now, the feeling of Anya being in immediate danger is very real. As is the belief that, *I mustn't fall asleep.*

Huffing, I throw off the duvet and sit on the edge of the bed, my head in my hands. I'd checked Anya's breathing often when she was a newborn eighteen years ago, but every new mum does the same, don't they? We all sleep with one ear cocked like a guard dog, alert for danger. Our fear unites us, this visceral need to keep our vulnerable new people alive.

'Why on earth do you need a breathing alarm?' my mother had asked when she'd reluctantly come to babysit a three-month-old Anya. 'There was nothing like that when you were a baby, we simply hoped for the best every time we put you to bed and were glad of the peace and quiet.'

'It's a precaution. A lot of the mums I know have one. Better to have it and not need it and all that.'

'You can't stop fate,' she'd said, switching off the breathing alarm after placing Anya in her cot.

Ignoring the echo of my mother's words I tiptoe across my bedroom, the soft carpet cushioning the soles of my feet. The door handle squeaks and the sound is as loud as if Big Ben had chimed in the hallway.

Anya's door is opposite mine. I press my ear against the cold wood, but only the thud of my heart fills my ears.

She's breathing. Go back to bed.

My chest is tight, as though her life hangs in the balance, and I lean against the wall to stop myself from falling to the floor. Grief squeezes my sternum and I put my hand there, my skin clammy and cold, angry at myself for not being able to control this.

Pressing my ear harder against the wood of the door I listen again. Silence. There is no other option. Like a compulsion to check I've locked the back door, I can't fight this urge to go into her room. Act now. Worry about what is causing me to be this insane later.

Unlike mine, Anya's door handle makes no sound. Fairy lights flicker around her wooden headboard. I've nagged her over and over again to switch them off; the fear of their heat making the entire house catch fire is genuine. But tonight, I am grateful they are on because they light up her face, her chest. Her breathing.

Curled up she faces the window and I sneak around the base of her bed, dodging the dirty clothes and empty glasses stuffed with crisp packets on the floor, a reversal of the days when I used to sneak out and pray she'd stay asleep.

Kneeling down beside her I want to reach out and stroke her face. Her lips are pursed and pink under wafts of her dyed brown, wavy fringe. Tiny freckles are splattered across her nose and cheeks. If I couldn't see the bulges of her long limbs hidden under the duvet I could almost pretend her face belonged to toddler Anya.

Her inhaler rests on the nightstand and my stomach twists, fearful that she's had to take her medication in the night. The heat of the summer always a trigger for the illness the doctors told me she'd grow out of.

Her eyelids flutter. I can't hear her breath entering and leaving her body, but the duvet rises and falls. My shoulders loosen. Of course she's breathing. Of course she is okay.

The tightness in my chest lifts. My heart rate slows.

She's alive.

I *can* sleep.

I smile and exhale a deep sigh.

And then Anya opens her eyes, stares at me, and screams.

'Shit, Mum.' She sits up in bed and I jump to my feet.

'Sorry, I–' I need to think of a reason for being in here again, and quick. 'I heard you cry out in your sleep. I wanted to check you're okay.'

Wiping a strand of her matted bed hair from her face Anya stares at me, deciding whether to believe me or not. Her chest rises and falls at a rate matching my own breathing, as if we've run a marathon.

She covers her face with her hands, groans and collapses back onto the bed.

'Whatever. But get out of my room. You know I've got an exam tomorrow.' She rubs her eyes and picks up her phone. The harsh light from the screen making her frown.

'Okay, sorry, sweetheart.'

'And do me a favour.' She looks at me as I reach her door, her expression mimicking the one I used to give her when she'd been naughty. 'Don't fucking come into my room in the middle of the night ever again, whatever noise you hear, right?'

'I won't,' I lie. 'I'm sorry.'

'Seriously. I mean it. You scared the shit out of me.' She checks her phone again. 'Oh.' She yawns and then mumbles, lying back on her bed, her eyes closed.

'Of course. Night, sweetheart,' I say, hoping she doesn't hear the tremor in my voice or see the tremble in my hand.

A faint scent of her coconut body spray sneaks out through the gap in the door as I close it. I want to cry. Maybe I'm not ready to lose her after all, even though she's more than ready to go. My behaviour tonight only pushing her away quicker.

Again anger makes me clench my fists. I'm furious with myself. The thought of her not breathing is a thought. A nasty, hideous, intrusive thought. Deep down I don't really believe she'd have died tonight if I hadn't checked on her, but a knowing inside me won't let the intrusive thought go.

Then a fresh fear grips me. Soon she won't be in the room across the hallway from mine. Soon she'll be in a house with eleven other people at university, two hours away from here.

Two hours away from me.

The branches on the ceiling above my bed shake as though berating me for going in to Anya's room. Maybe she should go to her dad's for a while, she deserves some peace.

But I'm worried I won't get any.

And I don't understand why.

3

CATHERINE

WEDNESDAY 5TH JUNE

'Hey, love. How was your day?'

The harsh light of the hallway emphasises the dark circles under her eyes. Her skin is pale; reminding me of the time she bought a foundation five shades too light. With the end of her A levels in sight, her intense studying is catching up with her.

'Fine.' Anya kicks off her shoes and dumps her rucksack at the base of the stairs. 'Just going to have a shower.'

Sighing, I slump at the kitchen table and wrap my hands around my iced tea, using the chill from the glass to cool my warm skin. Her hatred of water means she'll be in the shower briefly, music on, singing loudly. Maybe then we can go out and enjoy one of our remaining mother/daughter evenings; the countdown to her leaving for university looming on the horizon like a storm, one where you're excited to watch the lightning brighten up the dark sky, while petrified it will strike too close to home.

The shower stops and a few minutes later she is with me in the kitchen, her hair wet but brushed, her cheeks pink from the heat of the water she always has too hot, even in summer.

'What's for dinner?' she asks, opening the fridge. We still haven't discussed last night.

'I thought we could go out? Pizza? Or Wagamama? You can choose.'

She bites her lip, distracted by her phone and I close my eyes and take a deep breath. She tilts her head and snaps a quick pout to someone before replying to me. 'Sure. Wagas would be good.' Then she frowns. 'And we don't need to talk about last night, right? I want to forget about it. The exam was fine.'

'Okay.'

She heads to her room; presumably to put on some make-up and dry her hair. I'd stopped wearing make-up after some old mascara gave me an eye infection and my eyes watered non-stop for days. The habit of making myself look presentable was pointless with no man to impress and my line of work not being one where I have to go into an office and look the part. Dragging myself upstairs I sit at my dressing table.

A pot of blusher hidden in the drawer has a smidge left and I use my fingers to rub the powder along my cheekbones. Then I dab my lips with some clear gloss and brush my hair. That'll do.

'Anya, are you ready?' I call out and then count to ten in my head, clenching my teeth together. As I reach nine her bedroom door opens.

'Yup.'

'You look nice,' I say, knowing she'll be cross with me if I don't.

'Thanks.'

No 'you too', I notice.

The car journey passes quickly. Anya angles her phone every two seconds and pouts or grins. The early evening summer sunlight shines on her face through the window, giving her a warm glow. She hums along and taps her fingers as we listen to her music, and I remind myself that soon I'll be able to play nineties boyband hits in the car whenever I want.

We find a space to park and walk to the restaurant. The unique smell of exotic spices and fresh cooking greet us as we walk in. My empty stomach rumbles and the world around me blurs for a second. My lunch had been two boiled eggs and a handful of cashews in between meetings.

We don't take long to be seated, coming early always wise as the queue will be out the door within half an hour.

'Might have a different dish today.' I look at the menu and Anya laughs.

'Please don't, Mum. You always regret it.'

'Fine.' We giggle. 'But I'm definitely having all the side dishes.'

'Oh hell yeah.' Her voice goes high-pitched with a touch of sass. She's far more confident than I was at her age.

But Anya's cheeks blush pink when the waiter flirts with her while taking our order. I'm a crap flirt, but now I'm older I miss the attempts. The short intense bursts of acknowledgement. Although at Anya's age I'd have probably thought the waiter was angling for a large tip.

'Shall we have some Prosecco?' I suggest, eyebrows raised.

'Celebrating?' the waiter asks, a look of intrigue on his face, desperate for information so he can work it to his advantage.

'End of A levels soon,' Anya answers, the pink of her cheeks mutating into a fiery red.

'Ah I see. And then off to uni?'

'Yes, hopefully.'

'And is that why you're celebrating?' He faces me. 'My mum was the same when I left home. She couldn't wait to have the house to herself. But then, I wasn't the easiest kid.'

'Something like that,' I say. He's partly right. A little spark inside me ignites at the thought of being alone again. My heart races and I bite down a smile.

'So.' Anya rests her chin on her hands as the waiter walks off. 'I've been thinking.' Her thick, dark-brown eyebrows rise, her bright blue eyes wide.

Not sure where this is going I stay silent. Plates and pans clatter together as someone stacks them in the kitchen area. Each clash jolts through my body.

'I think you should start dating again, you know, after I go to university.'

'I am not going on Tinder.' I look her in the eye and shake my head.

'But.'

'No buts, Anya. It's hideous. I don't want to be sent dick pics.'

'It's not that bad,' she says with a grimace, but slumps back to her side of the table and I know then, with a sick feeling, she's been sent them. 'There are other apps you could try, Mum. Or maybe, I dunno, go to a pub or join a yoga class.'

'I don't want to date,' I say. I'd tried the marriage thing with her father. And we were doing okay until the day he told me he was leaving. Plenty of gadgets exist these days for me to be able to please myself in more ways than one.

I sit up tall and take a deep breath in. 'So, tell me, how many exams have you got left?'

'Can we just not, Mum.'

Before we descend into bickering one of our side dishes, the ebi katsu, arrives. Anya counts the breaded prawns even though we know there are always five and can't be shared equally.

'You have the extra prawn today,' I say. She doesn't argue and bites one whole leaving the tail in her hand, the fiery bright red sauce drips down her chin like blood. I wonder if she's washed her hands, but know she'll snap at me if I ask.

'Are we going to clear out Gran's house tomorrow?' She catches the sauce with her napkin.

'I was thinking Friday? Then it doesn't matter how late we stay as you won't have any revision to do.'

She shrugs.

'Okay?'

'Yep. I think I'm seeing Holly on Saturday so Friday's good.'

'Thanks for saying you'll come with me.'

'S'okay. I know it's hard, but it's not like there's anyone else to help.'

She's right. I have no siblings. My father is in a home. It's only me. It's always been me.

Anya's pad thai is placed in front of her. The meal contains peanuts and even though she isn't allergic, I'm on alert for any wheeze, swelling, or need for her inhaler. The lingering trauma from watching her foaming at the mouth and struggling for breath during an asthma attack when she was nine is never far away, even though she hasn't had another attack since.

'What's the betting Mrs Smith spies on us from next door like she usually does?' I say.

'Oh shit, of course she will. Maybe we should give her something to talk about, roll up a rug as though it's got a dead body inside.'

'Yes.' I laugh and spit a bit of food out, wiping it from the table before anyone notices. 'I could carry a spade and dig a hole in the garden, then you could help me bury the rug. Can you imagine what she'd do?'

'Call the police, probably. Be worth it though. Nosy old bag.'

'I won't turn into Mrs Smith when you're at uni, don't worry.' Long gone are the days where I'd sit at my bedroom window and make up imaginary lives for the people who walked below.

'Thank fuck for that.'

'Anya!'

'Sorry.'

There's a moment of silence from us where the sounds of the restaurant heighten. Deep laughter from a broad-shouldered man a few tables down. Sizzling from the woks as the chefs toss their stir fries. The buzz of a till receipt being printed. Crying from a baby in distress around the corner. We pick at our food with chopsticks, not knowing what to say.

We're like this a lot at the moment. Anya is excited about leaving for university, but is afraid to tell me in case she upsets me. I think forward a few weeks to when she's gone – to not being disappointed when I open the fridge and discover she's eaten the food I was saving for dinner. Or not shrieking when the shower suddenly turns cold as she's used the last of the hot water.

'I'll be fine, love.'

'I know you will.'

'Really, Anya. I want you to have an amazing time. I wish I'd gone to university. Now I can live vicariously through you.'

'Like I'm going to tell you everything I get up to.'

'You'd better, or you'll find me sat outside your house watching you.'

'Jeez, Mum. That's creepy.'

'I'm only joking.'

'You'd better be. I love you, Mum, but I can't wait to leave home.'

I'm surprised when that stings.

'Oh don't look so offended.' She rolls her eyes.

'I'm not looking like anything, Anya.'

'You're not going to make me feel guilty about being excited to go to uni, cos it ain't gonna happen.'

'I wasn't, and you know it.'

'Seriously, Mum, it's fucking hard work being your daughter sometimes.'

'What's that supposed to mean?'

'You're so intense. You've got nothing interesting in your life apart from me.'

'That's not true.'

'Is so. I bet if you had friends all you'd do is talk about me.' She leans forward and picks up another prawn. 'You do know you're the only person who finds stories about me interesting, right?' She bites the prawn in half.

Wanting to escape I look around, blinking at the bright lights and expecting the entire restaurant to be staring at us, but thankfully everyone is too engrossed in their own conversations, apart from a teenage boy on the table behind us staring at Anya. I glare at him and he looks down at the table in horror.

'Yes. I know,' I say, wanting to dilute the tension. 'I really am only joking.' Of course I am. There's no way I would spy on her at university. 'Don't worry. I've asked for more hours at work and will have plenty to occupy myself with.'

'Still think you should try dating.' She raises her eyebrows. In the time taken to snap a selfie she's switched back to normal.

Forcing a smile, I swallow the food stuck in my throat. 'We'll see.'

4

CATHERINE

Dust from the brown sofa clogs my nose. The blankets Mum had crocheted, thrown over the back, had gathered dirt too. Their bright colours faded beneath the grey mass of the dead skin she'd shed leaning against them, before passing away a few months ago. Her presence fills every inch, tainting the air with filth. Each breath fills my lungs with more pollution than any cigarette.

'Bloody hell,' says Anya, tying up her long hair. 'Did Gran ever clean?' Anya wipes a thick layer of dust off the top of the television – the screen so small teenagers these days would be horrified – with her sleeve. 'This place is gross.' She coughs into her elbow.

'Have you got your inhaler?'

'Yep.' She taps her rucksack on the sofa to imply it's in there. I'm not going to check.

My mother's lounge is full of crap. Three different rugs, all mismatched with clashing patterns and colours, overlap each other on top of the thick beige carpet. Books she'd probably never read cover the sideboard and empty teacups litter the coffee table. Mould spots the bottom of the empty cups, apart from one, which looks as though she's taken a sip before nipping out to the toilet and will be back at any moment to finish the last mouthful. The remaining contents are a mass of lumpy curdled milk.

'What the fuck is this?'

'Anya.' I wince. Then remind myself I'm not going to be sent to my room for swearing.

She holds a china dog, blows dust off its nose, and flaps her hand in front of her face to move the specks away. Her blue eyes squint as the dust dances before her in the sunlight.

'I thought Gran hated dogs after one bit her in the woods by the stream. She'd tell the story enough times, remember? It's why she'd never go walking in there with us. Oh shit, look, there's loads of them.'

On the top of the wooden cabinet seven china bulldogs sit side by side, all different sizes, all covered in dust. I have no idea why my mother would've had these. They certainly weren't here the last time I'd visited. Although I can't remember when that was.

Guilt pinches at me and I rub the base of my neck. Childhood homes are alive with happy memories, a colleague had once told me. With ornaments you can't bear to throw away. The dusty dogs will not be coming home with us.

Anya wheezes. I watch her chest swell as though fighting for clean air.

'Shall we begin in the kitchen and worry about this room later?' I ask. Why didn't I bring gloves? Or a mask? This dust will set off an asthma attack.

As if on cue, Anya coughs again and pulls her inhaler out of her bag. She takes a couple of puffs.

I push her towards the lounge door, closing it behind us to seal the filth in.

But the kitchen is no better.

'Jeez, Mum. What the–' Anya retches and pulls her top over her nose.

Rotting food ferments in dishes by the sink. Glasses with mould decorating the inside of them rest on the drainer. There's a sour taste on my tongue. I should've insisted my mother came to live with me after her stroke, even though neither of us would've been happy. The truth is I should've visited more. But this house, the memories, I'd wanted to leave them all behind.

'I'll be fine,' she'd said. 'A nurse will come in twice a day. I will not be a burden.'

'You wouldn't be a burden,' I'd repeated, but she must've heard the doubt in my voice because she'd waved her hand at me dismissing the very idea of living anywhere else.

'Shit.' Anya scrambles onto a chair and bursts out laughing. 'Mum. A rat.' She points to the floor by the sink.

'Oh my God, it's huge.' Without hesitating I join her on a chair. How can she laugh? The rat is gigantic. Thankfully it's too distracted by a half-empty can of beans to notice us. I pant as though in labour. I want a shower. Rats carry all sorts of germs and bacteria. A rustle from a cereal box on the table makes me jump.

'Let's go,' I say. 'Get the professionals in instead of cleaning everything up ourselves.'

'Look at its tail.' Anya peers closer to the rat. 'Finn at school had a pet rat. His was cute.'

'Anya, rats are not cute. Come on let's go. Please.'

I think about my bedroom upstairs, emptied when I'd escaped all those years ago and moved into my own beloved bedsit. A clearance company can take what's left.

'All right.' She jumps off the chair, knocking a stale loaf onto the floor. 'Come on, Mum.'

Holding each other's hands and screaming like school children being chased in the playground, we run through the hallway. Anya carries on as I bash into one of the cardboard boxes my mother had placed at the bottom of the stairs after an attempt to de-clutter with Mrs Smith from next door. The pink hand of a toy doll sticks out of the top. Pulling the doll out I grimace when I see one ghostly eye, winking at me, and a hole where the other should be. The white dress the doll wears is torn on the shoulder and lace frills surround the neck. This can't be one of mine from when I was younger because I never had any. Nor did my mother. Looking deeper into the box, photos cover the bottom. I reach in to pull them out when Anya reappears at the front door.

'Holly wants to catch up today, not tomorrow, so I'm going out with her before I go to Dad's, okay?'

Sensing her impatience I stuff the creepy doll back into the box and go outside.

Anya coughs. Her chest rises and falls too fast.

'You okay?' I ask, but she groans and walks off.

A midwife once told me, when Anya was hours old and curled up like she was still inside my stomach, how parents must nurture their children like birds, so when the time comes for them to leave the nest they can fly.

Every instinct in me wants to clip Anya's wings. But the feeling dissipates as quickly as it was formed.

For a second, I face the house. A two-up two-down end-of-terrace plot with a yellow exterior, like a sandcastle. The windows are double glazed now. Water no longer drips down the glass panes onto towels at the bottom. But I can still see black smudges on the lounge windowsill behind the grey net curtain hanging above it.

A movement catches my eye from a window of the house next door. A tiny nick in the curtain where two fingers pinch it, and the hint of a shadow. The hairs on the back of my neck prickle. Mrs Smith is watching. I blink and the curtain hangs freely again, the shadow vanished, as if she's clicked her fingers and teleported elsewhere in the house.

'Come on, Mum,' Anya shouts out of the car window, her oversized sunglasses hiding her freckles. 'I'm going out, remember?'

With a defeated sigh I tear myself away and get in the car beside her. She rolls her eyes. 'Finally.'

The sooner my mother's house is cleaned, gutted and sold, the better.

5

ANYA

SUNDAY 9TH JUNE

You heard me come home earlier this morning, Mum. I know you did because I made sure I said goodbye to Holly after she'd dropped me off using my loudest voice. You never sleep until I'm back and I hate not being able to have any fucking freedom and stay out all night like Holly. But then it sucks that her mum doesn't give a shit so maybe you checking I'm home safely isn't such a bad thing.

You did well not to come and interrogate me on where I'd been, although maybe you tracked me, and didn't need to ask.

Your bedroom curtains are open, as always, and I know you'll be lying on your bed, staring up at the ceiling. You won't have heard me creep downstairs and out of the back door into the garden for a cigarette.

You won't have realised what made the third stair down creak. You'll think it was the cat. And the security light switching on won't have alarmed you because the local fox always sets off the bright orange glow and so you wouldn't suspect that I'd triggered the sensor this time.

Do you feel like me? Like two hands are gripped tightly

around your neck? There's a permanent sensation of food stuck in my throat and no matter how many times I swallow or eat or drink the stubborn lump won't budge. I don't want to talk to you about my anxiety, but I'm afraid of failing my exams and not getting into uni and I can't breathe, as though I'm drowning even though I'm stood on dry land.

But the truth is, I haven't told you because I'm scared you'll use my anxiety to make me stay, not that you've ever actually said out loud you want me to, but either way I can't live here anymore because you're doing my fucking head in. You're always asking me where I'm going, who I'm going to be with and I know you say all mums are the same, but they're not. I reckon maybe you're actually looking forward to me going to uni so it's not your problem or responsibility anymore. Then if I get sick or run over or die you can't blame yourself. You can go back to being alone.

You've turned the main light in your bedroom on and I freeze by the fence, my cigarette sucked dry.

Stubbing out the last embers, I go into the kitchen. Shout to you that I woke up thirsty and needed a drink.

'Sorry, Mum,' I call to you, imagining your hand hovering over your bedroom door handle. 'Should've taken a glass up with me earlier.'

'Okay, love,' you shout down, a faint tremor in your voice. 'See you in the morning.'

'Night night,' I reply, hiding the frustration I feel even though I don't know if it's you making me frustrated or if it's me.

You've shut your bedroom door, but I know you'll be hiding behind the white painted wood, listening for me to come back to bed. I'll make sure my footsteps are heavy on the stairs, and then I'll yawn with meaning outside my room before closing the door with a firm hand.

A few weeks, that's how long until I leave for uni. A few weeks until I can escape this house, this garden, this street.

And you.

6

CATHERINE

MONDAY 10TH JUNE

No answer. Hours of my life have been spent standing on doorsteps waiting for doors to open. Sometimes the doorstep will offer information about the owner of the house. Dirty nappies and cigarettes butts might carpet the front lawn alongside cut off bits of wood and debris. Or there may be perfectly potted flowers full of colour and hope. Here there's nothing but a blank canvas in need of some love.

Turning to go I look up at a window and think someone is peeking from behind the net curtain before the light material falls again. They won't answer the door. After several years in this job as a peer support worker, supporting families who are affected by mental illness during and after pregnancy, I know I can't help someone who isn't ready.

There's an hour until my next appointment. Not enough time to go home, but too long to sit in my car in this heat. My T-shirt clings to my back. Maybe Anya is on her lunch break. The nursery she's doing work experience at is five minutes down the road.

Pulling my phone out of my bag I text my boss to say my

appointment had been a no-show, and then open up the Find Friends app.

My phone takes a while to locate Anya. I tense, but soon the blue dot and round photo of her face is on the map, a little off the main road in the local nursery. Then I wonder if she will want to have lunch with me. Maybe I'll wait in the car instead.

There's a park to my right. A young mum rocks to and fro on a swing doing the same as me, looking at her phone. Her child, a small boy of about two or three, tries to get her attention, and pulls at her skirt. A rush of empathy makes me smile; she's only grabbing a minute to herself while her child plays. Then the little boy's face lights up as his mum puts her phone in her pocket and follows him over to the slide.

Anya had always been happy to walk up to any child and play with them, while I'd sit on the grass at the edge of the play area and relax. Once, when she was about six, I'd lain down in the sunshine and fallen asleep.

Another mum had woken me up to tell me that Anya was stuck at the top of the climbing frame. I was mortified. Anything could've happened to her while I'd dozed, unaware. From then on, every time we went out, I was armed with coffee.

Screw it, I think. Anya might want lunch with me after all; at least I could give her the option. I switch the engine on and drive down the road to the nursery.

After a few rings of the buzzer and a couple of minutes' wait the main door opens.

'Hello. What do you want?' The woman who answers squints to block out the sunlight and I'm startled by her abruptness.

'Hi, I'm Anya's mum.'

She looks puzzled.

'Anya Williams? She's working here, getting experience before she goes to university to study teaching.' The woman's glare is making me feel uncomfortable and I hope she is nicer to the children she works with.

She doesn't say anything for a long time and I wonder if she is having some sort of seizure.

'Anya Williams?' I say again.

'I don't think we have any work experience people here with us at the moment.'

'But, I...' I am about to tell this woman I've checked Anya's phone and that I know she *is* here, but then realise I'd look crazy. 'Are you sure? She told me she's here all week.'

'I'm pretty sure, but I might be mistaken, not been here long. Either way I'm sorry, but I have to get back to the children.'

She shuts the door and for a second my hand hovers over the buzzer. Instead, I pull my phone out of my bag and open up the Find Friends app again. In an attempt to slow my heart rate I inhale deeply into my stomach like I would advise the anxious mums I support to do. I tell them to imagine placing their fears on a leaf and watch them being carried away on a stream. But all the leaves in my mind are brown and trodden upon.

Anya's photo shows she's here, or near here. The blue circle around her face has widened meaning the location is less precise.

Am I missing something? A shifting. I've not worried about her like this before. Yes, I like to know where she is, who she's with, but that's all. Usual mum of teenager stuff. Nothing more.

Shuffling from one foot to the other I dial Anya's number.

No answer.

A moped races by, the fumes from the exhaust blow up my nose and I cough as I dial her number again.

'Hello,' a voice I don't recognise answers, female, with a faint hint of a Scottish accent.

'Anya?'

'Hi, sorry, I found this phone, in the woods off Victoria Park, is it yours?'

'No, my daughter's. Are you still there?' Across the road, trees overflowing with green leaves line the outskirts of the park. The children from the nursery are often taken there to play, Anya has told me before. Maybe she was there with them today.

'Yes.'

'Okay, great. Can you meet me by the swings in five?'

Hanging up, I take a deep breath. My strange fears are unfounded. She's simply misplaced her phone while at work and will be grateful to me for getting it back.

Crossing the road to walk towards the woodland part of the park, a familiar wave of unease washes over me. My mother had hated the woods behind our house.

Every night, after putting me to bed, she'd open the curtains so the shadows of the branches would reach into my bedroom like fingers coming to snatch me away. Then she'd sit on my bed and tell stories of the witches and outcasts who dwelled beneath the dark canopy before shutting the curtains and keeping the witches out.

I can remember fragments, snippets of fairy tales where children got lost in the undergrowth never to come back. Then when she'd finished she would close the curtains and make me promise to never go into the woods.

Ahead of me a woman holds a young boy's hand, a phone in the other, standing by the swings. She looks from left to right as though searching for someone far more important than me.

'Hi,' I say. 'We spoke on the phone. That's my daughter's mobile.' I point to her hand.

'Yes, hi. Here.' She hands me the phone. 'I'm so glad I picked it up. Losing your phone is horrible.'

'She'll be so grateful you did. Where exactly did you find it?'

The small boy tugs at her arm and she leans sideways giving into the pull.

'Over there, towards the clearing. We were on a bear hunt weren't we, Leo?' The boy buries his face in her leg. 'I'm sorry, he's not good with strangers.'

'It's okay,' I say, thinking I should let her go instead of quizzing her like a detective searching for a missing person. 'Thank you.'

'No problem.' She smiles and walks into the woods.

My mouth is dry and I search for a bottle of water in my bag. The pathway into the woodland splits into two and winds through tall trees with ivy curling around their trunks. A mass of twigs and leaves carpet the floor, a fallen branch on the left with nettles at the base. For a second the world fades out behind me and all I can hear are the chirps of birds hiding in the hedgerow.

'Mum?'

A hand touches my shoulder and I turn, holding my bag in front of me like a shield.

'Oh my God, Anya.'

'Yay, my phone.' She snatches the mobile from my hand. 'I can't believe you have my phone. How the hell did that happen?'

'You tell me.' I look her squarely in the eye. 'Why was your phone here, in the park, without you?'

'We were here earlier with the children from the nursery. Must've fallen out of my pocket.'

Simple enough explanation. And I've never known her to lie before. My cheeks flush red.

'Sorry, Mum, but I need to get back to work. They only let me out to look for my phone.' She kisses me on the cheek, shouting over her shoulder as she goes. 'I'll be back around five.'

The leaves on the trees rustle as if they're trying to

communicate with me. A sudden gust of wind makes them call even louder.

But I don't listen to their warning that this had all been resolved a little too easily.

All I see is my daughter running away from me.

7

CATHERINE

TUESDAY 11TH JUNE

L ast night Anya had arrived home around five. During the afternoon, in between my appointments, I'd checked the app every few minutes, not being able to stop myself. In the past I'd only ever glanced at it if she was late home from a night out, or to check she was at her exam on time, but yesterday I'd been compelled to check more often.

Her photo had hovered above the nursery as though taunting me, making me wonder if the exchange with the cranky woman at the nursery door had even happened. I'd intended to discuss it with Anya at dinner, but chose not to as she'd suggested we play Monopoly, which we used to do on holiday together, and I hadn't wanted to spoil the mood.

Then this morning she'd left for work before I'd even got up.

Sipping my second coffee of the morning I check Google Maps then, realising I have to leave if I'm going to be on time for my first appointment, pour my coffee into the bamboo reusable mug Anya had given me for my birthday, pick up my bag and rush out the door.

Bang on time I pull up in to the driveway. The house reminds me of my mother's. The bay windows bulge, but there are no net curtains. And the front garden is tidy, unlike the mess that lines my mother's drive.

My thoughts turn to whoever might buy her house when I put it up for sale. They'd need to completely gut the place, stripping out every stale and painful whisper of past events with each speck of dirt.

After I text my boss I ring the doorbell. A baby cries inside. I imagine the mum shushing them and remember those days from when Anya was a baby. Pacing the floor. Rocking the pram to and fro in the hallway. Ignoring the cries at the end of the garden.

The door opens and I set my face into a warm smile.

'Hi,' I say. 'Leanne?'

She doesn't return my smile. 'Yes, hi.'

'I'm Catherine,' I hold up my lanyard with a jerk and the clasp snaps open behind my neck.

Taking a step back she ushers me inside. The air smells of fresh coffee.

'Excuse the mess.' Her hair is tied in a lump on top of her head, like Anya does when she can't be bothered to shower. There's no sign of the baby I heard.

'Oh goodness, that's okay. You should see my house.'

'Would you like a drink?' She rubs the black circles beneath her bloodshot eyes.

'No, thank you. I've just had one.'

We move into the lounge and I wonder where to sit. I opt for the sofa with her, then when she moves away from me I wish I'd chosen the chair.

'Are you okay if I take notes?'

She nods without blinking.

'Where would you like to start?'

This question often makes the mums go straight to what they believe their main problem is. A traumatic birth. A difficult pregnancy. A disordered relationship.

Leanne looks at the floor, her neck bent, and shrugs.

'It's all right,' I say. 'Take your time.'

Without being obvious I glance around the room. Photos hang on the wall behind the sofa. Smiling faces grin back at me from the beach, the moors and on a wedding day. That's odd. There is a photo of an older child, but her referral form said she only had one baby, four months old.

'That's Emily,' Leanne says, having caught me looking.

'She's gorgeous. Is she at nursery or school today?' I make a note that there's an older child in the house. Sometimes the referrer doesn't get all of the information initially.

Leanne puts her face in her hands. She shrinks in front of me.

A knot forms in my stomach and I lean back.

'Sorry,' she repeats and I hand her a tissue from my bag.

'Don't worry. Tell me when you feel ready.'

She takes some deep breaths, her eyes closed. Her nails are bitten down to the ends and flecks of dark red scabs surround them.

'Emily passed away. A few years ago.' She doesn't wipe away the tears now. She knows they are not going to stop.

Goosebumps pop up along my forearms. My mouth is dry and yet I keep needing to swallow.

'On holiday.'

'I'm so sorry.' Something weird is happening to me. My hands shake and I feel numb inside, as though I know how losing a child feels.

'And,' she points at a photo of a newborn and I refocus, 'now I'm terrified I'll lose Billy too.'

'That's understandable.' Tears pool in my eyes. I didn't even know her daughter. I'm here to support Leanne, so why do I feel like I'm the vulnerable one? I stare down at the packet of tissues in my hands and blink away the tears.

'I'm a horrible mother.' She tenses her jaw. 'Instead of wanting to keep him safe, I can't bear to be around him.' She scrunches up the tissue I gave her and then rips sections off and places them on the arm of the sofa.

'Where's Billy now?' I ask, my palms sweaty.

'In his cot. It's nap time.' There's no monitor near her like with the other mums I support. Leanne's eyes are wide, pleading, and I know she wants me to reassure her that Billy won't be harmed by her indifference. But I can't.

'Have you seen a bereavement counsellor?' My voice is flat. I feel heavy.

'Yes, but she told me to write it all down, in a journal. I couldn't do it.' She scrunches up her face. 'I turned my back for a fraction. I closed my eyes and she was gone.'

For the second time this visit I'm speechless, like these words have been taken right from my mouth and I have none left to use. My boundaries are normally spot on. I am able to separate their anxieties from any I may have. But with Leanne I'm already too close and out of my depth. Grief has sucked me in like a whirlpool and is dragging me down with her.

The rest of the session passes in a blur, time slowing and speeding with no rhythm. Leanne cries and says she is sorry over and over. I reassure her she has nothing to apologise for and suggest some therapy and a visit to the GP. And all the time a thick dark cloud hovers over me threatening to burst and drown me in grief that isn't mine.

On the way home I have to stop and pull over into a layby. My hands shake and I weep into them, tears landing on my skirt, the material absorbing them like ink blots. With the numbness gone, the pain in my stomach is raw, fresh. I pick at my lips until they bleed a little. My chest heaves and my head thumps.

We are taught that some visits might be triggering, but I have never experienced this before. My reaction must be to do with Anya leaving for university. I've read somewhere that a child moving out of home is a form of grief for the parents. But I thought I was okay about her going, a little nervous yes, but nothing out of the ordinary. Maybe I need to check in with my supervisor. I can't carry on working with vulnerable women if I am going to become an emotional wreck every time.

I reach into my bag and pull out a packet of tissues. Thankfully, I have no other appointments today.

But the grief isn't gone.

The pain nestles in my chest and rests there, heavy like a rock, weighing me down.

'Pull yourself together,' my mother would've said. 'Crying fixes nothing.'

But sucking your emotions up only makes them explode later.

And right now, I am a ticking time bomb.

When I was Anya's age the fuse inside me had been a slow burner. First lit when the realisation hit that my mother wasn't the same as the other mothers. Sighing as I lean forward and rest my head on the steering wheel, I remember my mother closing my bedroom door the day I'd got my mock A-level results.

They weren't bad, but lower than predicted. In truth, on the morning of the mock exam, I'd got my period. Not my first, but they were still unpredictable. There were no sanitary towels in the bathroom and I was too afraid to ask as last time the request had been met with an eye roll and a mutter of, 'you're seventeen now, surely you can buy these things yourself.'

That morning I'd stuffed my knickers with toilet paper and spent the entire exam convinced blood was dripping off the chair and onto the floor beneath me.

The clock on my bedroom wall had stopped ticking that evening. A branch outside had knocked against the window as a storm whipped the air. There would be no supper. Later, I'd have to sneak down to butter some bread and cut some chunks of cheese before sneaking back upstairs to eat.

How strange, I think now, that I'd chosen not to question my mother's behaviour. There were other girls in my class whose mothers got angry when their grades dipped. Or who cried alongside their daughters feeling the failure as though it were their own.

Whereas my mother showed little emotion. Instead there was a quiet sense of disappointment that hung around her like fog.

I'd leant out the window that evening and let my long hair dangle down pretending I were Rapunzel in a castle turret. But unlike the fairy tale, I hadn't wanted a prince to rescue me. No, it was my mother who I'd longed to climb up my braids, holding me as she reached the open window and admitting that when I'd come into this world I'd brought too much love with me and she hadn't known how to accept it.

———

Later that evening there was a knock at my door.

'Come in,' I'd called and she had. Her eyes red rimmed and puffy.

'Supper's ready,' she whispered.

A warm glow had spread across my chest.

That time the door remained open. A hint that she did care about me, if only I looked hard enough to find the clues she had left.

8

DAPHNE

'A stream, Mummy. Look.'

Quicker than I could keep up, she'd run along a pathway through the trees on the far side of the clearing. Tiny droplets of dew clung on to the blades of grass the sun hadn't yet reached. Beside the path, woven between tree trunks of different shapes and colours, were flowers and plants. Pinks and purples mixed with yellows and whites. I marvelled at life finding a way to survive even in the darkest of places.

At the end of the path I found her knee-deep in the stream. The bank provided a mossy seat and I sat down and caught my breath. A butterfly flew in front of us, its bright white wings standing out against the deep blue-grey of the water, which flowed over the rocks that lay beneath it.

'Are there fishes?' she asked. 'Can I catch them?'

'There might be. Here, why don't you sit next to me and we can look for them.'

My eyelids were heavy. They betrayed me and shut out the world.

A few minutes wouldn't hurt.

I wound my fingers around the hem of her skirt and held on tight.

Then I gave in to the exhaustion.

9

CATHERINE

FRIDAY 14TH JUNE

'See you tomorrow, Mum,' Anya calls up the stairs.

'Wait,' I shout back. 'Remind me where you're going.'

'My exams are done. I'm eighteen. An adult now. You don't need to know where I am going anymore. See you tomorrow.'

'Yes. I do. You know I do.'

Her body spray wafts towards me, musky and pungent.

She stands at the bottom of the stairs, one hand on the bannister, with a small rucksack on her back and a denim shoulder bag across her front. She wears too much dark smoky eye shadow and giant false lashes that make her eyes look as though spiders are crawling out of them. Her face is set in a grimace. I feel sick.

'Fine. What time will you be back?'

'Tomorrow sometime. I'm staying at Ruby's, remember? We're going to watch a couple of films and get a Domino's.'

Ruby is her closest friend from school. They turned eighteen in the same week and had a joint party. Her parents would text and let me know Anya had arrived safely, but the communication had petered out the older the girls had become.

'Okay.' I know there is nothing I can do to keep her here. A silent scream sticks in my throat. 'Have fun then.'

'I will,' she calls back, slamming the door behind her.

The heat has spent the day working its way outside in, the thick walls of our small home holding the stifling warmth inside no matter how many windows I open. Men with their tops off had sauntered down the road towards the river having parked across Mrs Taylor's drive. She'd leave them a note asking them to be more considerate in future. They'd urinate in her front garden before throwing the Post-it note off the windscreen without even looking at it when they'd returned.

Frozen, I stand at the top of the stairs unsure of what to do. Yesterday, I would've trusted Anya. Yesterday, I would've only checked her location once or twice. Yesterday I was calm. The night would still have been long and I would still have struggled to sleep, but Anya's blue dot above Ruby's house would've reassured me.

But not today. Before she left I'd tried to see if I could spot a tell on her face, either a curling of her upper lip, or an excessive blinking of her eyes. Those expressions had given the lie away every time when she was younger. But these days I have no idea what her *tell* is.

In the fridge there is a half-full bottle of dry white wine and I grab myself a large glass and pour all of the sharp alcohol in before taking a gulp. The shelves are empty apart from some eggs and a packet of wilting salad leaves. Shopping is always the last thing on my to-do list. Supermarkets are the work of the devil; aisle after aisle of too many decisions to be made.

Pasta and pesto for the fifth time this week will have to do.

My hands itch to pick up my phone and find out where Anya is, but her words from earlier ring in my ears.

An adult now.

An adult in age, yes. A person who knows about all the dangers the world has to offer, no.

Without wanting to, I think back to when I was eighteen. My mother had filled my head full of lies about the world. Paedophiles lived next door. Poisonous jellyfish swam in every wave. Toxins filled each plant I touched. Dogs would rip open my jugular with their teeth. The woods would swallow me whole.

Leaving the saucepan of water to boil I sink into the sofa and switch on the television. Underneath the screen is a thin layer of dust blanketing the DVD player. Dusting is Anya's job, but nagging her doesn't work. Grabbing the duster I wipe the flecks away myself.

My phone beeps with a text from a colleague wanting to know if I'm free for a chat tomorrow. But I ignore it. But while my phone is unlocked I'm compelled to tap on the Find Friends app.

Ruby lives about a mile away, in the next village. But the blue dot isn't there. In fact, the blue dot isn't anywhere.

No location found.

My breathing is shallow and fast. I refresh the screen, but get the same response.

Unable to sit still I pace. In the time it takes for my heart to skip a beat I am in fight or flight mode.

You aren't behaving normally, I tell myself, frustrated that I'm unable to let Anya go and make her own mistakes, safe in the knowledge that I've done my best to ensure she makes good choices in life. I was looking forward to the release of anxiety after she left, I don't understand why it's ramping up.

I refresh the screen again.

No location found.

Her phone will have run out of battery, that's what's happened. She's always forgetting to charge it. The blue circle will be back soon. She'll borrow a charger from Ruby. I gulp another large mouthful of wine, close my eyes, breathe.

She's not safe.

Working for a mental health charity I know about intrusive thoughts and how to deal with them. But right now, my thoughts are facts. Every bone in my body vibrates with the certainty that Anya is in danger. Fact. And I have to keep her safe. Fact.

Refreshing the phone for a third time is pointless. I already know what I'm going to do. It's what any mother would do.

The glass of wine is just under half full. I'm safe to drive.

Doubt creeps in. Maybe I am insane. Maybe no other mother would do this. If I do go and look for Anya I am unlikely to find her. Bristol is full of pubs and clubs. At times like this I wish I had more friends. More specifically, I wish I had friends with teenage daughters about to leave for university.

Even though my car keys are in my hand I hesitate and check one more time. *No location found* screams at me like an omen.

You need to find her location, my thoughts tell me, because technology has failed you. Go and do what your phone and GPS can't.

Save her.

Without a second thought I head out to the car.

The radio blares out at full volume and I jump and press the switch off. Then I take a second to compose myself. For some reason I feel as though *I* am sneaking out of the house. My heartbeat races and my eyesight is blurred, but I blink and pull away from the kerb.

The light from the sun tinges the sky with muted pinks and oranges. Wisps of cloud swim high up and I remember when Anya and I would lie in the garden, pointing at the white balls of fluff above us, finding elephants and bears. My hands grip the steering wheel. I miss the days when we were lost in our own bubble. When we hadn't needed anyone else. Well, I hadn't. The thought never occurred to me that Anya might've.

The roads into Bristol are empty, most people at home or settled in a pub garden enjoying the sunshine and weekend ahead.

Gloucester Road is busy. Everyone is dressed for summer in shorts and vests, or in some cases only shorts. Men not caring if their hairy chests and beer bellies hang over the waistlines of their low-slung jeans. T-shirts tucked in the back like a group of children playing a game of tag rugby at school. A sea of red washes over their shoulders and faces, too long spent in the sun without a care in the world.

With one eye on the road I scan the faces for Anya's. A girl ahead of me, facing away, has dark wavy hair like Anya, but when she turns I see brown eyes and no freckles. I release my breath before sucking air in again.

A car horn beeps and I jolt forward as I break, not having seen the car pull out in front of me. I throw my hands up into the air showing a bravado I don't feel as my eyes water.

And that's when I see her, Anya, looking at me, her mouth wide open, from the other side of the road. A cigarette dangles from her right hand, before she drops it, the tip burning her fingers. I pull over on to double yellow lines and switch off the engine.

Anya looks left and right before crossing over the road towards me, her face scrunched in confusion. I wind down the window, but she walks around the back of the car and gets into the passenger seat.

'What the fuck are you doing here?' she spits.

My mind is furry. Why *am* I here? A faint smell of cigarette smoke comes from her clothes, a hint of musk and vanilla diluting the stench. A realisation washes over me – she's used body spray to cover up the stale smell of cigarettes before.

'I thought you were going to Ruby's?'

Anya's expression reminds me of the character in *Inside Out*, whose head explodes in flames whenever he is angry.

'I was. And then we decided to come into Bristol. A load of mates from school were meeting up. So, like I said, what the fuck are you doing here?'

Don't say it, my brain urges me. Don't let her know you were tracking her. I can't believe I gave into my intrusive thoughts. A parasite has wormed into my mind and taken over all rational thinking.

'*Why* are you here, Mum?' she shouts. Her eyes don't twinkle with pleasure at seeing me like they used to when I picked her up from nursery. They burn with rage and confusion.

'It doesn't matter.'

'Yes it does.' Her chest rises and falls in short spurts and I can't stop myself from worrying if she has her inhaler.

My gaze drops down to my lap and my shoulders slump in defeat.

'So you *have* been tracking me.' Her tone is measured. 'I fucking knew it. You're stalking your own daughter. Your eighteen-year-old daughter. What the fuck is wrong with you?'

'Only since the park thing really. Before that I didn't track you all the time, I promise, only when you were due home, or were meant to be in an exam. Anyway, don't all mums use the app now?' I can't be the only one, surely.

'No. They. Do. Not.'

'How did you know I was?'

'I wasn't sure, so I gave my phone to that woman in the park the other day, the one with her shy little boy. I told her you'd probably call me in about five minutes and to tell you she'd found it by the swings. Don't know why she agreed, but she did. Didn't ask me any questions either. And I told the women at the nursery to say I wasn't working there once I saw you were at the door. Seriously, Mum. What's wrong with you? You're messed up.'

Who *is* this person in front of me? She isn't the loving girl I'd raised. The girl who used to say she loved me more than anything, even chocolate. The one who would make me cups of tea and bake a lemon drizzle cake to fix my PMT. Or snuggle with her head on my lap when watching a film. Or play with my hair and paint my nails. Where has that Anya gone?

'What's wrong with *me*?' I snap, my voice high-pitched. 'Who tricks their mum like that, Anya? Why would you pretend to lose your phone? Why would you make me think you were in danger? Why mess with my head like that?'

'I wouldn't have had to if you were normal.' Her voice is raised.

'I *am* normal.'

'Um no, basically, you're a psycho.'

I say nothing. My mind blank. My body numb.

'All my mates are over there.' She points across the road where her friends are trying not to stare at us. 'You've totally embarrassed me.'

'But Anya, I wouldn't even be here if you'd told me the truth about where you were going tonight. Or hadn't been so devious yesterday. I honestly thought you were in danger.'

'None of this is my fault. You've got problems and you need to sort yourself out. Sneaking into my bedroom at night is not normal. I couldn't get back to sleep after that and I'm pretty sure I've failed my exam because of it. You're suffocating me.' She opens the car door and as she shifts out of the seat a packet of cigarettes falls beside her.

'Go home, Mum.' She picks them up, shoving them back into her bag. 'And don't wait up.' Then she slams the car door and marches over the road to her friends.

Tears swim in my eyes, but I can't cry here.

Indicating, I pull out into the road, the sensation of a rock in my stomach weighing me down. And as I drive I wonder if my daughter is right.

Maybe I do need help.

10

CATHERINE

SATURDAY 15TH JUNE

Anya didn't come home last night, or this morning, and her blue dot is still absent from the Find Friends app. Location not found. Sleep had been fitful, but I remember hints of a dream, a small child running through the trees, out of reach.

Losing myself in paperwork offers no respite. I pack my bags and head into Bristol early for a meeting with my supervisor.

The traffic ahead of me stretches far into the distance and I sigh, glad that I'd left early and have time to waste. A gnawing in my stomach reminds me I haven't eaten this morning, too unsettled by last night. Anya must hate me. But I am angry at her too. If she is capable of deceiving me, what else is she capable of?

'Stop it!' I mutter, despising the way I'm behaving. I'd always encouraged Anya's independence and I don't understand why that's changed. But it can't continue. If it does, I'll lose her forever.

'Catherine, hi, come in.' Fiona opens the door to her private clinic with a grin that could put the Cheshire Cat out of business.

'Sorry I'm late, the traffic was awful again.'

'Don't worry. Tea?'

'Coffee, black, one sugar. Thanks.' My stomach rumbles and I rub the noise away hoping Fiona hasn't heard. Hearing someone's stomach gurgle is intimate, as though you are invited to listen to the inner workings of their digestive system when you didn't ask to be.

'How's Anya?' Fiona asks and I tense. I'm not ready to talk about Anya. This is supervision and I am here to discuss work and any cases I'm finding challenging.

Her counselling room smells damp. The clinic is in the basement of a large Victorian house; she lives in one of the flats above. Lights are placed around the room to detract from the fact that the only window is smaller than an envelope and high above normal eyeline.

There are other rooms here, but I understand why Fiona prefers to use the one out the back with a proper window as an office instead of this one. The soft lighting in here offers comfort and the feel of a place so safe that even your words can't float out of an open window and drift into the ears of people walking on the pavement above.

'So how is Anya?' Fiona repeats, looking at me with a frown nestled between her manicured eyebrows.

'Sorry.' I wave my hand and her concern away. 'I didn't get much sleep last night. Anya is fine. Excited about going to university.'

Fiona smiles and leans back in her chair. She sips her tea. I know what she's doing. Pausing. Inviting me to fill the awkward silence. Allowing me to say more.

'And how are *you*?'

'Tired, work has been a bit full on lately.'

Fiona sips her tea again. She must have a mouth made of asbestos; my mug is painful to touch.

'I meant about Anya going to university. It's a big change for you.'

'I'm fine.' I ignore my heart fluttering. 'Trying not to think about it.'

'Understandable. I was the same when Sam left, but in hindsight I wish I had taken the time to think about it before he moved out.'

My mind races. Fiona has been through this; she would be the perfect person to ask advice from. Be reassured that what I am experiencing is normal and all parents feel like this before their child leaves home. Empty nest syndrome. That's it. Maybe that's what this is.

'How did you feel?' I ask. 'When he went, before he went?'

Fiona narrows her eyes at me, unsure of what I am asking and always one step ahead, analysing my words and my body language.

'Grief,' she answers simply. 'I felt overwhelming grief.'

'Yes, that's it.' I lean forward. 'Me too. But ... did you feel an overriding sense of doom? Were you worried he was in danger at all?' There, I've told her how I feel. This can go one of two ways. Fiona will either think I am insane and I'll lose my job, or she'll validate my fears. I stare at my steaming cup of coffee, not wanting to meet her eyes.

'It's a while ago now, but I do remember worrying he wouldn't eat properly. Or sleep enough. Or that he would catch Fresher's Flu. Which he did. Is that what you mean?'

No. That isn't what I mean, but I can't explain how I feel because I don't understand it.

'I guess.' I pick up the coffee. 'Ever since Anya was born there has only ever been the two of us. I know her dad is around and she stays with him every other weekend, but, I don't know, maybe I'm frightened that *I* won't be okay on my own. She's like my security blanket, you know? She's why I do everything I do.'

We're silent while we unpick my words.

'What is it you're most concerned about?' Fiona asks. 'Because the grief you're feeling at the thought of Anya leaving can easily get muddled with apprehension about being alone once she has gone. And many parents worry about their children being in some kind of danger. We're programmed to protect our offspring from the minute they are born, but then, you know that working with the women you do.'

Many of the mums I support are overprotective of their babies. Then I think of Leanne and my visit with her.

'On that subject,' I say. 'Can we talk about a mum I saw recently?'

Fiona raises her eyebrows at the sudden change in topic, but doesn't stop me.

'She's got a young baby, a boy, but she lost a daughter not long ago. She was five and died while they were on holiday.' I blink to make the tears in my eyes go away.

'Take your time.' Fiona hands me a tissue, as I had done with Leanne.

'I don't know why, but it makes me so emotional.' The tears fall freely. I hate crying in front of people. I feel weak.

'You were triggered. It happens in your job. Hearing about a child who has died is incredibly hard.'

'Yes, listening to her tell me was horrible. It was like I was grieving for the little girl too.'

'In a way you are, you're grieving for five-year-old Anya now she's grown up.'

Of course. Of course that was why I felt her loss so acutely.

Fiona's so clever. My whole body tingles as if the tension is leaving it through my skin.

'But,' I continue, a lightness washing across my chest as Fiona draws the darkness out of me, 'I'm still not sure how to support Leanne. She said she doesn't want anything to do with her new baby and I'd expect her to be the opposite, more overprotective.'

Fiona leans forward in her chair. 'Grief doesn't always work like that. Sometimes the pain of the loss is so fierce the parent is terrified it'll happen again, and so pushes the new baby away so as not to form a close bond. They're trying to protect themselves.'

'That makes sense.'

'Has she seen a grief counsellor?'

'After it happened, yes. But not for long.'

'Okay. And she's with the specialist team?'

'The health visitor has done a referral, I think. I'll check.'

'I'm not surprised you're upset by this, Catherine. Especially at such a key moment in your life.'

Fiona has a way of validating my emotions, not only through her words, but also with her facial expressions. Her eye contact is intense, but not probing, as though she can read my mind and let me know she understands where I'm coming from simply through her stare.

'Do you know what's really good for you and can help you when you have difficult things to process?' she asks.

'I read, or take a bath. I also try not to drink all the wine in the house.' I laugh, but it comes out as more of a strangled sound.

'Why don't you take a walk in the woods? There's some near you, right?'

My chest tightens at the mention of woodland.

'Yes, the local woods are lovely at this time of year.' I hope she hasn't noticed my body stiffen. 'So cool under the trees and away from this heat.'

'Then stop and go for a walk in them on the way home. There is evidence that bathing in woodland is very healing. They have a wonderful energy. Might help you get some perspective.'

Like a puppet with no control over my body I nod.

'That's an order.' Fiona points her finger at me.

I hold my hands up in mock surrender. 'Okay, okay. I will, promise.'

The rest of the meeting is taken up with talk of new structures in place locally to support mums with psychosis, and then excitement, mostly from Fiona, over the charity's end-of-summer social event. I leave feeling lighter, and not simply because I still haven't eaten, refusing the biscuits Fiona offered alongside the coffee.

The journey back takes half the time that the journey in had taken and I hesitate as I reach the junction where I'll need to turn off to go to the woodland.

That's an order.

Fiona's words sound in my ears and I sigh. I'm uncomfortable with letting people down when I've made a promise, and so I put the indicator on and head towards the woods. My phone burns a hole in my pocket, but I refuse to look and see if Anya's blue circle has reappeared.

There are no cars parked at the entrance to the woodland. The midday sun blazes through the car windscreen and I scrabble about in the glove compartment for some sunglasses, grateful that my car isn't a complete tip and I usually find what I'm looking for. A cereal bar falls out into the footwell and I smile. That's lunch sorted. Then I grab onto the arm of a pair of old sunglasses with scratched lenses and pull them out.

The world looks broken and damaged with them on.

Hopefully bathing in the shadows and walking in the undergrowth will wash away the sense of unease settled around me like a bad smell. Anya, Leanne, all of them can soak into the soil beneath my feet and be absorbed and diluted by the roots of the trees.

The pathway leading in from the wooden gate is dry and dusty from a lack of rain and the welcome shade of the canopy washes over me. I look up at the abundance of green leaves. They dance and sway, the bright sun hidden behind them. I close my eyes and breathe deeply. The fear diminishes.

Birds chirp and a gust of wind whooshes through the trees. My nightmares of late featured branches like twisted, gnarled fingers that pulled and grabbed me and dragged me down. But here, in the heat of the midday sun, I know those nightmares are harmless.

'Mum, come on, catch up!'

I flinch at the sudden noise.

'Slow down,' someone calls. A little boy runs past and into the clearing ahead.

Behind me is a woman in a long floaty dress jogging down the wide path. She stops beside me, panting.

'He's too fast.' She laughs and rolls her eyes. 'And I'm so unfit.'

'They have boundless energy at that age, but be careful, there's a small stream up ahead if I remember rightly.'

'Oh is there? Thank you. I'd better catch him then.'

Her dress swishes and the colours blend with our surroundings and she disappears into the distance.

Standing still I exhale a long breath. A gust of wind forces a twig to fall to the ground. A rustle in the bushes to my right startles me and for a second I think I see a hint of blond curls, but I blink and they are gone.

This isn't working. I'm not calm. And I can't continue to

ignore the fact that I haven't seen or heard from Anya since last night.

Then, as I turn to leave, my phone beeps with a text.

Four short, direct words from Anya.

We need to talk.

11

ANYA

If you'd seen me in the nightclub last night you'd have dragged me home. Which is why I went.

For most of the evening I managed to eject you from my thoughts and danced and laughed and drank and smoked and was alive and free and excited. But, then, there was a second, a fucking fleeting moment, where you forced your way back in and flooded me with doubt.

Pulling apart from my friends, I'd stood in the corner of the dance floor, in a section where the disco lights didn't reach, and I watched. I watched one girl collapse onto a sofa to my right, her eyes closed, her head hanging forwards, her brain messed up with either booze or drugs, I didn't know which. Her cut-off top revealed a hint of her braless chest, a moon like curve where her right boob met her stomach.

I watched as other girls walked past and didn't even glance at her and I watched boys saunter after the girls and nudge each other and snigger when they saw her lying there. There was no one looking out for her and I wondered then if she had a mother like you who she wanted to escape from, or a mother who she was trying to prove that she could handle the adult world to.

Except a nightclub full of teenagers isn't the adult world, is it? It's the liminal space between childhood and responsibility and it is messy and out of control. We're playing at being grown-ups, us teenagers, drinking alcohol our bodies can't tolerate while convincing ourselves that we are nailing this new life, when it's terrifying us.

You never went clubbing, did you? Was that because you didn't want to, or because you weren't allowed? Not that I can imagine Gran giving two shits about what you did. Not that I know this for real because you never talk about her.

When I'd tried to find my friends, after seeing the unconscious girl's mates haul her to her feet, they'd gone and the only thing I could hear was your voice in my head, blaming me for having left them first.

I'd walked around and around the club, through the uncoordinated bodies on the dance floor, pushing sweat-drenched backs away from my face, looking for a top I recognised, or a shoe, or a bag. But they'd disappeared. I checked my phone but there was no signal and I knew I would have to leave the club to make the 4G bars reappear on the screen. The thump of the bass in the music pounded through me, boom, boom, boom and I couldn't hear myself think.

But even after wandering around in circles for ages, alone and scared, I didn't want you to save me. Satisfaction that I needed you after all was not a gift I was prepared to give you. I searched my wallet but found nothing, my money spent on cheap beer in plastic pint glasses and a packet of fags and the entrance fee to this shithole.

Did you sense I needed rescuing then? You were probably awake refreshing the fucking tracking app on your stupid phone and waiting for the front door to close behind me as always even though I told you I wasn't coming home.

You were the last person I wanted to call as I stood outside the club where, thank God, there was some signal and instead I rang all my friends to find out where the fuck they were while chain-smoking my cigarettes. They'd looked for me, they said, and then I remembered I'd been hiding in the shadows, watching the girl with no mates, not realising I was looking in a mirror.

My finger hovered above your number as some pissed bloke took a slash in the shop doorway next to me, but I knew if I called you I'd be enabling you further. You needed to think I was strong and capable, not stupid and weak or in danger.

So instead, and I knew you'd hate that I did, which is a little bit why I did it, but instead of calling you, I called Dad.

12

CATHERINE
SATURDAY 15TH JUNE

Opening the front door I hear two voices in the kitchen. One belongs to Anya and the other to a male.

The man laughs and like a punch to the stomach I realise she's with her dad. I can smell him too. He always did wear too much aftershave.

'Hi,' I call out and check my appearance in the hallway mirror. My roots are showing and my eyes are bloodshot. There isn't any time to pat on some powder so I pinch my cheeks to encourage the blood to flow and make them pink.

'Hey, you.' Sean kisses me on both cheeks. The familiar woody scent of the aftershave he's worn since we met twenty years ago wafts up my nose. If I close my eyes I'd be back there, falling for him when I didn't want to. 'You look well.'

'Thanks.' He's being polite.

I pull away. 'You too.'

Anya stands on the other side of the kitchen island and refuses to make eye contact with me. Smudges of mascara darken under her eyes and her hair looks like she's been caught in a hurricane without a brush.

'I didn't see your car outside,' I say to Sean.

'There was nowhere to park, it's round the corner.' He looks at Anya. Clearly I'm the only one who's missed the elephant in the room.

'So why are you here? And Anya why aren't you at school?'

'Exams finished, Mum.' She still doesn't look at me.

'I know that, but I thought you had some last lessons or tutor time that's all. Don't they do fun things at the end of term?' The summer term after my A levels was a challenging one as an outsider who had never penetrated any of the friendship groups. I remember a school trip to an amusement park, the seat next to me on the rollercoaster empty, no one there to hold my hand as I screamed. Maybe schools and parents don't have the funds to do that anymore. Or maybe teenagers aren't interested. Going by last night Anya would rather be out drinking and smoking with her friends.

'Sean?'

He looks at Anya again and then stares right into my eyes.

'Anya asked me to come so we could talk to you together.' He sighs. 'She's worried about you.'

'Look, if this is about last night, I made a mistake.' Best to be honest, this was already very awkward. Sean and I never discussed Anya. I made the decisions and he had no choice but to go along with them. That's what happens when you dump your pregnant partner.

'I shouldn't have followed her into Bristol,' I say. 'I don't really understand why I did. Bad instincts.'

I flinch as I speak. My instincts hadn't failed me before. When Anya fell off the corner of a sofa I knew her wrist was broken, even though she could use her arm as normal, and even though the nurse had at first diagnosed a sprain.

'Mum, this isn't about last night.' She throws her head back and rolls her eyes like a drama queen in full flow. 'You've snuck into my room at night too.'

'Anya,' Sean says with a stern look.

'Sorry, but I can't take it anymore, Dad. She's like a crazy woman. She's suffocating and it's weird. I'm eighteen for fuck's sake.'

My daughter's right. Sneaking into her bedroom is wrong, but if I explain that I have to know she is breathing, then they'd definitely question my sanity.

'Look.' I lean on the counter between us. 'I saw someone this morning. At work.' I'm bending the truth, but they need to hear this. 'She thinks I'm having an extreme reaction to Anya leaving for university. She mentioned something along the lines of pre-empting empty nest syndrome and being fearful of what life will be like when I'm here on my own.'

Placing a hand on my chest I try to catch my breath. I feel as though someone has me trapped in a huge bear hug. 'I'm going to miss you so much.' As the bear hug lifts the sob is forced out and my hand moves to my mouth to hold the emotion in. I hate this happening in front of Sean.

Anya's expression softens like a marshmallow being roasted over an open fire. The anger has gone, her freckles spreading out over her cheeks like pepper. Her eyes are sympathetic.

Then Anya and Sean stare at each other with a look I can't interpret.

'What?' My head swings between them. 'What's that look for?'

Sean's shoulders sag and Anya bites her lip. This reminds me of when the doctor came to find me to tell me my mother had passed away. Pity reeks from them like the smell of rotten eggs.

'Anya's going to come and stay with me for a while, only a few days, until things settle down with you.'

'Settle down? What's that meant to mean?' A dull ache

spreads across my chest. Why should *he* get to spend precious time with Anya before she leaves?

'Mum, you're too intense. We need a break from each other. Then we can spend some time together before I go to uni and things won't be so messed up.'

'Right, I see. And when was this arranged?'

'I stayed at Dad's last night.'

The rooms spins while I process this. Then, with as steady a voice as I can muster, I speak again. 'How did you get there?'

They look at the floor.

'You hitch-hiked, didn't you? For crying out loud, Anya.'

'I'm not listening to you anymore!' She storms out of the room.

'We've already spoken about it.' Sean's voice is a whisper. 'She knows it was wrong, but you'd pushed her so far.'

I walk around the other side of the island, grabbing a tea towel on my way. I wring it between my hands imagining it's his neck. They've convinced each other that I'm unhinged and need to sort myself out. Did they not hear what I said about my empty nest?

'Sean, you can't come in here after eighteen years and criticise my parenting.'

'Anya's got me involved now, Catherine. I have a say in this.'

'You know she smokes, right?'

'And?'

'And she's asthmatic.'

'I'm sure it's only social smoking, but okay, I'll talk to her about it.'

'And are you sure you can handle a teen and a newborn?'

As I say this I can hear laughter in my head. Of course he isn't looking after the baby. That will be Naomi's job.

'Look...' He holds out a hand and places it on top of mine and the gesture makes me cry again. I snatch my hand away.

'No, Sean. Don't do that. Anya will be getting impatient in the car. You'd better go. Can you check she's packed her inhalers? She needs to take the brown one twice a day. That's the preventative one, it's important.'

'Okay.' He goes to leave. I am empty, as though my heart has given up and stopped beating.

Then he reaches the kitchen door and turns to me. 'Maybe go and have a chat to your doctor. Might be a good idea to see someone.'

Shame washes over me like a tsunami and takes every emotion with it. Numbness settles in for the ride.

Sean sighs and walks away leaving me alone as he has done before. I notice with a wry smile that I hurt a little less each time he does.

On autopilot I go to the fridge and pull out a fresh bottle of rosé, unscrewing the cap and pouring most of the bright pink liquid into my largest wine glass, hearing Sean close the front door.

Maybe seeing a doctor is a good idea. My whole body aches with exhaustion. There has to be a tablet she can give me to help me sleep. I'm sure after a full night's slumber everything will be better. I'll feel more normal. Less out of control.

Then Anya will come home.

13

CATHERINE

WEDNESDAY 26TH JUNE

'So what brings you here today?'

The doctor doesn't look interested. She looks tired. Maybe she needs to see a doctor. The room smells strange, musty.

'I'm not sleeping well.'

She's young, in her late twenties maybe. Three piercings in each ear, one in her nose. I can't be sure, did she roll her eyes?

'Do you think I'm peri-menopausal?'

'Do you?'

Her computer screen takes her attention. I can't decide if I'm angry or want to cry. A gnawing feeling in my stomach spreads to my back.

'My periods are still regular, but everything aches. And I'm permanently anxious. I wake in the middle of the night and I can't drop off again.'

She scrolls through the notes on her computer. 'I see you've been on antidepressants before, would you like to have them again?'

'What? No. I'm not depressed. This is hormonal.'

Depression isn't causing my sleepless nights, I'm sure. After having Anya all I did was sleep.

'You're a little young to be peri-menopausal, and as you said yourself, your periods are still regular.'

Taking her fingers away from her keyboard she turns to me, a puzzled look on her face. 'Has anything happened recently? A big change?'

I bite the inside of my cheeks. I won't cry. My mother always said I was no good at being vulnerable.

'You suck everything up,' she'd say, 'right here.' Her fingers would dig deep into my diaphragm.

She'd laugh, but I'd always suspected I got my fear of being vulnerable from her. My mother was the master at sucking things up.

'You're an old soul,' she'd said. 'All deep-rooted knots, woven into you from the minute you took your first breath and inhaled your soul.'

The doctor coughs. I refocus.

'My daughter's moving to university soon. But she's more than ready.'

'And you?'

'I'll adjust.' I swallow hard.

'When did your symptoms start? Was it as her departure came closer?'

The doctor looks sympathetic, pleased with herself for diagnosing my problem within the allocated ten-minute slot no doubt.

'Maybe.'

Is that what this is? A strong reaction to Anya leaving? I feel stupid.

'Look,' the doctor leans forward. 'A child leaving home is a big change for anyone and can take a toll. We hold anxiety in our body without realising we're doing so. Have you tried mindfulness to help you sleep? Magnesium is also good.'

We sit in silence as she quickly writes down the websites I advise my clients to use down on a piece of paper.

'And if, in the meantime, your periods become erratic or you get any symptoms like hot flushes or headaches, then come back and see me, okay?'

'Right. Thank you.' I go to leave.

The doctor smiles, then turns to type up her notes.

One overprotective mother with no life of her own can't cope with her only child leaving home. I imagine her writing. *Refused antidepressants.*

Walking through the waiting area I feel everyone staring at me, even though when I look around they are engrossed in their phones. One mum has a sleeping toddler on her lap, dummy in mouth, flushed red cheeks. I smile at her, trying to convey that I've been there and know how she feels.

She doesn't smile back, probably too worried. And sleep deprived. I don't miss those days, but I do miss little Anya. The toddler who would suck her thumb and twiddle her hair. Gorgeous curls that would ping back up into corkscrews as soon as she let go.

'What you staring at?'

I jump.

'Oh nothing,' I mumble. 'My daughter, she's off to uni soon, but I remember when she was the same age as your little one.'

'Stop staring at me and go and bloody reminisce somewhere else.'

'Sorry. Hope she gets better soon.'

Pushing through the door to the surgery I rush out into the street.

Rain pelts down and I put my umbrella up and march to my

car. After I get in and shut the door I let the tears fall. Is this what every mother does when their child leaves home? Put on a fake smile and carry on when they're breaking bit by bit from the inside out. Or am I the only one who can't cope with the loss?

'She's not dead!' I shout. Anger taking over. 'She'll be a short way up the M5. For goodness' sake, Catherine. Get. A. Grip.'

I bang the steering wheel with my fists, before closing my eyes and groaning. My shoulders ache. I force them down, lengthening the distance between my back and my head, and rub the base of my neck.

Anya will be at university for the next three years. I have to find a way to deal with this.

The drive home passes in a blur.

Without thinking I call out, 'Hi, I'm home,' as I step inside the front door before a stab of grief hits me when there's no reply. The house smells different too as though preparing me for what's to come. Scentless.

In the kitchen I open a bottle of wine before firing up my laptop. Anya's Facebook page fills the screen. Her profile picture is one from a couple of summers ago when we went to Cornwall. She'd put her hair over her face and her sunglasses on top so she looked like a distorted Chewbacca. Happy times before freedom had beckoned and she'd started to lie to me in order to get some.

Where did I go wrong?

My phone beeps with a text from one of the removal men sorting out my mother's house. I'd not heard from them for a few days and assumed everything was going smoothly.

Some boxes in the hallway you might want to look at. Not sure what to do with them. Stuff looks sentimental. Photos, etc.

Frustrated as I'd told him I wanted nothing to be kept, a tingle of intrigue gnaws at me.

The doll.

That's the box he's talking about. That vile doll.

But he'd mentioned photos. I remember there being a few I'd wanted to look at. My mother had rarely used her camera. There were no photos in frames dotted around our house. Or in albums tucked away beside the drinks cabinet. I'd often thought she merely wanted to live her life and not reminisce over it. Each experience too painful for her to relive in photographic form.

On my way, I text and put my shoes back on, leaving my fresh glass of wine next to my laptop. The contents of the boxes a welcome distraction. Delving into the past preferable to imagining the future.

Stuck in traffic I drum my fingers on the steering wheel as red lights stretch out in front of me like baubles on a Christmas tree. My mother would go through the motions at Christmas. She'd tried to meet my levels of excitement and expectation, but the day always fell flat. The turkey burnt, the carrots mushy and the gravy lumpy. One year she'd attempted a stocking. She'd filled an old pair of tights with small gifts, unwrapped. But I could tell she'd shoved them in without any care because the gifts would get caught in the ladders as I pulled them out.

My father would visit in the afternoon and bring presents and that was the best part of the day. He always knew what I'd wanted and I thought he was magic, as though the elves had let him sneak a peek at my Christmas list.

Urgent beeping from behind makes me realise I've zoned

out again and the cars in front of me have moved. The red lights vanish along with the Christmas memories.

A few minutes later and I am at my mother's house. Dave, the clearance man, is vaping in the porch. The sickly strawberry scent filters inside the car and I turn my nose up. I miss tobacco catching at the back of my throat as I suck on a cigarette.

'All right,' Dave says and I dash through a sudden rain shower to greet him. 'The boxes are in here, want me to carry them to the car for you?'

'That would be great, thanks.'

He opens the front door and I catch a glance of the house as it used to be before my mother had stopped cleaning and started hoarding. The tiles of the hallway floor are able to breathe again.

'Wow, you've made some headway.'

'We've binned some stuff already as you can see from the skips. A few broken things. Her clothes really weren't up to passing on to anyone either.'

'Oh God, don't worry. I'm pretty confident her style of fashion won't be popular again.'

Dave goes inside and comes out with two boxes balanced on top of each other. He peeks around the side of them to see where he's going. My hands itch to look inside.

'There's one more in there if you want to grab it.' He nods towards the hallway.

The rain has eased, but we still rush to the car to save the boxes and their contents getting wet. Dave salutes me before heading back into the house.

'Speak soon,' I call after him.

Without hesitating I set off home, praying the traffic has

eased with people instead sipping wine in bars or cuppas in kitchens.

The journey back doesn't take long. I carry the boxes inside. My heart skips a beat, a feeling I am getting used to and one that doesn't alarm me anymore, knowing the flutters simply mean I'm tense.

The boxes are dusty. I cough as I open one of them up. A spider crawls across my fingers and I jump. Leaning back against the stairs I catch my breath and try to stop my hands shaking. The doctor's offer of antidepressants comes into my thoughts, but I shake her suggestion away. This is situational. A period of time I have to live through until the emotions blur and the sting in Anya's departure's tail is harmless.

The spider runs away and under a small crack in the skirting board. No doubt more terrified than I am.

I think about all of the items the clearance team have already removed and I frown. I'm sure my mother had secrets buried with her, but maybe her home also held secrets like those in this box. What if there are more?

Inside the first box is the doll. She stares at me with her only eye as though offended I have no recollection of her. Sniffing the dress I close my eyes and try to let the scent transport me back, but there is nothing but a faint damp smell. I put her to one side, facing her away from me so her judging eye can't stare.

Digging deeper I find a notebook and flick through. Much of the handwriting is scrawled and illegible. Shorthand maybe, I can't tell having never followed my mother's advice to take lessons. But other pages are clearer. I attempt to decipher the swirls of the cursive writing.

Your father has gone now. He could not look me in the eye. Blame and hatred poured from him. I soaked it up. I deserved it. I hate myself too. And I miss you. I keep thinking I can smell you, or hear you. I catch sight of your blue dungarees, of you running with the lace of your doll's dress gripped in your hand, her arms dangling beside you. And for a split second, I forget.

Feeling like I'm intruding into someone's private thoughts I put the notebook down.

Nostalgia gnaws at me and I think of my father. I haven't visited him in the home for too long. He hadn't recognised me the last time – my visit causing him more stress than comfort – so I'd stayed away. Tiredness sweeps over me like a blanket. The photos will have to wait.

My legs creak as I get up from the hallway floor and go to the kitchen. Staring at the fridge I decide to have more wine and some toast instead of dinner. No wonder Anya was keen to go to her dad's. He's an amazing cook; she'll be well fed there.

After eating the toast without bothering to get a plate, I take the wine up to my bedroom and get into bed, phone in hand. The blue circle on the app is above Anya's dad's house. Maybe the alcohol will help me sleep tonight and I won't wake screaming and sweating.

There's always hope, someone at work had once told me.

But lying in my bed and in my house alone, there is none.

14

DAPHNE

Birdsong filled my ears. Demanding my attention. I opened my eyes, squinting at the bright sunshine.

Above me the branches swayed and I was transfixed, stuck halfway between sleep and waking. The green leaves merged together; hiding the gnarly wooden twigs they grew from. A small brown bird flew above me, chirruping.

Reaching out I patted the ground around me, reaching for her dress, her smooth skin, her curled hair. But my hand met grass, each blade as sharp as a knife.

The skin on the back of my neck prickled.

She was gone.

'Darling!' I screamed and scrambled to my feet. 'Darling, where are you?'

The bushes rustled, berating me.

The sun disappeared, hidden behind menacing clouds. How long had I fallen asleep for? I looked at my wrist for reassurance that it hadn't been long, but there was nothing there except faint tan lines and a strip of lighter skin in between them.

The leaves above roared at me as the wind flew through them

and fresh raindrops pounded them. I swung around and around the clearing by the stream.

'Mummy's coming,' I called.

Mud splattered my trousers as I raced back along the path. Panic surged through me, infused in my blood. How could I have been so careless? What if she's been taken? But these woods are quiet. No one walked their dog here, instead they went to the local park. We'd never seen anyone else. Only the odd fox.

A fox.

'Darling,' I called again and again. 'Darling, where are you?' I slipped on the muddy pathway. I'd run in the forest as a child, with my dad, intrigued by what was hidden beneath the canopy, discovering hidden pathways and endless hiding places. I'd run without thinking, without awareness of danger, convinced my dad would know where I was. Is that how she felt, safe because she thought I'd find her?

But what if I couldn't find her?

'Darling? Mummy's getting scared. Please stop hiding.'

Branches looked like fingers pointing at a terrible mother who'd fallen asleep and lost her child.

I panted, my breath coming in rasps as I tried to catch it.

Back at the clearing I was sheltered from the worst of the rain by the thick green leaves above.

But the space was still empty.

There was no laughter. No blonde curls or speckled freckles.

She was gone.

I sank to my knees, grasped at my hair and pulled each strand tight.

'Darling!' I screamed again. 'WHERE ARE YOU?'

Where was she? Where was she? Where was she?

I couldn't order the thoughts in my head. It was as though I were in front of a group of children all screaming at me for attention, each one raising their voice louder than the other. I didn't know what to do.

I'd been told as a child that if you ever got lost you needed to stay where you were and someone would find you. But I wasn't the one who was lost. I knew where I was. She was the one who was lost. Gone.

Taken?

15

CATHERINE

WEDNESDAY 14TH AUGUST

Grounding myself by pressing my feet on the soft carpet, I can tell by Leanne's face that she agrees with me – colouring in is boring. Staying between the lines. Shading. A walk by the sea is much more my thing. Woodlands used to calm me, but not anymore. Instead I worry that if I catch my finger on a rogue thorn then sepsis is inevitable. Slathering on antibacterial cream lessens the panic, but the fear never fully leaves until the redness burning around the wound fades to pale pink.

'Colouring books?' she asks, face screwed up in disgust. 'When the hell would I have time to do that?'

'When Billy's napping?'

'But then when would I empty the dishwasher? Or do the laundry? Or prepare the bottles?'

She picks at her leggings and shuffles in the chair opposite me. There is a small worn patch of fabric on its arm, as though she has picked away at it, thread by thread, like a scab lifting at the edges.

'It's okay.' I smile at her to show I mean it. 'Colouring is not for everyone. But being creative can help people who are feeling low. I've got lots of other suggestions.'

'What, to fix me?'

Sighing, I supress the urge to clench my fists. 'I'm not trying to fix you.'

'I know. I know.' She waves her hands at me. 'I'm sorry.'

This meeting could go one of two ways. I am aware my emotions may cloud any advice I give her. Maybe I do want to fix her because her grief is so visceral.

'Okay.' I refocus. 'What do you think might help?'

'I don't know.' Leanne stands and runs her hands through her hair. 'Nothing is helping so far. The talking. The medication. None of it.' She's crying and her breathing is fast and uneven.

Grief isn't that simple, I want to tell her. Talking about the loss doesn't lessen the pain. Grief never goes away, but you learn to live with the pain somehow, time blurring the rawness.

'Why don't we take a break,' I suggest. 'Would you like a cup of tea? Or some fresh air?'

She sniffs and I follow her into the kitchen where she tells me to sit at the table outside while she makes the tea.

The garden is overgrown. Weeds peek out from every crack in the paving of the patio. Pots along the fence are filled with dead dark-brown leaves, large cracks running down the side of the blue pottery. There was once love here, I think. A haven full of flowers. Their neglect represents Leanne. The colourful well-tended woman she was being left to the weeds to feed on.

A stray piece of hair flies into my mouth and I reach into my bag for a band. This morning I styled it to appease Anya, even though she's still at her dad's. I'm hoping that the neat presentation of my exterior will hide the slow crumbling of my interior.

As I manipulate my hair into a messy bun I realise I am fooling no one. Screw Leanne. Maybe this garden is a visual representation of me. Like the flowers, with every text from Anya saying she's staying at her dad's for longer, I wilt and wither a little more.

Pulling the hairband out again I'm struck with anxiety that I'm not well enough to support anyone. I consider leaving, then Leanne appears with two mugs of tea.

'I didn't know if you took sugar?' She raises her eyebrows at me.

'I take cups of tea as they come,' I answer. In truth, I rarely get offered one. 'Thank you.'

Leanne looks to the bottom of the garden. 'Don't come out here anymore.' She sips her tea and winces, as it's still too hot. 'When we moved in, there was a pond, by the back gate. We got rid of it because I was paranoid about drowning. Full of fish it was. Bright gold ones that the previous owners couldn't take with them as they were moving to Spain.'

Hugging my mug I don't ask what happened to the fish.

'Stupid isn't it? We were so careful here at home. Never left Emily for a second in the bath. Or when she was eating in case she choked. Held her hand across every road. But on holiday it's different. You let your guard down as though the heat and the sun wraps you in this false sense of security.'

'Her death wasn't your fault, Leanne.'

She places her mug down on the table and rests her hands in her lap. 'The fault is all mine,' she whispers. 'Trust me.'

I sense there is more than grief behind her words. Revealed in the way her eyes flick from side to side as if recalling important information, or attempting to forget it.

Bits of milk float over the top of my tea like oil slicks and I blow them away before taking a sip.

Leanne concentrates on me. 'What about you? You ever put your child in danger?'

Goosebumps prickle on my arms. We're not meant to talk about our lives during these meetings. Our clients can become too attached or take on board our anxieties. But then there are times when being human offers comfort.

'Only once,' I reply, staring into the mug of tea and watching the milk float around.

'And?' Her eyes are wide, hungry for details.

'Just an incident with a busy road,' I lie. 'She was three and ran off to cross without me. I grabbed her arm, yanked her back, and dislocated her elbow.' I look at the ground as though ashamed. 'I'd been on my phone. Not paying attention.'

She stares towards the end of the garden again, lost in her own world. 'It wasn't like that with Emily.'

Leanne's words blur and I think of Anya. From deep inside me I have an urge to check where she is, but my phone isn't on the table.

'Where's my phone?' I say, a ringing in my ears. 'It's not here.'

'Sorry, what?' Leanne looks at me blankly. 'I was talking about Emily.'

'My phone, I had it a second ago, didn't I?' Or had I left it in the car? I can't remember.

'I'm not sure.'

'Did you see me with it or not, in my hand, did I put it in my bag can you remember?' I shouldn't snap, not her fault. But Anya.

'I ... I think maybe ... no, I can't remember. I'm sorry. Try under the chair.'

'No. Not there.' I throw the cushion to the floor. 'I need to find it. I need to see where...'

'How about under the table?'

'We'd have heard it thud, wouldn't we?' But I look anyway. Nothing but half a rice cake and some brown leaves.

'Your handbag then?'

'I've checked. Can you ring it?'

'My phone is on charge, upstairs, I don't want to wake Billy.'

'Are they in the same room?'

'No, but the stairs, they creak, he always, and I mean always, hears one of us if we go upstairs.'

'So you never go upstairs when he's asleep, not even to wee?'

She shakes her head.

'Do you have a landline?'

'A what?'

I close my eyes and rub my temples. 'Never mind, look could you please get your phone and call mine? I wouldn't normally ask, but I need to see where she ... when my next appointment is. I have to let work know.'

'Okay.' She sighs and hesitates.

'Please?'

Jiggling my legs I wait for either her to come back, or for my phone to ring wherever it is hiding. I wipe my sweaty hands on my trousers.

Then I hear the creak of a stair, and the wail of a baby.

Leanne returns with her mobile and calls mine. Her jaw is tense. She looks at her watch. There is a vibration from the back pocket of my jeans. I sigh with relief.

'Thank you,' I say, quickly opening up the phone and checking Anya's location. The dot shows she's at Sean's.

'He's awake now.' Leanne has an edge to her voice. 'That was a short nap.'

My stomach drops. 'I'm sorry. I really did need my phone. Maybe he'll drop back off?'

'He never does. You know I find everything so hard when

he's awake. He might fall and bang his head or swallow something he shouldn't or ... or...'

I reach out and rest my hand on hers, but she pulls it away.

'Probably best if you leave us to it,' she says without looking at me. 'I've got to get to the post office before they close.'

Full of guilt, I get up from the table and go into the lounge to fetch my bag.

'Do you want to arrange another appointment?' I ask. I shouldn't have made her go upstairs. I've made everything worse. The already-fragile bond between us broken.

'Can you text me in a week or so?' she replies, the same as always.

'Of course. Take care then. You know where I am.'

As I leave, Billy is still crying. Leanne hasn't rushed to him. Maybe she's hoping he'll soothe himself back to sleep so she can sit downstairs knowing he's safe in his cot after all.

I pull out my phone and open the Find Friends app again. Anya's blue circle hovers over her dad's house as it has done for several weeks now. Without doubt some of the loneliest weeks of my life so far.

She's safe.

Her A-level results are tomorrow and I am picking her up and taking her to the school to collect them first thing. She's been talking about going to Newquay to stay with her mates in a caravan after she gets them. I'd googled the campsite. My brain conjured up images of mould in the caravan's bathroom, seeping into her lungs, crusty milk in the fridge, the cloying smell of sweat and hangovers.

She knows I don't want her to go. And I know she won't stay home because of me. The other parents obviously approve, not that I can ask as I don't know any of them. Maybe I still have Ruby's mum's number on my phone. I can call her. Talk through my concerns and see if she shares them and then maybe we can persuade the girls to put up tents in someone's garden and camp there for the week instead.

Fat chance, a voice in my head says, and I know the voice is right.

I can't call Ruby's mum. I can't stop Anya going anywhere. And I can't get over the fear that I'm losing control.

16

ANYA

THURSDAY 15TH AUGUST

You've done something different to your hair. Like you've tried too hard and I know you want me to tell you I think you look good, but I can't bring myself to.

'You're not coming in to get my results with me,' I say and watch as your face falls. You didn't think you'd be allowed, did you?

'Fine.' You shrug. 'I'll wait in the car then.'

'No, Mum. Please don't. I might be ages and me and my mates want to go and celebrate somewhere, you know? Why don't you go home and I'll see you later, yeah?'

You glare at me, and the spark of guilt you ignite in me every single time we are together, which thanks to Dad isn't that often, flares. He's been great letting me stay for so long. Shame he has to work today and can't have been the one to bring me to collect my results because I would've been calmer with him here instead of you, even though we already know my university place is secure.

My acceptance email came first thing this morning before I knew my results. Not like it was in your day, you'd told me. You got a phone call and Gran hadn't even been there with you, she'd gone to church.

I stand back and watch you pull away from the pavement, a slight wave of your hand as if you are the one to dismiss me. For a minute, I think about turning my location services off so you can't see where I am, but then I feel the spark of guilt again and decide not to. Rocking the boat this close to me leaving for uni probably isn't wise. You're already on the edge.

Your behaviour reminds me of Gran. A long time ago she whispered to me, when you'd left the room to make yet another cup of tea, that she knew you didn't love her.

'Your mum doesn't know how to love,' Gran had whispered, her breath stale like gone-off milk. 'I guess that's my fault.'

Too young to understand at the time, I'd laughed.

'You're funny, Gran. Mummy loves me, she tells me all the time. More than anything she says. That means more than you.'

You'd come back in the room then and had missed Gran wiping away a tear. I'd jumped on your lap and squeezed you tight. And do you remember what I said then? I asked you, out loud, in my best and most clearest voice, I asked you if you loved Gran because she'd said you didn't. Then I asked if every bit of your love was used up on me instead and so that was why there was none left for her. I can't remember what you said. But I do remember there being cake.

You've driven out onto the main road now and I want to check your location to see if you really are heading home. I wouldn't be surprised if you were in the road parallel to this one, waiting, watching, but I think me being at Dad's for so long might have done you good, if your fancy hair is anything to go by. Maybe you're beginning to be able to see that without me you can be okay. Removing myself from your life bit by bit is the right thing to do.

Newquay is cancelled, but I haven't told you yet. The

caravan park got shut down. Rumours of rats and food poisoning. Story of my life. Will get our money back, thank fuck, but it's too late to book anywhere else and I don't really mind as I couldn't really afford the holiday anyway. I can have a mad Freshers Fortnight instead. Not long now. I'll spend the summer at Dad's. Don't care if that upsets you. I'm doing it because he gets me and understands what I need right now. He listens and you don't. He lets me breathe when all you do is drown me with your fears.

Across the road my friends wave at me to join them and I stop thinking about you and cross over. But then I look down the road opposite and I swear for a second, only a second, I can see your red car disappearing into the distance.

But I blink and the car is gone.

17

CATHERINE

FRIDAY 13TH SEPTEMBER

No one in the car speaks. The air fizzes with different emotions. The last few weeks have been horrible. And today is the day I've dreaded. She's really leaving me and going to university. I struggle not to vomit into my lap.

'Turn left here,' Anya says to her dad. She's in the front next to him; I am a mere passenger in the back. 'There it is, park here,' she instructs and he does as he's told. His knuckles whiten as he reverses the car into the space.

Students carry boxes and bags with their parents everywhere we look. Others wear blue T-shirts and lanyards and as soon as we get out of the car one bounds over with the energy of a toddler after a nap.

'Hi, I'm Matt and I am here to help you with anything you need today.'

'Hi, Matt,' Anya says, 'I'm Anya.'

'Cool, what are you studying?'

'Teaching.'

'Cool.' His face is splattered with acne. He rubs his chin, dislodging some scabs.

'Do you know where you're staying?'

'In one of the townhouses.'

'Cool.' He looks at his clipboard. I wonder how his parents feel about his extensive vocabulary after having been at university for at least one year already.

'Right, let's get your keys first and then a group of us can help you take your stuff up there. Follow me.'

'Cool,' Anya says. I roll my eyes.

He bounces along. Anya walks beside him and they talk and laugh. I want to cry. I'm loathed to admit it, but a part of me is jealous.

Anya throws her hair back, giggles and places her hand on Matt's arm, pushing him away, her cheeks flushed. Sean looks at me, eyebrows raised.

And so it begins.

A myriad of emotions run through me. I'm proud she's here and of everything she's achieved. When she was younger I wondered if she'd have the confidence to follow her dreams. Anxiety had hit when Sean remarried and her first half-sibling was born.

Anya would vomit, anxious he'd love the new baby more than he loved her. As an only child myself I never worried, but the joy she gets from playing with her half-siblings makes my heart sad she never had a full one.

'Hold this.' Anya bounds over from one of the many tables set up in the student union foyer. She hands me a brown envelope. 'It's for the doctor's. There's a form I need to fill in to register.'

'Okay, but shouldn't we do it now?' I have visions of this envelope being lost under piles of empty vodka bottles and cigarette packets. 'You'll need a repeat prescription for your inhalers soon.'

But her and Sean have moved on to the next table, the student union information section. There, blue T-shirted students secure wristbands on her left arm and pass her purple T-shirts and endless leaflets about Freshers events. Sean rubs in between her shoulder blades looking every bit the devoted dad. I'm an outsider. Here to hold the unimportant stuff.

At the next table she picks up the key card to her room and Matt rounds up a group of other blue T-shirted students who place their clipboards in a pile and declare themselves ready to assist. Whatever drugs they are taking to make them so happy and bouncy, I decide I want some.

Lagging behind I swallow hard. This is the start of a new amazing phase for Anya, but I'm hollow inside, as though I've given birth and my belly is empty and bloated. Fear creeps inside me and fills the space Anya has left.

I want to bundle her in the car and bring her back to the bedroom she has slept in since she was a baby. I want to watch her sleep night after night.

I want to keep her safe.

A metal gate clangs open and I snap back to the present. I can't ruin this day with my paranoia. If Anya and I argue now there'll be nothing left. No weekly phone calls or holiday visits home. Voicing my fears will mean losing her for good.

'What can I take?' I force a smile. Anya looks at me like I've asked her to work out what twelve times fifty-two is.

'Anything you can carry.' She waves her arm towards the contents of the boot. 'Everything in there needs to come.'

She grabs a large box and hands it to Matt who walks in the direction of the gated halls of residence.

'No one can get in or out without their key card,' Matt explains. 'So don't lose yours. They cost a lot of money to replace and if you're here without it at 3am, you're screwed.'

A knot tightens in my stomach.

'Are you listening, Anya?' Her back is to me, but I know she's rolling her eyes.

'Isn't there night-time security?' I picture her sleeping her drunkenness off on the metal bench beside us.

'Yup,' says Matt. 'But unless you've got ID they won't let you in anyway. I once spent the night on that bench right there in the middle of winter. Wouldn't recommend the experience.'

They laugh and Anya looks at me, putting the key card in her back pocket with intent.

'Don't stress, Mum. I won't lose it. Promise.' She purses her lips and air kisses me. My head is about to explode.

Although no one can enter without a key card, as the gate slams shut I realise with a jolt – there's no stopping a stranger who doesn't live here coming in alongside a person who does.

'She's settled in already.' Sean appears beside me.

'She's just excited.'

He frowns, but whatever he's thinking he chooses not to voice it.

We're stood outside a row of townhouses, five of them squeezed in together as though the architect messed up his measurements, but carried on and built them anyway.

'What's your room number?' Matt asks.

Anya looks up to the sky in thought. '203.' She clicks her fingers into a point.

'Second floor.'

Counting, I look up at the building. It's a long way down from the second-floor window. As if reading my mind Matt puts a hand on my shoulder. He's too close and I can't help but shrug him off.

'It's all right,' he says. 'Every window has a safety catch. Can't even lean out for a fag.'

'Good to know.' I laugh awkwardly.

After lugging what feels like far too much stuff for one person up to her room, we stand there panting. The heavy fire door is wedged open with her suitcase; bags and boxes surround us on the floor and the bed.

A strong scent of bleach permeates the air and I wonder if the mattress is new. A flimsy protector lies on the top and I'm convinced it's only been put there to hide any rogue stains.

'Look at the view.' Sean walks over to the large window at the far end of the room. Beyond the road below is a vast hill with a small crop of trees at the top. But Anya doesn't look up from the box she's unpacking. She takes out a photo of her and her school friends and places it on the desk.

Another student opens the hallway door and carries a large television into the room opposite. My stomach drops before I remember that I'm not the one who'll be listening to him gaming through the walls all night.

'Shall I make a start in the kitchen?' I ask.

'Choose a cupboard for your food and a shelf in the fridge,' Matt says.

'I'll come with you. Here,' Anya hands me a bag. 'This is for the kitchen.'

Downstairs, six bottles of Fairy Liquid line the draining board alongside more sponges than I'd go through in a year. I wonder if Sean thought to get Anya some too.

Anya opens cupboard doors, but they all have food in them already. Tins of baked beans and tuna line shelf after shelf. Finally, she finds an empty one.

'Mum? Can you put my food in there and I'll go and get my plates and stuff?'

She disappears and I unload the food Sean has bought her, silently judging him for the choices he's allowed her to make. Not one single tin of sweetcorn or anything that contains vitamins or nutrients. I'll do an online shop for her next week.

A young lad walks through the door behind me, his tracksuit bottoms several inches below his waistline revealing well-worn black pants. 'All right,' he says, chest puffed out like a bird attracting a mate.

'Hi,' I say. 'I'm Anya's mum.'

'Jamie.'

He walks past and unpacks three bottles of vodka and several cans of cider onto a white dresser. On top of cupboards and fridge shelves it would seem the students also have booze shelves. Has Sean bought Anya vodka too?

She crashes in with a heavy box. Jamie rushes over to help her and I'm reminded not to judge people by how they look. He doesn't pull his trousers up to cover his pants though.

'Thanks.' She tucks her hair behind her ears, a sure sign she's feeling embarrassed. Her cheeks flush a faint pink.

'No worries. I'm Jamie.'

'Anya.' They smile. A hint of attraction buzzing around them like fireflies.

'Where are you from?' he asks.

'Bristol. You?'

'Just outside London.'

'Cool.'

I'm an intruder. Her new life has begun and I'm watching the events unfold on a screen in front of me.

'What course you doing?'

'Teaching. You?'

'Geography.'

'Cool.'

Anya unpacks her fresh food into the fridge.

'If you're a veggie put your stuff on the top shelf,' Jamie says. 'Won't get any meat juices dripping on it that way, that's what I've done.'

'Good plan, cheers,' Anya says.

'I'm done here.' A sudden urge to stay and cook her one last meal overwhelms me. 'I'll go back up and start unpacking in the bedroom, shall I?'

Anya nods. Jamie shows her where the booze dresser is and I leave them alone.

Matt and his posse have left Sean by himself in Anya's bedroom. He's sat on the bed with his head in his hands.

'You okay?' I ask.

He looks up. His eyes are red and puffy. I feel a flutter of irritation. She's not leaving him.

'I can't believe how fast it's gone.'

I keep my mouth closed and sigh. I will *not* start an argument with anyone today, no matter how hard this is.

'They do say the days are long, but the years are short.' I cringe at resorting to clichés. 'It's as though I brought her home from the hospital yesterday.'

His face flinches as I mention her birth. And the fact he wasn't there.

'She's met another housemate downstairs. Jamie. He's nice, but I haven't met his parents. They might've gone already, I think.'

'That's good. A girl went into the room next door, but she hasn't come out since.'

The thought of living with eleven other people makes me break out in a cold sweat and I don't envy Anya the nerves of meeting everyone after we leave.

'We should probably go,' Sean says and a sharp pain flashes across my chest.

I can't leave her here.

As though she sensed our departure, Anya appears at the doorway.

'I'm ready for you to go,' she says and smiles. 'Most of the other parents have left.'

'Okay.' Sean gets up from the bed. 'We won't stay and

embarrass you. Although, I think your mum wants to move in too.'

They laugh and I try to join in, but every part of me is on fire.

Of course I want to move in with her.

'Bye, Mum,' she says, her face full of emotion. 'Don't worry, I'll take my inhalers twice a day.'

We embrace. I struggle to let go.

'Love you,' she whispers in my ear.

'Love you too,' I reply, wiping the tears from my cheeks.

Sean and Anya hug too and I want to scream. She's in danger. Why can't they feel it? But I don't speak.

Sean and I walk back to the car in silence.

'She'll be okay, you know.' He pats me on the shoulder.

And I wish I could believe him.

Opening up the tracking app, Anya's blue circle pulses above the halls of residence.

And suddenly, as though someone has waited until this moment to plant the thought there, I know what I have to do. I'll keep track of her all the time. Check she's home after a night out. Has gone to lectures. Watch her social media for signs of illness or risky behaviours. Join Snapchat and find her on Snapmaps, in case she ever turns her location services off.

Stalking my daughter isn't an option.

Stalking my daughter is a must.

18

CATHERINE

SATURDAY 14TH SEPTEMBER

L ying in my bed I stare up at the ceiling, anxiety my new
night-time companion.

I haven't slept. Necking loads of alcohol in order to pass out
is rubbish, I've discovered. A bottle and a half of wine have not
helped me fall into a calm slumber. Instead the alcohol has
caused my heart to race and a sweat to break out across my chest
and drip in between my breasts.

Anya's blue circle hovers above her student house. She
hasn't been anywhere else since Sean and I had left her there,
which is both a blessing and a curse. At least if she'd left her
halls I'd know she was alive. This way I have visions of her
having choked on her own vomit in her bedroom after a wild
start to her new life and no one thinking to check on her.

The clock on my phone says 5am and I conclude that I
might as well get up and make a triple espresso. Luckily, I had
the foresight to take a week's unpaid leave. I put my dressing
gown on and wander down to the kitchen, only briefly stopping
outside Anya's bedroom door and fighting back the tears.

At the bottom of the stairs I stare at the boxes from my
mother's house and decide maybe it would be as good a time as

any to look through them again. The contents will distract me from images of Anya covered in her own vomit that play on a loop in my head. They'll also stop me from jumping in my car and driving up to her halls of residence to check she's alive.

I put three sugars into my coffee for good measure and take the full mug and the notebook through to the lounge. Dust along the mantlepiece and around the fire grate taunts me. Cleaning is not top of my priorities now I don't need to worry about dirt triggering an asthma attack in Anya.

I wonder if that's why my mother stopped cleaning her house. With only her there, she felt no need.

I open up the notebook. There are no dates on any of the pages. Just the same scrawling handwriting in bright blue ink and patches of blurred words, as though the author had been crying when they wrote.

I wish I could turn back the clock to that day. I wouldn't fall asleep. You wouldn't leave me to go and explore. I'm cross with you too. You knew the rules. You knew you weren't allowed to go off alone and yet you did. Your father called me cruel, for blaming you when we knew what happened was my fault. I'm so sorry, Heather.

The sunlight from through the window rests on the page I'm reading and reminds me of the time my dad had pretended to capture the rays from the sun in a jar. We'd put the jar in the garden to keep the fairies safe at night, under the cherry tree. With magic and wonder alive in my innocent head, I'd looked out of my bedroom window after dark and had sworn I could see the jar lit up beside the tree trunk.

Several months have passed since I last visited him. He

doesn't know about my mother yet. Telling him when he'd been so distressed at my last visit would've been cruel.

But he has a right to know she has died.

Maybe he can help solve the mystery of the notebook too, I think, as he often lives in the past.

While making myself another coffee I check the tracking app again. No movement. The dot hangs above Anya's halls taunting me as though saying, *I know where she is all the time, do you?* But I push the sick feeling away.

I'm going to go and see my father. At times like this I wish I had a sibling to share the burden. I scribble on a piece of paper to remind myself to contact the house removal people and see how they are getting on and stick it to the fridge. Maybe I'll pop by after visiting him.

One more check on the app shows Anya is on the move, hopefully off to the main campus to register. Tension leaves my body with the proof she survived the night, until a thought enters my head telling me she could have had her phone stolen and that's why the blue dot is moving. Groaning I pop the notebook from my mother's house in my handbag, before showering and heading off to see my father.

My father's nursing home is a twenty-minute drive away, and I'm glad the journey doesn't take long because I'm becoming increasingly anxious whenever I get behind the wheel of my car. There's no reason as to why this has started to happen – no crash or near miss – yet every time I sit in my driving seat, my hands hold on to the steering wheel a little tighter than is necessary. And my breathing quickens.

The car park at the home is not too busy and I park in my usual space, closest to the entrance. As I get out, a gust of wind reaches under my skirt and blows the thin material in the air. The flowers I'd picked up on the way fall from my hands and are blown around the tarmac like confetti. Damn.

I'm frightened at how something usually so insignificant makes me want to collapse in a heap. I scramble around to pick up the flowers, leaving the battered ones for the wind.

'Good Morning, Catherine,' greets a nurse walking past as I enter the building. Scent from a large vase of lilies placed on a table in the entrance hall fills the air around me and hides the stench of cleaning products and the waft of urine that never fully leaves no matter how much they clean.

All of the regular staff here know me and I'm always made to feel welcome. When my father first moved here I visited him every week. While the place isn't exactly home from home – for there is not really anything terribly homely about the place – it has become familiar.

Over the years I'd pray for him to have a good day, but they are diminishing fast. On bad days he recognises no one and is, at times, rude and aggressive. I've often felt as though I am watching a seventy-five-year-old man experience a toddler tantrum.

They have changed the artwork hung outside of his room on the ground floor. Where there used to be a painting of a generic seaside scene, there now hangs a piece of 'abstract' art. Blobs of oranges and reds blend into swirls of green. Hints of blues and flicks of yellows. Maybe the painting would look better from a distance and not so close up. I'm unsure as to how the artwork should be interpreted.

A card is stuck on the wall at the bottom, which tells me the painting is called *The Sleeping Mind*. Maybe the artist had been asleep when they had created the masterpiece.

'Hi, he's having a good day today,' one of the care workers

says as we pass each other at his door. 'He'll be pleased you've popped in.'

My father is in a chair facing the window, a yellow blanket draped over his legs. The window looks out over the expansive gardens at the back of the home, which are very well tended to.

His hair is bushier and shinier than when I had last seen him. He used to pride himself on his hair, the only one of his friends not to have gone bald, but he's let that go too.

As he stares into the distance he hums to himself and taps his fingers against the wooden arm of the chair. Music has been such an important part of his life, a piano teacher for many years after retiring early. Humming and 'finger'-playing his favourite piano pieces often means he's having a good day, which is wonderful, even though he can be lost in a concerto or a minuet for several minutes mid conversation. I sit in the chair opposite him, by the window, and wait for him to finish.

He opens his eyes after a few moments, and smiles, in what I hope is recognition.

'Hi, Dad,' I say. 'I brought you some flowers.' He'd probably have preferred chocolate.

Grabbing the flowers with an outstretched hand, he holds them to his chest, and grins.

'So, how are you, Dad?'

A frown appears across his forehead. 'I miss her,' he says.

'I know.' Except, I didn't know, but experience has taught me that it is always best to agree with him. 'Me too.'

'She came to see me a couple of weeks ago and then she hasn't been back since. We had a lovely time catching up. Dreadful what happened. All her mother's fault, you know.'

Sometimes this happens. He'll have dreams and believe they are real. Or hallucinate. He looks in pain.

He doesn't appear to be having a good day after all. But my

interest is piqued by what he has said, maybe from reading the notebook earlier, and so I go with my gut.

'She left a long time ago, didn't she? Are you sure it was her who came to see you?'

'Oh yes, dear. She was wearing the dress she always does. You know, the one with the swirls, which makes your eyes ache if you spend too long looking at the pattern. Definitely her. I'd know her face anywhere.' He closes his eyes and begins humming again. Shutting himself off from me.

Outside one of my lost flowers dances across the grass. I pour myself a glass of water from the jug that is on the table next to his bed. The tea trolley will be along soon. I could do with a cup.

He stops humming and is looking at me. 'You're a lot like her you know. You have the same blue eyes. Transparent. They can't hide how you feel. Her eyes were sad eyes the day she came to visit too. I told her so.' He pauses and smooths the blanket over his knees. His hands tremble. 'Why are you sad today?'

He stares at me with a strange intensity I've not seen before, frowning with his head tilting to one side as though he is looking inside me. Unlike mine his eyes are impenetrable. Anya has inherited them. Her eyes give nothing away.

'I'm not sad, Dad,' I keep the tone of my voice light. 'I have been very busy though, maybe my eyes are showing you I'm tired.'

He doesn't remember Anya, he doesn't need to know she's left home.

'That is what *she* said, you know. She said, I'm tired, too.' He shakes his head. 'Such a worry. You never stop worrying.' He pauses and leans forward. 'You know, you do remind me of her.'

Then he closes his eyes and becomes lost in his world of music once more.

Leaning back in my chair I watch him and order my thoughts. Maybe showing him the notebook isn't a good idea. He often rambles on about things that make no sense. And I've always accepted his quirks.

But today is different.

I know no one would've visited him two weeks ago because there is no one left to visit him. His only sister died thirty-two years ago in an accident and his parents are also deceased. Other than my mother and me, he has nobody. And I can't ever remember a time she'd visited him; their divorce, which happened when I was too young to remember, was not an amicable one.

Maybe the receptionist will be able to look at the visitors log and tell me if someone had come to see him. The truth is that he is probably having a bad day after all, but there is a new feeling inside me after visiting him today, like being on a boat in the middle of a storm. I'm unbalanced.

'I'm going to go now, Dad,' I say, but he doesn't open his eyes. His fingers strum on the arms of the chair and his humming intensifies.

Then, as I reach the door to his room, I hear him cough.

'Goodbye, Heather,' he calls, and I stop dead. He's looking at me, a smile as wide as his face, his eyes glistening. 'Thank you for coming.'

He closes his eyes again, and I'm left holding my breath and wondering if I misheard him.

The reception desk is empty and I hang around for several minutes, but no one returns. I consider sneaking a look at the visitor's book even though it is against the rules.

Could it be coincidence, I think, as I walk back to my car, him calling me the name from the notebook? He could've had a friend called Heather. Or one of the nurses here could be called Heather. Heather isn't an uncommon name. But a nagging sensation tells me I've hit on the truth, like a spade bashing against the corner of buried treasure.

Treasure I want to dig up.

19

CATHERINE

MONDAY 23RD SEPTEMBER

'All right, love,' the removal man says. 'It's one hell of a mess in there.'

Outside my mother's house are two skips, each half full, and a long line of black bin bags full and tied closed at the top. It's more of a state than the last time I was here.

'Rick got bitten by a rat yesterday, he's on antibiotics now, tells me he's fine to work, but I've told him to take the day off. So it's just me and Pete, might take a bit longer.'

'Oh shit,' I say.

He looks at me with a mix of pity and confusion. 'You knew she lived like this?'

Shaking my head I peer into the nearest skip. 'No.'

'Happens more than you'd think. Either they stop caring or they can't clean up after themselves. They don't like to be a burden, the older generation, do they?'

'I did ask her to come and live with me, but she refused.' Guilt compels me to defend myself.

'My ma's the same.' He sticks his hands in his pockets.

'Is everything you've found rubbish then? Apart from the boxes I've already got?' I point at the skips and black bags.

'Yeah, we're working through clearing out all the crap, sorry, I mean debris, and then we start looking at the rest. See what can go to charity, that sort of thing. Not every removal company works the same, but that's the way we do it.'

Which is why I'd chosen them above the others.

'You still sure there's nothing you want?'

Shielding my eyes from the sun I look up at the house. I don't know how to answer him. They've already uncovered more than I realised was here.

'I don't know,' I say. 'I guess if there are letters or photos then yes, I'd like them. Or any more notebooks, diaries or journals.'

'What about jewellery? People normally want to keep that.'

My mother hadn't worn jewellery that I could remember. She'd told me she'd thrown her wedding ring into a stream in the woods.

'I don't think you'll find any, but yes okay, if you do then thank you.'

'Look, I'll tell you what; before we chuck anything we think is important away I'll give you a bell, yeah? I've been doing this a fair few years and so I'm pretty good at recognising what's special and what isn't, you know?' He laughs and then sighs as if he finds himself hilarious.

'Dave, there's another rat up here, mate,' someone who I assume is Pete shouts from the upstairs bedroom window. My old bedroom.

'We're probably going to have to call in the pest control people,' he says. 'One or two we can handle, but any more than that and it's above our remit, you know?'

'Of course, do whatever it is you need to do. I don't want anyone else getting bitten.' Least of all me, I didn't add for fear of sounding self-absorbed. Looks like I am not going to be able to go inside and uncover any hidden secrets today.

'All right, I'll give you a call tomorrow, let you know what's happening.'

'Thanks, speak then.'

Walking back to my car I check the tracking app. The blue circle is back over her halls. I want to text her and ask how she is, but I don't want to intrude.

It's five o'clock, a perfectly acceptable time to have a glass of wine, or a double gin and tonic even though it's a Monday. I don't want to go home. The place smells different without Anya's body spray haunting the hallway. And it feels different too, more than empty, as though the walls have stopped breathing since fresh life is not being injected into the space between them anymore. I miss the sound of her stomping up the stairs and slamming doors. I even miss the dirty dishes and stale smell of gone-off milk emanating from her bedroom.

No, I can't go home. I won't be the stereotypical single mother with empty nest syndrome, licking her wounds like a cat after a fight.

My mother's house isn't far from the town centre and I remember seeing an advert for a new bar there pop up on Anya's Facebook feed earlier when I was looking to see if she'd uploaded any photos. She hadn't. Maybe I could pop in for one. There might be a nice man there. That would show Anya. Show her that I'm not some sad, lonely old woman who stalks her daughter on social media, hell no.

Butterflies flutter in my stomach as I walk into the bar. I don't ever remember having done this by myself before. Large iron lampshades hang down from the ceiling lighting up a mismatch of wooden tables and seating.

A group of young girls are standing by the bar, they hop

from one foot to the other, the bottom half of them showing their nerves, while the top half displays confidence and eyebrows a tad too thick and dark accentuating make-up at the top end of subtle. They laugh at each other and check their phones, before laughing again and looking around the room.

A dull thud of music spills out of speakers on the walls. A tune I don't recognise. A family in the far corner are having their dinner, a young couple and their baby. They watch me as I walk over to the bar and I smile at them as if apologising for being here alone.

'Hey, what can I get you?' a guy who looks young enough to be my son says from behind the bar.

'White wine, please, dry.'

'Medium or large?' He raises his eyebrows and looks at me. 'I'm gonna guess large, right?'

Is he flirting with me? Or do I look so dreadful that he thinks I need all the alcohol?

'Do I look that bad?' I ask, raising my eyebrows in return.

'Not at all.' He laughs. 'You look like someone who's had a long day. My job is to suss these things out.'

'As it happens I have had a difficult day. So yes, a large, please.'

'Coming right up.' He takes a half-empty bottle out the fridge behind him and I consider telling him to shove a straw in it, before stopping myself.

I prop myself up on the bar stool and sit like a small child with my legs dangling. The wine tastes like vinegar, but I take a couple of gulps anyway. A few more people have propped up the bar beside me, a couple of men in suits. I wonder if their wives know they are in the pub and not in the office. Tracking Sean when he used to tell me he was working late would've been handy.

Pulling my phone out of my bag I flick through Twitter and

Facebook. There are no updates from Anya. Although she could've started a new private account I don't know about and be posting what she likes.

After draining the first one I order another glass of wine and mull over the events of the day. My father calling me Heather has unnerved me.

'This one's on me,' says a deep voice to my left.

One of the men in a suit who'd walked in earlier stands grinning at me. He has a dimple on his left cheek that reminds me of a boy I had a crush on in secondary school.

'No, you don't have to do that,' I say, but he waves his hands at me.

'I insist,' he says. 'I've been stood up before too and it sucks.'

Oh the shame.

'No, no, I'm not meeting anyone here. My daughter's moved to university and I couldn't bear to go home to an empty house.'

His expression tells me he's got the information he wanted and I scan his left hand for a ring. A faint dent and lighter patch on his ring finger implies he's not long taken it off.

'Ah, I see.' He rubs his chin. 'That might call for something stronger. Tequila chaser maybe?'

Shaking my head and laughing, I lean away from him.

'God, no.' I hold up my hand like a policeman stopping traffic. 'Wine will do fine, thank you.'

He perches on the bar stool next to me, clearly not getting the hint.

'My eldest daughter left last year and I cried nearly every day for the first six months.' He looks down at his pint and wipes condensation off the side.

'Really?' I have no idea if I'm being played or fed a line, but I don't care. I need to talk to someone about how I am feeling and he is the only person willing to listen. I can purge my soul without having to wake up tomorrow awash with regret and anxiety that I've made a fool out of myself in front of someone I know.

'Really.' He nods solemnly. 'She's in London training to be a vet and I have to say this year, when she went back in September, I found her leaving easier. I only cried for a week. Here–' He gets a photo out of his wallet and hands it to me. His daughter is beautiful. In the photo she stands tall and smiles with her whole face. Confidence radiates from her and enhances her natural beauty.

'She's gorgeous,' I say. 'Did you worry that she was in danger after she'd left? Like a little part of you was walking around on its own without you there as a safety net?'

He laughs. 'Absolutely. I've got a mate in the police force in London and I even considered paying him to look out for her for a while. I had to stop myself from driving down to London the weekend she left and following her around.'

Tension oozes from me like oil. My shoulders drop several inches and there is space in my chest again. I can breathe. The extreme emotions I have been experiencing are normal. *I* am normal.

'That's it exactly.' I point at him and nearly fall off my stool in excitement. 'The worry started not long before she left. I'd wake in the middle of the night terrified she was in danger.'

'Oh I know. Most nights I wake briefly at some point and worry about her. You know there's an app you can use to see where they are, don't you?'

'Yes.' I look down, ashamed at myself, and at the same time relieved I'm not the only one.

'I'm embarrassed to admit this to a stranger, but I followed her on that app for a while,' he says. 'Until she found out and blocked me.'

As though my soul is being cleansed I suddenly feel tearful.

He leans forward and puts his hand on my knee. 'Them not

being at home does get easier, I promise. Each day that goes by where she is safe, and she is safe, the anxiety lessens. Currently, my worry is a vague ache that washes over my chest every now and again.'

'I hurt everywhere,' I say. 'My whole body aches with the tension. And I'm on edge, convinced I'm about to get bad news, and then there are these flashes of utter terror and I know I'm about to die right there and then on the spot.'

He nods and I take it as encouragement to carry on.

'I have these nightmares too, every night. I wake sweating and my heart is racing. I have to check my phone to see where she is like a woman possessed. I feel like this part of me that used to be sewn onto my body has been ripped off and the wound is open and raw and nothing is fixing it.'

I breathe in sharply and look up at the ceiling to blink the tears away. Everything I've been thinking has poured out of me like water, the tap that was rusty and stuck forced open by a man in a suit and two large glasses of wine.

His hand is still on my knee. He squeezes it.

I continue. 'I thought I was going mad. I don't know anyone else going through the same. And I'm so lonely.' Regretting those last words as soon as they are out of my mouth I move my knee away from his hand.

'Of course you are,' he says. 'How does your husband feel?'

Clever, I think. Very clever. We don't even know each other's names and already he knows more about me than my colleagues.

'Her dad doesn't really talk to me about this kind of stuff,' I neglect to give the answer he is looking for.

We sit in silence for a few minutes and I gulp the rest of my wine.

'Look, I'd better get going. And you ought to get back to your mate.'

He looks crestfallen and I wonder if they had a dare about him pulling me and he's lost twenty quid.

'Thank you for listening though,' I say with meaning. Regardless of whether what he said was true or not he's made me feel less alone and less of a crazy, obsessive, helicopter mum.

'Anytime. I'm not usually here on a Monday, we closed a big deal, but I am here most Fridays after work if you ever want to avoid an empty house,' he says, but we know I won't be here again.

I grab my bag and smile as I jump off the barstool. He puts out a hand to steady me as I stumble forward into his lap. My face brushes his neck. He smells like Sean and I recoil.

'Sorry,' I say and he waves the apology away before I run from the bar. High heels and wine do not make a good combination. Taking my car keys from my bag I realise I'm over the limit and shouldn't drive.

'Fuck,' I mutter, not normally one to swear. The app tells me an Uber is a few minutes away and so I sit at the local bus stop, track Anya, and cry.

20

DAPHNE

My neighbour's dog had found her, in the stream not far from where I'd fallen asleep. He'd barked and barked until he had my attention. Then my neighbour pulled her out. Told me to call an ambulance. Gave her mouth-to-mouth.

But I'd frozen. Leaving her to find a phone was not an option. She needed me here, beside her, holding her hand.

'I can feel a pulse,' he said and she coughed and spluttered and spat out a load of water. He lifted her up in his arms.

'We need to get her to the hospital, now.'

We rushed through the woodland, along the pathway, my breath coming in fits. Twigs snagged my hair and clothes and nicked my skin as I brushed them out of the way. I could not keep up. My stomach twinged.

The baby.

A wood pigeon called above us.

'It's her fault,' I imagined them saying. 'She fell asleep.'

I placed my hands over my ears to drown them out.

Ahead of me my neighbour turned. 'Come on,' he called.

But my legs were heavy. He was moving too fast, even with

her in his arms. His dog ran to and fro between us as though binding us together with invisible string.

We emerged from under the canopy and I fell to my knees, panting. Bright lights flickered in front of me.

Then everything went black.

21

CATHERINE

THURSDAY 3RD OCTOBER

A couple of weeks ago Leanne and I agreed via text to go on a buggy walk today. The plan was to help introduce her to some other mums and build her confidence.

However, this morning I've already had two panic attacks and am currently swallowing Rescue Remedy straight from the bottle instead of spraying the liquid onto my tongue.

Last night was one of the worse nights I've had since Anya left. I'd slept, but the nightmares had penetrated my sleep every hour. At one point I'd jerked awake thinking I could smell smoke. I'd raced downstairs thinking that Anya must be having a midnight snack and burning some toast, but was greeted by a dark kitchen, no Anya and no toast.

The smell vanished and I'd gone back to bed too wired to sleep. For a minute I wonder if purging my sins to the stranger in the bar has unlocked an area of my brain and caused the anxiety to worsen.

At least I'll be able to empathise with the sleep-deprived mums on the buggy walk. The notebook from my mother's house is on the kitchen counter beside me. I'd picked it up when I'd got in last night and had not been able to put it down. It was like reading a memoir and I'd stayed awake far too late flicking through the pages. But there was still no clarity as to who Heather was, or what had happened to her. I put the notebook into my handbag thinking I might have a chance to sneak a peek of some more pages at some point during the day.

Draining the rest of my coffee I head out the door. I go to shout up to Anya that I am leaving before remembering she isn't here to tell. The coffee swirls in my stomach and I run back in, ignoring the silence, to grab a banana.

At the entrance to the park several mums rock their babies in buggies, to and fro. They stand in groups of two or three. Talks of teething, nappy rash and sleepless nights fill the air around them. Leanne is stood alone, a little way back from the others. She bites her nails and sways from one leg to another as though rocking an invisible baby.

'Hi,' I go over to her. 'How are you doing?'

'I'm fine,' she snaps, but I don't believe her. 'I hope he stays asleep for the whole of the walk, he had me up all night and I've had enough.'

'That's tough. Is he teething?' I look in the pram, his cheeks are red and flushed, a sure sign that his teeth are on the move.

'I have no idea, and at 4am I stopped caring and left him to cry.' She leans forward and hisses at me. 'I'm a horrible mother. He deserves better.'

'Those kind of thoughts are very common, Leanne. You're not horrible, you're tired. Babies are hard work. And having no sleep is torture.'

I remember when Anya was a newborn. One night I left her crying in her cot and stood at the bottom of the garden where I couldn't hear her wails. And then I'd panicked that she'd somehow managed to climb out of the cot and was lying on the floor with a broken neck. I'd rushed back in, scooped her up from her cot and told her I was sorry over and over again.

'Come on,' I say as everyone else starts to walk. 'Let's take it slowly. You'll feel better for the fresh air, I promise.'

She moves beside me, her feet dragging behind her like a toddler having a strop. Exercise has been proven to help lift the mood, but even I feel like saying, 'Screw it, shall we go and get a coffee instead?' But I know she needs this, and so do I.

We don't talk as we walk up the steep hill towards the top of the park. I offer to push the heavy buggy for her, but Leanne declines. She huffs and puffs at the top as she tries to catch her breath.

The sun creeps out from behind a cloud but offers little warmth, the heat of the summer fading along with the lighter evenings. There are a couple of mums ahead with babies the same age as Leanne's, but there is no easy way to get talking to them. Introducing two mums is like setting up a blind date, but so much harder. We need to stop and sit around together in order for new conversations to start. At the moment the mums are sticking with the people they know. People are naïve to think that having a baby in common is the only quality they need to bond.

'How have you found the relaxation recordings?' I ask.

Leanne shakes her head. 'I tried a couple of times, but he screams most evenings and I'm always on edge. I can tense my muscles perfectly, I just can't relax them again afterwards.' She laughs, testing the feeling out before deciding she doesn't like the sound and her face sets into a frown again.

She looks exhausted, black shadows sit under her eyes, which are red and bloodshot and I suspect she's been crying throughout the night alongside her baby. Her shoulders slump and her head droops. Maybe I should speak to her health visitor, she seems worse than the last time I met her. This often happens. The mums put up a front on my first visit, and then as they get to know me their guard lowers and they are more honest.

'Keep going with it,' I say, 'these things can take practice.'

She shrugs.

'Why don't we try a bit of grounding as we walk round?'

'Grounding doesn't work,' she says. 'I've tried counting what I can see or hear or taste and nothing. My brain is too busy. I'm too tired.'

'That's okay,' I say. Her baby stirs in the buggy and I see her grip the handle tight with both hands, her knuckles white. 'Is your husband at home today? Do you have anyone who could take the baby and give you a break?'

'He's coming home from work early. He's going to take the baby out for a drive so I can't hear him.' And then she speaks so quietly I struggle to hear her. 'It would've been her birthday today.' Her tears fall freely, wiping at them only when they drip onto the buggy's handles.

'Oh, Leanne, I'm so sorry. I never would've suggested this if I'd known.'

'No, it's okay. I thought it would be a good thing to do, instead of moping all day at home.'

She pauses for a moment, unable to speak.

'Last year we held a memorial,' she blurts out in between shuddered breaths. 'I had these expectations of how the day would be and then it rained and the flowers were ruined and everything made me feel worse.'

The world fades around me and in its place is a flash of a recollection in the corner of my brain, of me holding flowers, red and yellow roses. I can smell their scent, I remember wanting to pick the petals off. The smell of the flowers is so vivid. Looking around I search to see if we are walking past any, but there aren't even any daisies poking through the grass beside the pathway where we walk.

'Catherine?' Leanne is looking at me and for a second I'm unable to recall what we were talking about.

'Gosh, I'm sorry,' I say. 'You reminded me to send a friend some flowers. I got distracted, I'm so sorry.'

'Oh. Okay.' She looks sad. I'm frustrated at myself for buggering up again. My relationship with my clients is often fragile. One wrong turn and I can break any trust I've built up with them in seconds. I can see that I've lost her.

'Please, carry on telling me about Emily. The memorial being a washout wasn't your fault at all. You can't control the weather.'

'I can't control anything at the moment,' she says, and I know I'm getting her back, like there might be another way in.

'Not the big things, maybe, but there will be something that you will be able to feel you have control of right now. Lowering your expectations isn't a bad thing. Look at today, for example, it would've been okay for you to be a mess, to not shower, to hide under the duvet.'

'But that feels like I'm failing. Like I'm letting her down.'

We stop to cross over a bridge at the bottom of the park and there is a natural pause in our conversation. A weir roars to our right. Plus the pathway is narrow and we have to go in single file as the buggy and I can't fit side by side.

My phone buzzes in my pocket. If I take a break to answer the call I will lose Leanne for good. I can't allow that to happen.

'What would you say if it was your best friend going through this?' I ask, not knowing what I'd say to my best friend as I don't have one. 'What advice would you give her?'

Leanne sighs. Her face looks like a child's does when they don't get what they want; her bottom lip sticks out, her frown is exaggerated. The pain inside her fighting to get out. We're still at the back of the long line of mums and buggies so no one sees. I suspect she isn't the only one crying here today anyway.

'I'd tell her that it wasn't her fault. That accidents happen. All the old clichés, you know? I'd tell her to be a bit kinder to herself. To let some of the guilt go.'

Those words feel familiar, but instead of falling into another flashback I can't fully reach, I force myself to remain in the present. 'I think that sounds like excellent advice.'

'My psychologist said the same thing. She also told me to write a journal, to my daughter. But I've not been able to start it yet, every time I do I cry and cry.'

'Maybe that's not such a bad thing. It's good to let emotions out.'

'Gives me a headache,' she says and tries out the laugh for the second time.

My phone vibrates in my pocket again and I hold it tight in my hand. What if Anya is the one calling? I can't bear the thought of her call going unanswered.

'You seem distracted today,' Leanne says.

'I'm sorry. My daughter left for university recently and I've not been myself.' I wouldn't normally divulge such personal information, but Leanne deserves the truth.

'Oh.' Her expression darkens.

'I know, I know, I should be thrilled she's having the time of her life. But I'm finding her leaving really hard, I'm not sure why.'

'Emily always said she wanted to be a doctor. I'm angry she didn't get the chance to follow her dreams like your daughter.' Her lip curls. Looks like maybe honesty wasn't the best policy on this occasion.

'I'm sorry.'

Leanne shakes her head. 'No, I'm sorry, I shouldn't be

taking my grief out on you, I hate it when people moan about things I'm not going to get to experience.'

I feel scolded. My phone vibrates again and this time I pull it out and look at the screen. Anya.

'Is that her?'

'Yes.'

'Answer. It's okay, really.'

'Thank you.' I'm already swiping right. I hold the phone up to my ear, still alongside Leanne. I can't leave her on this buggy walk alone.

'Anya, hey how are you?'

She coughs on the other end of the line. I haven't heard my daughter's voice for over a week, I haven't heard her cough like this for years. It's a poor connection.

'Anya?'

'Hi, Mum,' she croaks. 'How ... you?'

'I'm fine, darling. Are you?' Have you taken your inhaler? I want to ask: When did you last eat some fruit or vegetables? Have you drunk enough water today? Slept?

'I'm all right.' She coughs again, then says something I can't understand.

'You keep cutting out, I can't hear you.'

'Hang on.' A shuffling sound fills my ear and I imagine her moving closer to the window. Another cough down the line.

'That better?'

'Yes, that's better. Were you coughing then?'

'Nah I'm fine, just a tickle. Not gonna lie, this place is sick.'

And so are you, I think.

'Have you–'

'Yes, I have been using my inhaler,' she interrupts. 'It's only a cough, don't stress.'

'I'm not stressed.'

Leanne stops to put her baby's dummy back in his mouth.

He looks as though he is about to burst into a full-on screaming mode.

'Shall I come up? Take you out for lunch?' Make sure you have at least one good meal. Some water.

'No. I'm fine. Basically, I phoned for a chat, that's all. Don't start.'

I bite my tongue. 'Okay. Look, sweetheart, I'm actually at work right now.' And I can't concentrate on you fully, I want to add, and I need to. 'Can I call you back in a bit?'

'Yeah, cool.'

Hanging up I look at Leanne. Tears stream down her face. Her baby whimpers in his buggy. 'Leanne, do you want to go home?' I ask.

She nods and we tail off from the rest of the group. Our cars are parked in different directions and I say goodbye to her at the pedestrian crossing, a heavy feeling weighing me down.

As she walks off, her shoulders judder. I'm ashamed that I can't give her the attention she craves today.

But I'm glad she wanted to go home because I need to call Anya back. Actually, I think I need to see for myself that she's okay.

Getting in my car I call her over the handsfree Bluetooth. And instead of heading for home, I drive to her halls of residence.

22

CATHERINE

THURSDAY 3RD OCTOBER

The sun is setting and my back aches. I rub my shoulders and stretch the muscles in my neck. The need for a toilet is acute, but Anya has not come out of her university halls since I've been here and I can't leave yet.

When I'd spoken to her in the car as I drove here earlier, she'd said she was going out tonight to somewhere in town. But I wasn't reassured. Intrusive thoughts had battered my mind. And at this moment I feel as though I am trying to solve a riddle in order to unlock the cage I am trapped in. The endless cycle of checking the tracking app to see where Anya is and then panicking when her blue dot doesn't move or panicking when it does is exhausting. And today my obsession encroached on my job and I was unprofessional. I have to make the pattern stop.

I'm parked outside the back of the student village, beside the small shop I know Anya visits at least once a day. Thick black railings edge her accommodation, and a few students stumble out and wander off in the direction of the town centre. Anya is not one of them.

Her bedroom window, ahead of me on the second floor, is closed. The light is off and there isn't even so much as a shadow inside. She must be in the kitchen having pre-drinks. She told me her housemates and her do this most days whether they go out or not.

The darkness wraps around me like a blanket, but then a street light comes on, encircling my car in a spotlight. If she does come out of this gate she'll see my car. And I dread to think the response that would provoke.

I move the car further away and come back on foot, hiding behind a bush next to the nearby shop. The bright lights from inside spill out onto the pavement and highlight a couple of stubbed out cigarette butts. No one other than the person behind the till is in there.

Laughter returns my attention to the black iron railings. A group of students push through the gate in hysterics. Several boys in baggy T-shirts and tight jeans stagger behind them, some with long hair, some short. One of them smokes what looks like a joint, but is probably a roll-up.

And then there she is.

My daughter.

Her dark wavy hair is tied up in a messy bun and she's wearing a black crop top with a grey skirt and trainers. Over her shoulder is a small bag, enough room for a phone, a credit card and a packet of cigarettes, I think. Not an inhaler as well.

She holds on to the arm of one of the boys and I recognise him as Jamie, the boy I met on her first day. They stop and embrace and he bends down to kiss her. She tilts her head back, reaches up to join her hands behind his neck and allows his tongue to probe her mouth. My breath feels as though it's been knocked out of me.

The rest of the group pile in and wrap their arms around them before they fall apart in hysterics again. Sadness envelops me. I can't remember the last time I laughed with such carefree abandon.

In fact, I can't ever remember laughing like that.

Peaking out from the side of the bush I inspect Anya. The light is dim. She looks a little pale, unless the glow of the distant street light is draining her skin of its colour. There's no sign of the cough I heard on the phone and I breathe a sigh of relief.

She's alive. And she's happy.

'Wait!' she calls. 'I need some fags.'

Shit.

I hold my breath as she looks to cross the road. She's walking towards the little shop.

Shit. Shit. Shit.

Looking around I have one option. Squeezing myself between the hedge and the shop I pray there's no CCTV. The last thing I need is the owner coming out and asking me what the hell I'm playing at.

Anya's body spray wafts in the air around me after she dashes inside. The smell makes me want to rush in there and hold her and sod the consequences. But my feet won't move. Closing my eyes I breathe her in, the scent of her teenage years very different to those of her younger days when she mostly smelt of chocolate or suntan lotion. Before the first hints of body odour and puberty hit.

She steps out of the shop and runs over the road, back to her friends.

Lowering my gaze to the ground I'm ashamed of myself. I don't know why I can't rationalise my fears.

The sounds of Anya and her friends fade as they skip off into town and I'm left in the dark with a deep emptiness inside me. There's no need to follow her into town. I've seen all I need to see without fully understanding why I needed to see it.

Making my way back to my car I sigh and wonder if this is happening because I haven't grieved for my mother and am focusing on Anya instead.

Fiona might hold the answers but I'm not due another session with her for a month or so. And the doctor had been no help. Working for a mental health charity I know all of the people I can call to have some therapy, but I don't know what I need therapy for. Grief? Childhood issues? Or are my problems more complex than that? I'm pretty sure they're interlinked and entwined like ivy wrapping around a tree trunk and taking hold so it becomes part of the tree, part of me.

At the moment I have too many questions and no answers.

The drive back passes in a blur. All I want is my bed even though I know when I'm under my duvet sleep will be hard to find. I'm having less sleep now than when Anya was a newborn.

The house is dark when I arrive home, and is cold when I walk in. Some post sits on the doormat, but I walk over the envelopes and fliers and head straight up to bed.

The curtains to my bedroom are open as they always are. My mother kept them closed when I was a child. My bedroom overlooked the woodland behind our house and she said she was keeping the witches out.

They'd been closed during the day too and so as soon as I'd left home I'd vowed to always keep my curtains open, to banish the remnants of her fear-inducing tales. There are no such things as witches, I'd tell myself as I lay in bed, those first few nights full of terror without her there.

There are no such things as witches. The woods are safe. There are no such things as witches. The woods are safe.

Over and over again, every night, I would whisper these words until the panic subsided and I slept. And to this day I believe them. The swaying of the branches on the ceiling calms me and soothes me into, if not sleep, a calmer state.

With a shudder I think back to those nights as a child, where my mother would tell me about Hansel and Gretel, or Little Red Riding Hood and make me promise, night after night, that I'd never go into the woods.

'I won't go!' I used to scream at her.

'You promise!' she'd shout back.

'I promise. I promise I won't go. I won't.'

But then, one night she'd left my room straight after my bedtime story and had forgotten to make me promise. I didn't call after her. Instead, I'd snuck out of bed and looked behind the curtain at the sprawling woodland beyond our back garden.

The moonlight had shone and made the trees look full of magic. I'd imagined fairies dancing at the base of the tree trunks, their little fairy doors open, bright lights twinkling around them. I pictured Moon Face and Silky. I daren't let my mother know I'd borrowed *The Magic Faraway Tree* books from school. She'd said they were too scary for me, but they weren't scary at all.

The Enchanted Wood was full of wonder. I wanted to delve deep into them and find the Faraway Tree. Climb the branches and venture into every single world hovering above the hole in the cloud.

That night I'd sat on my windowsill for hours watching the trees sway. Shadows danced on the grass in our garden, willing me to join them. My mother was asleep, she went straight to bed every night after reading me a story. She wouldn't hear me, or come and fetch me back to bed. I could sneak out and go deep into the woods to find fairies and magic.

I'd put on my warmest jumper and socks and opened my bedroom door as quietly as I could. The soft sound of my mother's snoring seeped from under her bedroom door. The fact that I was breaking the rules didn't cross my mind. I hadn't promised anything that night. My mother had made the woodland so forbidden I wanted to go in there even more.

The back door was locked, but I knew where she kept the key. I stood on a kitchen chair and reached up on to the top of the fridge. Giggles burst from my mouth as the excitement I was feeling escaped. I put my hand over my mouth to trap the laughter in. My stomach gurgled as if I'd swallowed the giggles and I wondered if I should pack a snack. No, not this time. I wouldn't go too far in, only a little way to have a look. The next time my mother forgot to make me promise, I'd be more prepared.

A slap of cold air blew the hair from my face and I shivered on the back doorstep. I'd never left the house alone before. My hand was always in my mother's, sometimes held by hers so tight my skin hurt. That night, I'd held my own hands in front of my chest and crept into the garden. The shadows of the trees looked like fingers beckoning me forwards. A smell of smoke in the air tickled my nose. I didn't like it.

Walking towards the gate at the bottom of the garden that led to the woodland made the world get darker. A new smell appeared, like a wet towel, or dirty dishcloth. The wind blew around me and I wrapped my hands around my body in a hug. I was too cold. This wasn't fun.

And then I heard her scream from inside the house. My mother.

As fast as I could I ran back into the kitchen and shut the door, putting the key into my pocket as she raced in.

'Where have you been?' she shouted. 'Tell me, where have you been?' She looked at the back door and then to me. 'Why are your cheeks so flushed?' She touched my forehead. 'You're freezing. Have you been outside? Have you?'

I stayed silent; my internal voice begged her not to check if the back door was locked.

Without waiting for me to speak she went to the back door, and opened it with no effort. Her shoulders slumped and she paused for a second before turning to face me. She licked her lips and for a minute I wondered if she was a wolf in my mother's skin about to eat me.

With my heart in my throat I took the key out of my pocket and held it out to her. Her eyes widened and she snatched the key from my hand. Her cheeks were wet.

'You broke our promise, didn't you?' she hissed at me and I wanted to shout that she didn't make me promise today.

But I didn't get the chance.

She grabbed my arm and dragged me back to my bedroom. Then she threw me onto the bed and stood looming in my doorway. She was swollen with anger; bloated like a body left in the sea for too long.

Without exhaling she turned and locked the door.

And I didn't leave my bedroom for days.

23

ANYA

You think I didn't see you, don't you, but I did. I saw your car from my bedroom window before you parked somewhere else. Fuck, I even saw you hiding between the shop and the bush. I let Jamie stick his tongue in as far as he could because I knew you were there, even though he'd had garlic bread for tea and his breath stunk.

Were you here spying on me because I was coughing when I called you yesterday because if that is the reason then you are fucking ridiculous. The coughing was because I was having a fag and didn't want you to know. So each time I exhaled, I coughed to cover the sound up. I forgot you caught me smoking when you followed me into Bristol, so you already know about one of my dirty little habits.

Your worrying is making me paranoid too, you know, and now I think about it, maybe my cough is a bit worse than usual, a bit more wheezy or phlegmy, and I've had to take my inhaler more often too, but not much. No, it's not that bad. I'm tired, that's all, and smoking more than normal. I'm fine. See what you're doing to me?

Did you tense when I came over to buy some fags? I hope

so. For a second there was an urge deep inside of me, like I was one of those bears chained and desperate to escape, to confront you, but then I changed my mind. Exposing you would've been stupid. I need these new friends. I need them to think I am cool and calm and collected and don't have a weirdo mum. That kind of shit can do damage, you know?

You didn't follow us into town. I kept looking back to check and even though I thought I saw you a couple of times I was glad when the shadow in the distance was a young man, or a new mum with her baby in a sling.

You're fucking annoying me, Mum, and maybe next time, fuck I hope there isn't a next time, but if there is I won't hesitate to call you out. Because what you need to know is that *of course* I'd reach out to you for help if I was in trouble. Not gonna lie, if I'm in trouble, real trouble, then I promise, hand on heart, swear to die promise, that *you* will be the person I ring.

But until then, for the love of fuck, I need you to leave. Me. Alone.

Please.

24

CATHERINE

SATURDAY 12TH OCTOBER

The bar is noisy and stuffy and I have no idea why I agreed to come to the work end-of-summer 'do'. The charity always has a night out at some point in autumn, but I've never gone. The excuses have been easy in the past: my mother needed me, my daughter was unwell. But this year, with my life the way it is, I figure I have nothing to lose. Do something every day that scares you and all that bollocks.

My eyes sting, objecting to the vast amounts of glitter I slathered over them earlier. I keep wiping away globs of eyeliner from the inner corners of my sockets.

'You scrub up well,' Sarah said when I'd arrived. I'd taken it as a compliment.

Wriggling, I pull at the centre of my push-up bra where it digs into my upper stomach, a centimetre or two above where my hold-it-all-in pants end. They'd been in my cupboard, unused, since the Christmas party. Holding everything in is making me want to fart. Adjusting my bra again I can feel myself glistening with sweat.

'So, how is life without Anya?' a colleague, Penny, asks with an expectant look on her face, which I interpret as her wanting me to say I've been having one-night stands every night since she left.

'Quiet,' I answer, and her stance changes. I've bored her, but she doesn't know how to end the conversation so soon after its started.

'Some guy did try to pull me the other night,' I add, and she perks up like a dog being offered a treat, tongue hanging out and reaching for the straw sticking from her drink.

'Ooo, tell me more.' She takes a sip and leans in. 'Was he fit?'

'Totally, fit as,' I say and cringe. This isn't me. 'About my age, never found out his name.'

'Any snogging action?' She winks at me.

Penny is a lot younger than I am, but I'm not sure people her age call it *snogging* and then I get that she's speaking in a language she thinks I'll understand.

'Yep. Lots. All the tonguing.' Oh God.

'Sweet.'

Small talk has always been painful for me. Every word tonight is an effort. Emptying my glass of wine I ask her if she'd like another drink.

'Sex on the Beach, please,' she says and winks again.

Sex, no thanks, I think, and wonder if this is where I'm going wrong.

The barman raises an eyebrow at me when I order.

'It's not for me.' I force a smile. 'Mine's a large glass of dry white wine, please.'

'Ah,' he says, as though everything makes sense. Maybe everyone but me knows that once you're past forty 'sex on the beach' is no longer available to you in any shape or form.

Music pumps out from loudspeakers in each corner of the bar. Several people move their feet or jiggle in time to the beat.

My father would be tapping his fingers if he were here, playing a melody in his head along with the rhythm.

'Eleven seventy-five,' the barman says and I gasp. 'It's the cocktail.' He shrugs. 'They ain't cheap.'

I make a mental note not to offer anyone else a drink this evening.

'Thanks.' Penny grins as I hand her the orangey pink drink that looks full of sugar and not much booze. 'OMG, I love this song.' She sticks her hand in the air and shimmies onto the dance floor.

I want to go home. The wine isn't numbing me. Instead, I fizz as though bubbles are tightly packed inside me and popping one by one. My phone burns a hole in my handbag, calling me to have a look and see where Anya is. I've deleted the app and then reinstalled it three times already today. Without hesitating, I pull my phone from my bag and delete the app again, then I down the rest of my glass of wine and order another.

'Hi.' Fiona is stood beside me. She looks at me with a mixture of concern and pity. 'You're not enjoying this, are you?'

'You know me well, Fiona,' I say and pay the barman. 'But being here beats being alone in an empty house.'

'I hear you.' She orders her own drink, a double gin and tonic, and then indicates towards an empty table where we could sit.

'I was thinking about you the other day,' she starts. 'And how you're feeling now Anya has left.'

'And?' If Fiona's discovered some psychological reason as to why I am feeling the way I am then I'm all ears, even if discussing my issues on a night out is a tad unprofessional.

'I've been doing some research for the charity into the effects of epigenetics. About mothers and trauma.'

'Yes,' I say, it's hard to hear her over the music. I lean in closer. 'We did some training on it last year.'

For a second I'm taken out of the bar and I wonder if a traumatic event happened to my mother. Then the thud of the music brings me back.

'Your grandmother died young, is that right?'

'Yes, when I was five.'

I never knew either of my grandmothers. I have vague recollections of the smell of talcum powder and curly grey hair, wet kisses on my cheek and tears, but they'd both died by the time I was six.

'It's only a theory, but you can also inherit trauma through behaviours. Maybe your mum didn't cope with her death, and if that's the case then you may have inherited some of her unresolved grief, which is why you're struggling with Anya leaving home so much. You are feeling your mother's grief as well as your own.'

This makes sense.

'Anyway,' Fiona continues, 'not a topic to discuss in depth now, but I'm going to look into it and research some more.'

I'm glad she's ending the conversation, it doesn't feel right discussing this kind of stuff here. We should be in her office.

'If I find out anything else interesting I'll let you know.'

'Please do,' I say, and mean it.

'Oh and I've got the number of an amazing grief counsellor I was going to give to you for that mum.'

'Thanks, that would be great. She's really struggling.' A sense of unease washes over me as I remember my last, awful meeting with Leanne. We haven't spoken since.

'Right, enough shop talk,' Fiona says. 'I've signed up to Tinder so help me God, and I need a partner in crime, you up for it?'

Resisting the urge to make retching sounds I shake my head. Then I wave my hands around as though flapping away a wasp. 'No. Hell, no.'

'Oh go on, it'll be fun. Look...' She gets her phone out of her bag and opens the app. 'It'll show us if there are any available men nearby.' She starts swiping with a grimace on her face, which makes me even less inclined to join her.

The truth is I have no desire to be with a man. No urge to be dependent on another and have another dependent on me. Men don't like women with baggage and I'm carrying enough to move to Australia. Why everyone thinks I need sex I don't know. I'm perfectly capable of amusing myself without a man. Less messy on all counts.

'Yes there are some idiots on here.' Fiona chuckles. 'But some serve a purpose, if you know what I mean.' She winks at me and I recoil. What's with everyone winking tonight? Social Fiona is very different to work Fiona, I think. 'Look at this one.' She hands me her phone. 'Now he's hot.'

My mind whirs with what she's told me about my possible inherited grief and I can't focus on whether I find a photo of some random man attractive or not. What if I'd passed on any learnt behaviours to Anya? Will the cycle ever end? When I'd been pregnant with her I'd wished for a son so there would be no danger of me turning into my mother and damaging a daughter instead of nurturing her.

'Fiona, seriously. I thought Tinder was for young people.'

'Oi, what are you saying? I'm not old. There are loads of blokes on here my age.'

'Sorry, of course you're not. It just seems a weird way to meet people to me.' I think back to the man at the bar the other day. That was how to meet people, I used to think, when fate pushed them into your path. Not that our meeting had been destined to go any further.

'Right, he's messaged me. He's round the corner, I'm off.' She finishes her drink and gets up, adjusting her skirt and smoothing her hair. 'Say goodbye to everyone for me. Tell them I had a family emergency.'

'Okay. Have fun.'

She skips towards the door and I don't know how she does it. My legs haven't been shaved for at least three weeks and as for the state of what's in my knickers, there are probably cobwebs down there.

I clutch my chest and have a vision of my mother's hands doing the same, reaching for her necklace; her stress patterns alive and well inside me. What else did I do subconsciously that was hers? What else had she handed down?

Without making Fiona's excuses, or mine, I sneak off home, confident that no one will notice or miss me. They are dancing and already very, very drunk.

Back at home I sit on my bed and stare out of the window at the trees in the distance. I feel like a saucepan of water threatening to boil. Emotions and thoughts have stirred inside me even further this evening. I am hot and flustered.

After what Fiona told me I'm wondering if the emotions and feelings I have supressed over my life are coming to the surface. And maybe I have no choice but to face them. Many of my early childhood experiences, most of which I don't remember or understand, are being forced to the forefront of my mind whether I like it or not.

The trees sway and whisper to each other. Even under the canopy there is a clearing, light where all else is dark. Exposure where shelter is gone.

The tracking app, reinstalled as soon as I got home, shows me that Anya is out again, this time in the middle of town. The blue circle out of which her profile picture comes, hovers above the pub I tracked her to after I saw her the other night. Down by the river. I'm surprised she likes going there given her fear of water, but maybe peer pressure is sweeping her along and making her forget about her anxieties.

If only I'd allowed tonight's work do to have the same effect on me.

Closing my eyes I take some deep breaths and pray I'm able to sleep before I'm inevitably jolted awake.

'Please let her be home and safe by then,' I whisper. 'Please, please let her be safe.'

25

CATHERINE

SUNDAY 13TH OCTOBER

The dust in my mother's loft is not as bad as I was expecting and there's no sign of the rats. This whole process is taking far longer than I'd anticipated. But Dave is happy for me to come up here while his team still work through the rest of the house. I think he is pleased that I am showing some interest; I get the impression he finds relatives who don't appear to care hard to understand.

I pause at the top of the loft hatch and realise I'm not sure what I am looking for. Fiona's words last night had stuck with me and I'd woken determined to find evidence of how my mother had dealt with my grandmother's death as well as uncovering any possible trauma I'd suffered as a child that I can't remember. I'd looked through the notebook again before I'd left, but it was more of the same rambling nonsense and for some reason I'd felt compelled to be here.

Boxes cover the floor. I look in some and find my old clothes, corduroy trousers, a couple of yellowing Babygros. And then, as I explore some more, I discover paintings behind the boxes and under a dusty sheet; acrylic landscapes of woodlands and bluebells. My breath catches in my throat as I pull one out.

The picture is of a clearing by a stream, a white butterfly in the forefront – its wings wide and open – heading towards the sunlight filtering through the branches above. The water in the stream glistens over the grey and black rocks below. Flowers blanket the grassy bank; pinks and yellows swim together to make orange and peach tones. In the right-hand corner there is a squiggle of a signature. My mother's initials.

My mother was an artist. And I didn't know. Why these beautiful works of art are hidden here in the dark and gloom of the attic I don't know either. At no point in my life do I remember my mother ever picking up a paintbrush. And for me anything creative was reserved for nursery and school only. My GCSE teacher had said I'd had a natural talent, but art brought me no joy, even when I'd produced work I'd been proud of. And after my exam I hadn't painted or drawn again.

Delving deeper under the dustsheets reveals several more woodland canvases, capturing the trees in different seasons or at different times of the day. Rain-splashed scenes stand next to ones containing the first signs of spring, filled with white wild garlic and purple bluebells. In order to paint these with such detail my mother must have spent a lot of time in woodland, yet she'd claimed to hate them.

'Need a hand up here, love?' One of the removal men's heads appears at the top of the ladder and I don't know how to answer. I can't let these paintings go to a charity shop and yet I have no space for them at home.

'How long until you'll get around to the attic do you think?' I ask and he scratches his head and shrugs.

'Few days yet I reckon. The rats have gone, but there's still a fair amount in the bedrooms. We've found a box of old children's clothes and toys if you want to take a look, might bring back some memories, you know?'

'Oh, okay.' I'm not sure how to feel. For my own sanity I

wonder if I should stop delving. Then the undiscovered memories and trauma can be laid to rest alongside my mother. Curiosity gets the better of me and I climb down the ladder and head towards my bedroom.

But he stops me.

'They're not in there, love. In here.' He points to my mother's bedroom and a chill slides down my spine. I was never allowed in my mother's bedroom. Not even in an emergency. I remember one night when I was about seven, I had woken up and been sick all over my bed. My stomach had cramped and I was clammy. Scared, I'd crawled along the hallway to my mother's bedroom. But I couldn't go in. I knew I would be told off for disturbing her sleep.

Instead, I'd sat outside her bedroom door for hours, in and out of consciousness, shivering with a temperature and sweating. After several painful hours, the morning light had filtered through the curtains of the landing window and from under the crack at the bottom of her door. My mouth was dry and my tongue stuck to my teeth.

She groaned when she opened the door and saw me lying at her feet. Her hand had reached out and touched my forehead and I'd then been plonked into a cold bath and scrubbed clean from head to toe before being placed back in my bed and left alone.

'You need to sleep to get better.' She'd clutched her necklace. Her breathing came in bursts.

Later that evening tomato soup had been left on a tray outside my bedroom door with dry toast. I'd eaten the warm red liquid before throwing it back up and straight into the bowl.

I thought I'd heard my mother sobbing at the top of the stairs when she'd come up to collect the tray, but I couldn't be sure. She'd always made me feel guilty for being unwell, like illness was a thing to be ashamed of. But maybe she'd been frightened. Fear consumes me whenever Anya has an asthma attack, but I never leave her alone, no matter how hard watching her struggle is.

Most of the furniture from my mother's bedroom has been removed.

'Her mattress was beyond saving,' Dave says. 'And the bedframe was falling apart too so we've chucked it, but the chest of drawers might be good for someone to upcycle.'

I step into my mother's bedroom. A chill settles on the back of my neck as though she is here, watching me. Her floral perfume tinged with cigarette smoke hangs in the air, mingled with dust.

On the floor under the bay window is a pile of children's clothing and I go over and pick through it. I find small dungarees and stripy T-shirts I don't remember wearing, with some knitted yellow cardigans.

'Thanks,' I say, and without needing to be asked he leaves the room.

The box of toys is full of treasures I know aren't mine. As a child my toys were scarce, and mostly made from plastic, none of which are here. These toys are immaculate. A painted tea set encased in a beautiful leather case has been carefully packed away next to wooden jigsaw puzzles and some more dolls with the freaky eyes that blink without you touching them.

A feeling of sadness creeps over me. Maybe these were my mother's toys and for some reason she'd felt compelled to keep them, yet not hand them down to either Anya or me.

Walking out of her room I pause at the top of the stairs as I had done so many times as a child. Wanting to call down after a nightmare, knowing that if I did my cries would be met with anger, not comfort.

'Can you keep the paintings in the attic for me?' I ask, meeting Dave at the bottom of the stairs.

'Course, love. You keeping any of the toys? The grandkids might like them someday instead of this plastic tat we have nowadays.'

I smile at the thought of Anya having children.

'No, you take them for your future grandchildren if you like.' I wonder how often he gets to keep stuff he likes from the houses he clears out. Not a bad job after all.

'You sure? My daughter's expecting in December actually.'

'Of course. I'd like to think of them going to a good home.'

'Smashing, thank you.'

I hope my mother would approve, although I suspect she wouldn't. She may not have let me play with these toys, but there's nothing she can do about me giving them to a new family who will treasure them. A dark cloud swallows the sun and for a second the hallway and stairs are blanketed in shadows.

'Right, better crack on,' Dave says and we slide past each other as the sunlight reappears.

For some reason I salute him as though he is a solitary magpie. 'Speak soon.'

And as I always do these days, I stand on the driveway and look at the house. The paintings are another piece of a jigsaw puzzle I didn't ask to solve. And with no guidance the picture is unclear.

My mother's home stands in front of me, unassuming, holding secrets behind the ripped wallpaper and within the tight weave of the carpets, trapped between the crumbling floorboards and Artex ceilings. Suffocated by the dust.

Secrets I don't think I want to uncover.

26

DAPHNE

My hand rested on my lower abdomen, creating heat and warmth. The baby within me was safe, but we were no longer connected. With so many days, weeks, and months still to go there was no need to bond now. Then, if the birthing room wasn't filled with the fresh energy new life brought with its first breath, the loss wouldn't be deep, as I'd never allowed myself to love that life in the first place.

I fell asleep, and now she'd die.

Although the doctors told me she was already gone. Under too long. Suffocated by the water from the stream filling her lungs, breaking them. There was no cure, no mending, no hope.

My fault.

Her father had already said goodbye. He demanded I wasn't in the room when he did so. He hadn't shouted at me to release the anger holding him in a powerful grip. He'd remained mute.

The ventilator beeped over and over. Her chest rose and fell on demand as air was forced in and sucked out.

I couldn't let the doctors switch the machine off. I didn't want to go home and bury my face in her clothes, her bedding, her scent. And not her.

Numbness enveloped me and I floated above my body. Why didn't I cry? Or scream? The woman I saw below was an empty shell, even though new life grew inside her. Her painful emotions were locked in a box with the key thrown away.

As I leant against the hospital bed, my head beside her hand in mine, I decided that getting close to another soul was not an option. From this day forward there would be a wall between myself and everyone else.

Including the unborn baby inside me.

That wall would be the thickest of them all.

27

CATHERINE

MONDAY 14TH OCTOBER

Dad's nursing home car park is full today. Some God-awful oversized car is in my usual space, which means I've had to park further away. Silly to get bothered by such a simple thing, but at the moment the little things bother me more and more, as though my tolerance moved out with Anya.

On arrival it is obvious that my father isn't having a good day. He's agitated and wringing his blanket through his fingers revealing his thin frail legs underneath.

'Can I get you a cup of tea?' I ask. Tea usually calms him when he is having a day like this, although not always.

'Where is she? Have you heard from her? Why aren't they home yet?'

Reaching out to hold his hand I sit down in the chair next to his bed, which always faces the window. He lets go of the wrung blanket and takes my hand.

'Who are you talking about?' I ask.

'Catherine. Have they found her yet?'

'Dad.' I look him in the eyes. 'I'm Catherine. I'm here.'

'Yes, you do look like her, dear. But she's gone missing you see, and her mother is beside herself with worry.' His juddering hands release mine and he twists the blanket once more. 'She can't find her. You know, you really do look like her. Your eyes, they are the same.'

My stomach aches when my father is like this.

'Dad,' I say, although calling him that often muddles him further. 'I am Catherine. I am here. Everything is okay.'

'No!' he shouts. 'Please find her.' He rocks in his chair and grips the blanket with his fingers, which are as twisted and frail as the material he manipulates with them.

Unable to handle this by myself I go to get a nurse. They often give him medicine to calm him when he is like this, but he grabs my arm with surprising strength.

'Your mother deserves this,' he says, spittle on his lips. 'She did wrong. Not you. She drove you away.' He lets go and shakes his head, tears trailing across his face. 'Oh, Catherine.'

'Dad. I'm going to get a nurse. I'll be back, I promise.'

In the corridor, I stand against the wall, shaking. I can't catch my breath and I pull at the scarf around my neck, a present from Anya last Mother's Day. I hold it to my face and bury my head into the soft material. My skin is thin, as though several layers have been stripped away by grief. Scratch the surface or nip my skin and I am on edge. Strangled by emotion.

'Are you okay?' A warm voice makes its way through the scarf and the sobs. I shake my head, unable to speak.

'Come with me, I'll make us a cuppa.' She guides me towards the lounge where some of the residents spend their days. In an array of chairs sit women and men all of whom time has not been kind to. I wonder what secrets their pasts hold. Are they, like me, harbouring an all-consuming grief for a part of their past they don't understand? Or are they too ill to remember what their names are let alone what happened to them thirty years ago?

'There you are.' The care worker hands me a cup of milky

tea. I glance at her name badge. Heather. A coincidence after all. 'I added a couple of sugars,' she says. 'Always good for when you're upset, I think.'

We sit in silence for a bit and guilt for not telling her how distressed my father is bites me. Someone will have checked on him by now, I am sure. He is never left alone for long.

'Are you okay?' she asks again.

I sniff and nod.

She smiles. 'I sometimes sit with your father. He talks about you a lot.'

'Oh that is kind of you, thank you.' I am not going to ask what they talk about. 'Is he having a bad day? He wasn't himself when I last saw him. Troubled.'

Right then and there I know I'm going to tell this perfect stranger about what's been happening to me and I can't explain why.

'I think his mood and confusion today is my fault,' I say. 'Every time I see him at the moment I unnerve him.'

'Oh come now, I'm sure that's not true.'

'Oh, but it is.' I breathe in and out slowly, attempting to calm the panic. 'My mother died not long ago and I've been trying to tell him, but it's as if he senses it anyway, but doesn't understand.'

'Go on.'

Sighing, I hold the scarf to my chest and rest my chin on the bulk as I breathe out.

'And my daughter, my only child, left for university in September. She used to come and visit him with me. He keeps asking about someone who's gone missing. Sometimes I wonder if he's talking about her.'

'Having children leave home is hard, it's normal for it to take time to adjust.'

'I know. But, you see, I feel like it's more than that. This might sound stupid, but my reaction to her going has been overwhelming. Somehow I feel as though I've lost a child, or at least the grief of her going is what I imagine that to be like. I've been tracking her too. God, that makes me sound awful, doesn't it? But I have this intense need to check she's alive every minute of every day. I know I sound crazy, but I believe that if I don't check on her, if I don't do everything I can to keep her safe, then, then she'll die.'

One of the old ladies in a chair on the opposite side of the room stands up and claps three times before sitting back down. Does she want to snap me out of this? But I can't stop, the words come out of my mouth and I can't control them.

'I think she's in danger all of the time, and no one believes me.'

'I believe you,' Heather says.

Feeling understood for the first time in months I look at her. 'You do?'

'Yes.'

'I'm sorry. I don't know why I am telling you any of this.'

'It's okay. I'm here to listen.'

'But to the people who live here, not me.'

'I'm here for everyone.'

'I should check he's okay.' I go to get up but she holds out a hand and directs me to stay where I am.

'I told another nurse what had happened when I got your tea and they are with him. He's okay. Go on.' Her face is soft and encouraging, and she smells of lavender, which calms me. It's as though I'm in a confession box in church and everything I say will be kept a secret.

The lady opposite stands up again, but doesn't clap this time. The deep gnawing in my stomach has subsided. The relief at talking to a stranger removing the extra blanket of anxiety I've been wearing.

'Have you grieved for your mum?' she asks, and I'm confused. How can you grieve for someone you don't miss? She offered little comfort and so I learnt to comfort myself. The one time I lowered the barrier was when I met Anya's dad, and look how that turned out. Maybe it isn't my mother I'm grieving for, but a release from years of pent-up resentment and hurt.

'We didn't have a great relationship. Maybe I don't know how to grieve for her. I didn't cry when they told me she'd passed away. I didn't even cry at the funeral.'

We sit in silence for a few minutes and I sip at my tea, which is lukewarm.

'Have you thought that maybe your sadness at your daughter going to university is probably linked to your mother's death. A bit like you've projected those emotions so this is why your daughter going feels so visceral. You have lost before; you've lost your mother. Your feelings are valid.' She reaches out and squeezes my hand.

'Thank you. I thought I was going crazy.' Of course. I'm grieving for my mother. The doctor. Fiona. Everyone is right.

'Our minds are very powerful; they often try to protect us from painful emotions and memories. It doesn't always work though.' Heather looks at the floor and I wonder what her mind has tried to protect her from.

A sudden chill enters the room as though a window has been opened.

'Right,' she says. 'I ought to get back to work. Are you feeling better?'

'Yes, thank you for listening.'

I pick at fluff on my skirt in an attempt to rid myself of the shame I feel in having told a stranger about tracking Anya.

The residents of the home sat in this room with me are silent and for a minute my life flashes before my eyes. I imagine myself as one of them, mute and trapped inside my failing body. Would Anya come and visit me? There is no one else.

For a second I consider driving to the bar where the man in the suit, whose name I don't know, might be. But I won't. After years of shutting out the world a brief glimpse of my future isn't enough to change the habits of a lifetime.

I walk back into my father's room to find him asleep in his bed. Standing over him I watch him breathe. His hands are balled into fists and he is curled up like a small child sitting on their parent's lap. His last good day was so long ago that I'm sure they're gone forever.

'Bye, Dad.' I kiss him on the forehead. He doesn't stir.

Heather is nowhere to be seen as I leave and I contemplate hanging around to thank her again before deciding not to.

Rain lashes down outside the front door of the home and I rush to my car. Once inside I check my phone. There are no new messages or missed calls. I open up the tracking app. Anya's blue circle is at her halls of residence where it's been all day. Anxiety surges in me, starting like a spark in my chest, before flaming across my body.

I could call her and check she's okay, but I don't want her to know how worried I am.

Maybe I'll go home and get drunk instead.

28

CATHERINE

TUESDAY 15TH OCTOBER

My bedroom is smaller, the contents are squashed together and the walls are moving closer. And what's that banging noise? I need to get out, but my hangover has pinned me to my bed. Part of me is desperate to breathe air that blows freely around me instead of the stale fog that hangs in the room, occasionally diffused with a clean gust from the open window, but a bigger part of me feels sick.

I have no meetings today, thank goodness. I cancelled them all, including one with Leanne, which I don't feel great about.

A niggle stirs at the back of my mind, uncomfortable like an ill-fitting bra. Putting the pillow over my head to block out the harsh light of the room, I imagine the water from a shower washing the weight of my darkness as well as cleansing my filthy body. I scrape a nail across the skin on my arm expecting it to fill with dirt, yet when I look there is none. No visible sign of my personal neglect.

'Laziness breeds laziness,' my mother used to say, and she was right. The less I move the more effort it takes when I have to and the more exhausted I feel afterwards. Earlier this morning when I'd ventured to the toilet I'd rubbed the top of my thighs as

I sat there, but the dull ache in them persisted. Then, as the sunlight had started to filter through the window, and my breathing rapid, I'd crawled back into bed and slept for a further three hours.

But I've rested enough now. The unnerving niggle rises in me again and I think back to last night, wondering if I did go to the bar and hunt the suited man down after all, before blacking out. No, I came straight home. I do have a vague memory of sitting on the lounge floor surrounded by photos from the boxes from my mother's house though. But I didn't go out, I am sure of it and yet an uncomfortable feeling still pulls at me, inviting me to remember.

Getting out of bed is a huge effort and my breathing speeds up again. My head pounds and I am grateful for pissed Catherine for having the foresight to put a large glass of water and two paracetamol on my bedside table.

There is a fresh towel, the fluffy white ones you normally find in overpriced hotels, on the chair beside my bed and after downing the water and tablets in several loud gulps I grab it and walk to the bathroom.

The air is cold and I turn the dial on the shower to the hottest setting. Then I face the mirror. Looking back at me is someone I don't recognise. This woman is frowning, and a deep line carves through the centre of her forehead. Her eyes lack any sign of life and she clenches her jaw. Her hair hangs beside her cheekbones that stand out too far making it look like her skin has been stretched behind her ears.

This can't be me. My hair bounces. This woman's hangs limp. I have bright blue eyes and this woman's are grey. Steam from the shower clings to the mirror and slowly fades my reflection until I am a blur.

Removing my clothes I realise I've been wearing them since yesterday, and that's when the memory of me pulling my phone out of my back pocket hits me. I shake the unease away. I didn't speak to anyone last night. Did I?

The hot water stings my skin. The pain is good; I need to be cleansed. I hurt all over as if I am being pierced by millions of needles. My eyes close and my teeth grind together. My skin turns red and I wash my hair and body. Everything smells artificial and I scratch my arms, my shoulders, my neck, my head. I claw at my skin, my nails jagged from being bitten. Small drops of fresh blood mix with bubbles and froth at my feet.

I switch the shower off and wrap my arms around me, burying my face into my left shoulder.

When Anya had been a toddler, whenever I'd switched off the shower, she would hand my towel to me. Ever since she learned to walk she would follow me into the bathroom and sit on the toilet waiting for the water to stop and for my arm to appear around the edge of the shower curtain.

Today I pick up my own towel. Then I walk back to my bed, lie down, and cry.

You're crazy, Mum.

Anya's words come back to haunt me and I sit up.

Oh shit.

I grab my phone from the bedside table and open up the recent call list.

Shit shit shit.

Oh God. I called her. And not only once. The list is here. Ten, fifteen calls to her phone between midnight and four in the morning.

A bubble of nausea forms at the back of my throat and I swallow and pop it.

Leave me alone. You need help.

My chest constricts at the thought of her feeling the same way about me as I did about my mother. I've worked so hard to make sure that didn't happen.

But she does. She hates me. I'm so stupid. I can't even look after myself anymore. I used to get annoyed when people gave that as an excuse for not having children, but after all these years I finally understand what they mean. When you have a child you have to be prepared to give yourself wholly – no ifs, no buts, no compromise – and I'd been a shit mother right from the start. My hand trails across my C-section scar. I'd failed to even get Anya here safely.

The doorbell rings and I dive under the pillow and groan. The only people who ever ring my doorbell are deliverymen, or Anya's dad. And I do not need to see Sean today.

Hoping it is a cold-caller I ignore the ringing and knocking. But the person on my doorstep is persistent and that can mean only one thing.

That the person doing the ringing and knocking is Sean.

Anya must have called him and told him about my drunken phone calls. Shame washes over me like a giant wave in the middle of a storm and reminds me of all the times I'd called Sean after he'd left me, always after I'd drunk too much. I'd cry down the phone for hours. Begging him to list my faults, knowing that phoning him while drunk and looking after Anya was at the top of that list. There'd been a period of time where I'd worried he was going to try to get custody so I'd stopped drinking and deleted his number from my phone. But I couldn't ever delete Anya's number.

The doorbell rings again. He won't stop until I answer. Facing him will be harder than facing Anya. I feel like a child who's been caught stealing penny sweets from the local shop by her father. Sean will make me feel even more ashamed of myself than I already do.

Seriously, don't call me again.

I cringe and get out of bed, pressure in my head causing it to throb.

At least Anya cares enough to send Sean round and not leave me to wallow in my own pity. Unless he's come of his own accord.

Pinching my cheeks to put some colour in them I'm grateful he's arrived after I showered, but when I walk past the mirror to get my dressing gown there's no hiding the fact that I am hungover and exhausted. My blotchy skin has a green tinge, and the dark circles under my eyes look like they've been sketched on with charcoal.

Without saying a word I open the door and step back to let him in, his aftershave paving the way for him. The muscles in his jaw tense and I know he is literally biting his tongue. We walk through to the kitchen.

'Coffee?' I ask and he nods.

We don't speak as the kettle boils. I busy myself with stacking the dishwasher.

'What's going on?' he asks without warning.

With my head in the mug cupboard I clench and unclench my fists and take some deep breaths. How dare he be so direct; so uncaring.

Taking my time, I pour the hot water into mugs, add milk and a sugar to his before placing it in front of him on the breakfast bar. The smell of fresh coffee covers the stench of his aftershave.

'What's going on?' I struggle to keep my voice measured. 'Let me see. My father no longer knows who I am and is constantly in a state of anxiety over the thought that I've gone missing, even though I am right there in the room talking to him.

'My mother is dead and her house is full of all sorts of shit I have no idea what to do with. And I'm pretty sure she had secrets I don't know about and don't know if I want to know or if I want them to remain buried with her. Oh and then Anya, my only child has left home and doesn't ever talk to me anymore. So in short, I'm grieving for three people in three different ways and funnily enough I am a tad overwhelmed by it all.'

A small piece of skin next to my thumbnail comes away as I pick and pick at it until blood seeps out. The fleshy part around my nails is worn down and red. Small scabs ask to be dug at so the blood can ooze and my pain can be soothed. I bite at my short nails, numb.

Sean sighs. I feel like I'm a naughty puppy chewing his shoe and he doesn't know what to do with me.

'The last few months have been really tough for you, I know.'

'No, you don't know, Sean. You're too busy with your new wife and baby. God, my life is such a fricking cliché.'

'Why don't you ever ask me for help?'

Holy fuck, he really doesn't know me. If he did, he would know I never ask anyone for help. Ever.

He carries on. 'It's one of the reasons we split up. You'd never let me in. There was always an edge to you, like you had your very own army of soldiers defending the fort. Hard to love someone like that, you know.' He looks down at his coffee and wipes a drip off the side of the mug. He's never said any of this before. And then he whispers, like a disposal expert tiptoeing around a bomb that might explode if his words are heard. 'You're exactly like your mother.'

'I'm *nothing* like my mother.'

'Then what are you so afraid of?'

'I don't know! That's the problem. I have no idea, but there's this fear inside me. A fear that goes off like a warning siren every time I get too close to someone to try and protect me from any kind of loss. But I've lost you all anyway.'

'Like your mother,' Sean says again, with more projection this time.

'Does Anya hate me?'

He shakes his head. 'No, but she had you on speakerphone before she realised you were drunk, and her friends heard you.'

'Oh God.' I'm going to be sick. I lean over the sink.

'Apparently you were quizzing Jamie, her housemate, about his intentions towards her. You called him a gaslighting arsehole.'

Closing my eyes, I rub my forehead with my fingers. What had made me say that?

'Don't tell me any more.' I put my hand up. 'I don't want to know.'

'She'll be fine, Catherine. She needs a bit of space.'

A voice in my head suggests that if I give Anya space then I'm not doing the right thing. I'm not protecting her. I could give her physical space and still track her. Or I could drive up to the halls again and watch. Like a guardian angel she can't see.

'Okay,' I say. 'You can tell her I won't call her again, but that she can call me anytime she wants to. And tell her I'm sorry. *Really* sorry. And that I'll speak to the counsellor at work again. About everything.'

'You can speak to *me.*'

'No I can't. The counsellor and I have already touched on this so I'd rather talk to her.' He stares at me. 'I will call her as soon as you've gone, I promise.' I'm pushing him away again, but I need him out of my house.

He sighs. 'Okay. You know where I am.' He walks around to my side of the breakfast bar and wraps his arms around me.

For a second I think I'm going to dissolve into tears, but I bite my bottom lip and blink them away. Then I pat him on the back and we pull apart.

'I need to get ready for work,' I lie.

'You might want to put some make-up on.' He smiles at me. 'And some deodorant.'

After he's gone I sink into the sofa under a blanket and let the tears fall until the soft material is sodden.

Then I look at the tracking app. Anya's right where she should be, at her halls of residence. I'm surprised to find she hasn't blocked me and am grateful for her not having done so.

Sleep nips at the corners of my hungover brain, and reassured that she is safe for now, I close my eyes and give in to the nightmare I know awaits.

29

ANYA

You've outdone yourself this time, Mum. Ringing me up fucked out of your head was bloody stupid. You rambled on and on and, even though I told you everyone could hear you, you didn't care and then started talking even louder. Talking utter crap as well. I've never been so embarrassed even that time when you stalked me into the middle of Bristol.

Plus, you're making my asthma worse. This morning I woke up after hardly any sleep because of you and I couldn't breathe. My lungs are infected by your constant worry, like a twisted kind of self-fulfilling prophecy. You're making me ill, do you know that? You. The person who is obsessed with my health and my safety, not me, the teenager who knows how to look after herself and do her inhalers and watch for signs of infection. You taught me to be responsible for all of those things so you didn't have to be anymore. That's how growing up works, Mum, or at least that's how it's supposed to work when it's done right.

I can imagine you at home now as I talk to you in my head, nestled on the sofa full of shame and guilt with your hands wrapped around a mug of tea, your knuckles white where you are gripping it so hard. And are you tracking me right now? I considered blocking you this morning after you made a total twat out of us both last night, but what good would that do? I don't want to be responsible for making you any more bonkers than you already are because that would be really fucking unfair.

Jamie wasn't impressed with you phoning either and at first I didn't give a shit what he thought because he's got a dark side to him I don't really like and so I was glad when I thought you might've made him break up with me, but he didn't, and he's been really supportive all day bringing me cans of Coke and packets of sweets while I watch Netflix on my iPad and try to get rid of my wheezing, and so maybe I'll stay with him after all to spite you.

I miss the days when the fear that has gripped you didn't exist and you were made up of love and normal motherly worries and nothing else. The mum who would sing to me as she combed my hair after a bath, or would let me lick the bowl after making a cake, or agree to travelling first class to London because I'd asked for a whole day where I could be in charge of the decisions for once.

That's the mum I miss. Not the one from last night.

Not her. Not one little bit.

30

CATHERINE
WEDNESDAY 16TH OCTOBER

Signs frame the entrance to the crèche part of the local Children's Centre, but one that always catches my eye is about having courage. The quote, by Maya Angelou, is nestled beneath a multitude of rainbow pictures the children have painted or drawn. I'd love to have been a fly on the wall for that session; to hear what three- and four-year-olds thought having courage meant.

I'm in my forties and I have no idea what it means. People told me I was courageous having Anya by myself. But in my mind that wasn't courage, it was fear. Fear of who I would become if I didn't have her. Fear of God striking me down. Of guilt drowning me for the rest of my life. Of dates coming and going uncelebrated. Of milestones never met. Fear that I'd see the child's face every time I looked at mine. Fear of losing someone I'd never know. Fear of grief beckoning me ever closer, enveloping me and holding me so I couldn't ever break free.

'Morning, Catherine.'

Vicky, the receptionist, has an uplifting sing-song tone to her voice, as though nothing ever gets her down.

'Morning, Vicky,' I say and sign in. I'm here to give a talk to pregnant women about the service the charity I work for offers. The crèche is empty and through a slither of glass in a set of double doors I can see the antenatal group has already started. One of the health visitors holds a baby doll and mimics winding it. I scrunch up my nose, relieved that I don't have to do that part of the talk. No one ever listens, the only thing first-time parents are concerned with is labour; they naively think that's the hard part.

'Can I have a quick word?' Vicky is beside me, a fresh cup of tea held out in front of her for me to take. She always adds two sugars and I have to find a way to throw the overly sweet liquid down the sink without her realising I haven't drunk any. I've been doing this for too long to tell her I don't take sugar.

'Of course, what's up?'

'One of the mums in the group came to me this morning, before it started. I think she might need a referral, but also might need some encouragement to do one.'

'Okay. I can have a chat to her, hang around after the meeting if you like?'

'That would be great. She's on her own, not sure if she has a partner. I think she feels a bit left out.'

Nineteen years ago I'd felt the same. The massage session at my antenatal group had been what tipped me over the edge. Everyone else had loving partners to pretend to soothe their imminent labour pains by rubbing their backs, while I had to contend with the health visitor leading the group massaging me.

Ever since I can remember I've struggled with touch; when people I don't know well grab me for hugs when we are introduced, or others stand too close to me in a queue so I can feel their warm breath on my neck, I want to push them away.

The health visitor's hands had burned my skin even though she'd pressed on my lower back through my clothing. I'd wanted to shrug her off. Shout at her to leave me alone. But hadn't.

Instead, I'd sat there, leaning forward and clutching my handbag on my lap as she'd massaged me. My jaw had ached for a full twenty-four hours afterwards.

'She's also got issues with her mother, I heard.'

Ha. Speaking to her will be like looking in a mirror.

'These things often come up during pregnancy,' I say. 'No worries. Point out who she is and I'll be subtle, don't worry.' I take a quick sip of my tea and supress the urge to grimace at the sweetness.

'Thanks,' Vicky says. 'Right, I'm nipping to the loo.'

She disappears out the door and I hurry round to the sink to dispose of the tea, then I knock on the door to the meeting to let them know I am here.

The talk goes as usual and I do my best to balance the truth about how your mental health can decline after a baby is born with a bit of humour so the parents aren't terrified. One man has his arm wrapped around his partner and squeezes her shoulder. I toy with wondering if he's controlling, and then release that thought. I'm not here to judge.

He's probably the anxious one and is squeezing her shoulder as a way of trying to communicate that he's nervous and needs some affection and comfort. Looking around it soon becomes apparent that Vicky won't need to point out the nervous mum-to-be.

I can tell straight away who she is. The pregnant woman on her own picks fluff off her leggings and doesn't make eye contact with me like the others do. Nor does she rub her stomach like the others. Her eyes are glazed over and focus past her bump to a spot on the floor.

I wrap the session up by handing out some leaflets and saying I'll be hanging around for a bit while they have tea and biscuits if anyone has any questions. This is normally the best way I find, as often no one asks questions for fear of looking like they have a problem.

After leaving everyone to gather their belongings and move through to the crèche room for tea and biscuits I approach the woman on her own, pleased she hasn't taken the first opportunity she had to leave the building.

'Would you like a biscuit?' I ask and she smiles and takes two Bourbons from the plate I hold out to her.

'Thanks.' She dunks one in her tea and takes a bite of the soggy end before it drops into the cup.

'Do you have long to go?' I ask. I know most pregnant women are tired of answering the same questions – When are you due? Do you know what you're having? Is it your first? – and yet I always find myself asking them anyway.

'Three weeks. Can't wait to not be pregnant anymore.' She has an expression that reminds me of Anya when she is trying to provoke or challenge me.

'Oh I know how that feels. I was drinking raspberry leaf tea and eating hot curries from about thirty-five weeks,' I say, but I don't add that Anya was still two weeks late and that I had to be induced. 'Late-stage pregnancy is hard.'

The woman's features soften as though she has decided to trust me instead of being suspicious. 'Everything aches. And my mum won't leave me alone.'

'Do you live with her?' There's no wedding band on her third finger. From experience I always preferred it when people assumed I was single instead of the other way around.

'Yes. My partner, he's in prison.'

'Oh okay, has he been there for long?'

'No. But he'll be in there for a while. That's why I'm staying with her. Couldn't afford the rent on my own at our flat. Got kicked out.'

Every bone in my body wants to ask what he's in for, but I

resist the temptation. Whatever he's done he's not a danger to Anya. He's locked up. This woman's mum must be so worried about her.

'That's tough.'

'Yes,' she says again.

'So, talk to me more about your mum. You said she won't leave you alone.'

I was expecting her to tell me her mum had never approved of the partner. That she didn't want him to be involved with the baby. That she wanted to shield her daughter from someone who could break the law and hurt her.

My tongue sticks to the roof of my mouth and I wish I had one of Vicky's sweet teas to lubricate my throat. Even the thought of Anya being with someone violent has triggered my fight or flight response.

'She's too nice, you know? I'm worried I'm not going to be as good a mum as her. She's so bloody understanding and decent. Visits him she does, my partner, all the time. But I won't. She says she understands why he did what he did. His own mum killed herself when he was seven and he's been fucked-up ever since. Sorry.' She covers her mouth like the monkey who speaks no evil, even though she has already blurted everything out.

'How does that make you feel? Her visiting him?'

'I dunno. It's not like she's choosing him over me, she's so lovely to me too, she's like a giant comfort blanket. I feel totally safe around her, but it's a bit suffocating at times, you know?'

No. I don't know, but keep my mouth closed and my expression neutral. When I fell pregnant with Anya worrying that I wouldn't live up to the kind of parent my mother had been was never a concern. But did Anya feel suffocated by me?

'She's probably worried about you,' I say, 'especially with the baby due so soon.'

'I know. And I know I'm lucky to have her. But I'm scared.

159

What if loving this baby doesn't happen? What if the baby reminds me too much of him and makes me angry?'

'That's a lot of what ifs. Have you spoken to the midwife about bonding with the baby, they can offer a lot of really good advice and tell you some techniques to try that might help.'

'I'm seeing them tomorrow, maybe I could ask then.'

'That's a great idea. And you've got one of the leaflets I handed out, right? If you feel you need any more support then give us a call and I can come to your house and chat through what we do with you. There are lots of courses and resources to help.'

'Yep, I got one. Thanks.' Her phone buzzes in her pocket and she pulls it out and looks at the screen. 'It's Mum; she's outside. We're off to buy a pram.'

'Oh how lovely.'

She smiles as she puts down the cup of tea on the side and stuffs the last Bourbon in her mouth.

'Thanks again.' She turns to leave.

'My pleasure.' I wave my hand as though flapping away her thanks and smile.

Maybe daughters are the problem, not the mothers, I think. Even those with loving mothers don't fully appreciate what they've got. Or maybe that's until they have their own daughter and they start to realise everything their mother has been through. We don't always view our parents as people in their own right. We don't take into account their pasts, their experiences, or their beliefs. We don't understand who they really are. Maybe I should've paid my mother more attention.

'Did you get to speak to her?' Vicky makes me jump. My hand goes to my heart and I shake it off.

'Sorry, was miles away. Yes I did. And I think she'll be okay.'

Me though, I'm not so sure.

'Are you okay if I go now?' I'm already putting my coat on and my bag over my shoulder.

'Of course, see you next time.'

In the car my stomach churns as though I've eaten a spicy curry. I can't leave it any longer before phoning Anya to say I'm sorry. Sean told me to give her space, but surely I should apologise over the phone and not by text?

Perhaps I should check she's at home and not in a lecture first.

Holding my breath I open the app, expecting to see her blue dot over her halls. The circle next to her name whirs around, unable to locate her, and I swallow a lump in my throat. I refresh the page, but the circle still spins. The information under her name informs me she was in her halls forty-two minutes ago, but that isn't good enough. I need to know where she is right now.

And then the app finds her.

She is in a location I don't recognise.

Park Street, in the centre of town.

My hands shake. I zoom in to where she is. The building's name below her picture becomes clear.

The Park Surgery.

Shit.

31

CATHERINE
WEDNESDAY 16TH OCTOBER

My first instinct is to race to my car and drive to her. Why is she at the surgery? My mind races with the possibilities. Maybe she is simply getting a repeat prescription for her inhalers. Or she could be registering with the surgery. While tracking her I hadn't seen her picture hovering over the doctor's surgery before and so this could definitely be what she is doing. There might be nothing wrong after all. My heart rate slows a little, but I am still on edge.

Breathing into my abdomen I contemplate calling her. Is there any chance she has calmed down after my drunken call? Probably not. Twenty-four hours isn't long enough. I look at my phone again. She's still there. Not popping in and out to register then. That wouldn't take this long. Should I call Sean and ask him?

No.

And then, as I sit in my car on the verge of a panic attack, the edge of my vision flashing with black and yellow orbs, my phone rings.

'Anya?'

'Mum.' She coughs and my body tenses. 'I'm at the doctors.'

Without thinking I nearly tell her that I know, but I stop myself.

'Are you okay?' But she's not okay, she can't be.

I hear a whistle as she breathes on the other end of the line. She coughs again.

'I've got a chest infection. Feel like shit.' The whistling is louder as she struggles to breathe and talk to me.

Blood pulses through my head. 'Oh, sweetheart. Why didn't you tell me?' You said you'd call me if you needed me, I want to shout at her, you promised.

'I'm telling you now. The cough only really came on today. I was managing, but this morning everything ached when I woke up and I'm ...' she pauses to take a deep breath in before coughing, unable to catch her breath, 'I'm so tired.'

'Do you want me to come and get you?'

Please say yes. Please say yes. Please say yes.

'I don't know if I could sit in the car for that long, Mum. Jamie's here; he came with me to see the doctor. But I think he might be getting ill too. And the doctor did advise me that some time at home might be a good idea.'

My heartbeat quickens and I'm no longer panicked. I'm ready to pounce. My reactions are always at the top of their game in an emergency. It's only after the challenge is over that everything catches up with me. I'm a soldier ready for battle, gun loaded and poised.

'Anya, I can be with you in an hour. Didn't you say next week was a reading week anyway?'

'Yes it is.' She whistles. 'I don't have lectures, but I do have an assignment.'

'Don't worry about that. We can get you an extension. Right, I'm on my way.'

'Are you sure?' I detect a wobble in her voice and I think she's crying. Ever since she was a baby her emotions had always been linked to mine. If she cried, I cried, as though her sadness not only made my breast milk flow, but also my tears.

'Of course I'm sure. Pack a few things and I'll call you when I'm there.'

A mix of emotions swirl inside me. I'm anxious she's unwell, but I get to bring her home where I can keep her safe and this excites me. I can watch her breathing in the middle of the night instead of lying awake helpless, praying that she is okay.

The drive to her university takes a little under an hour. Students mill around the little shop where I'd hidden a while back. The motivation for needing to do that still evades me, but it had felt like life or death at the time.

Anya answers her phone after one ring.

'I'm outside, sweetheart.' My voice is high-pitched. I sound too happy. My daughter being unwell and needing to come home isn't something that should be celebrated, so why do I feel victorious? My fingers buzz with pins and needles from grasping the steering wheel on the way here.

'Okay, Mum. I'll come down now.'

Several minutes pass where I wait for the gate to open. Leaves on the pavement swirl as an invisible person sweeps them away. And then, there she is, opening the gate.

My hand flies to my mouth at the sight of her. A grey tinge blankets her skin. And she is so thin, like someone has peeled several outer layers off her, or eaten her insides so there is less for her skin to cover.

Jamie carries her bags with one hand, the other holding her up like a knight in shining armour. Her hair is scraped into a bun on the top of her head and I can see flashes of her pale scalp in between the greasy hairs.

For a moment I am frozen in the car, before I realise I need to get out and meet her.

Her eyes fill with tears when she catches sight of me and a sob escapes her mouth.

'Oh, darling.' Together Jamie and I help her into the car. Not knowing him well I can't tell if his pale skin is genetic or due to the same infection ravaging Anya.

'Here are her antibiotics.' He hands me a cold bag. 'They need to be kept in the fridge.'

'Thanks,' I say and lean into the car. 'Do you have your inhalers?'

Anya nods and closes her eyes.

'Thank you for going to the doctors with her today, Jamie. You look after yourself, okay?'

'I will. I'm not asthmatic like Anya so hopefully it won't be as bad. Her cough came on so sudden, she was *sweet as* yesterday.'

His words remind me of when Anya had first had an asthma attack. Out of nowhere her lips were tinged blue and she'd crawled on her hands and her knees to the toilet, froth at the edges of her mouth. The GP had given her a nebuliser full of steroids before urging me to take her straight to the children's ward at the local hospital, where they'd been expecting us. Over the years I've learnt to look out for the early telltale signs that her airways are closing, but there isn't always a warning.

In the car I glance over at her, her chest rising and falling at a rate that is too quick. Beads of sweat glisten on her forehead. She looks away from Jamie, which I find strange. They haven't said goodbye to each other either. Maybe they're too exhausted, or already said farewell before coming to meet me.

'When did you last have any painkillers?' I ask and she shrugs. 'Before or after the doctors?'

'Before.'

'Paracetamol or Ibuprofen?'

'Paracetamol.'

'Right, wait there. I won't be long.'

Grabbing my purse I head over to the shop and get a bottle of water and some Ibuprofen. I cover my lower face with my scarf, suddenly fearful that they do have CCTV and have been waiting for me, the lurker, to come in so they can ask me what the hell I'd been doing that night. But the cashier doesn't even look up as I pay.

Back in the car the windows have steamed up. I make Anya take two tablets with the water and then set off home.

A short way into the journey Anya's breathing calms as the medicine begins to work and her fever is cooled. She sleeps, her head resting on the window beside her, and I think back to the nights when we would drive around when she was a baby, desperate to soothe her endless cries.

She'd been so difficult to calm. I remember thinking her upset was because she was missing a part of herself I couldn't fill; a part of her soul that was caught elsewhere and without it she was unable to feel safe.

In those early days I tried everything: breastfeeding, co-sleeping, slings. Bath time was the worse, as though she knew it signified the start of me trying to get her to go to sleep, or that I was going to go to sleep and leave her awake, alone and fearful.

Every time her skin touched the water she would scream, so much that I had to check and check again that the water wasn't too hot. Even now she never bathes, only showers and even then she is in and out as quickly as possible, and always with the distraction of music.

We arrive home as the sun turns blood orange, the house dark and menacing with no lights on inside. My head throbs at the temples. The car smells of illness, the air thick and warm. Shaking Anya by the arm she stirs and I help her into the house and up to her bedroom. She crawls, fully clothed, under her duvet and I switch on the fairy lights that wind around her headboard before opening the window a crack. A slither of the fading sunlight cuts across her face. The freckles that pepper her skin in summer have faded, a small smattering rests along the top of her cheeks as if someone has painted them there and then tried to rub them off.

She breathes quickly, in and out, in and out. The rest of her is still. Her energy keeping her breath going. I pray the antibiotics kick in soon.

A twinge at the base of my neck unnerves me. Even with her home I'm not as calm as I thought I would be. My anxiety is heightened. To me there is a real and present danger. My body is preparing to do battle. My hearing is more alert. My senses are in overdrive. I thought this would make everything better, having her here, but I feel worse. This has fixed nothing.

Downstairs in the kitchen I pour myself a large glass of wine and take some deep breaths. Rubbing the base of my neck, knots in my shoulders crackle under my fingers.

She's here. She's with me. Upstairs. And yet I'm still convinced she's in danger. And I can do nothing to save her. I should've checked on her more, driven up, made sure she had enough food and had taken her vitamins. This is my fault. I haven't prepared her for life away from me.

Sean was right when he said I'd indulged her too much and not given her enough freedom. She was never allowed to cross the road alone, or cook without me hovering over her. I'd tried so hard not to be as distant and controlling as my mother, but instead I'd taken away her independence and controlled her anyway.

'Mum?' Her feeble voice floats down the stairs like wind swirling through trees.

'I'm coming,' I call back. My heart picks up the pace in response to her voice. At the bottom of the stairs I find her sat at the top, out of breath, her hair stuck to her forehead, her hand grasping the bannister railings. A shadow of purple bruising circles around her wrist, but she pulls her sleeve down and the image leaves me.

'What's the matter? Are you in pain?'

Slowly, she shakes her head, then winces. 'No, I think I left my inhalers in the car. Can you get them for me?'

'Of course. Go back to bed. I'll bring them up.'

They're in the footwell of the car and I sigh with relief, not wanting to think about what I'd have had to do in the middle of the night if she'd needed them and they hadn't been there.

In her bedroom she's fallen back to sleep and I stroke her fringe away from her face. The inhalers aren't needed for now. Her breathing has calmed.

But *my* breaths are as though I have run a marathon.

I won't sleep tonight. The need to stay awake is overwhelming.

As though, if I fall asleep, she'll die.

32

DAPHNE

The mossy bank was cold beneath me. The stream carried away the flowers I'd scattered in. Pinks and reds vanished into the darkness beneath the trees where the stream retreated. Swallowed whole and spat out further down where the pathway didn't weave.

I held my hand over my newborn's chest. In and out she breathed. I'd check again in a few seconds. Sometimes I waited for a few minutes. But I always checked. In. Out. In. Out.

The midwives visited me daily. They usually did when there was a birth after child loss, so I was told. And because I was on my own they were even more concerned. But they needn't have worried. We were surviving. One day at a time.

Through practise I had perfected hiding the truth from the health visitors and my family. I suffocated my dark feelings for fear that my daughter would be taken away from me too if I spoke of them, but I had prepared myself for that event. Lightning strikes twice after all. They asked me how I was, if I'd bonded with her and I lied, I told them I thought she was beautiful. That she had eyes like her sister, the colour of the sea.

I lay down, the trees and branches and leaves swayed above

me. The blue sky was dotted above as though the leaves were bristles of paintbrushes, sweeping the bright colour onto a blank canvas.

I held out my hand again. Her chest rose and fell.

I wouldn't fall asleep.

She wouldn't die.

33

CATHERINE

MONDAY 21ST OCTOBER

'I'm sorry I'm late.' I am stood on Leanne's doorstep. 'My daughter's home from university, she's not well, I had to give her some medicine before I left.' Stop talking, I tell myself. Leanne does not need anything else to worry about. I should've cancelled really, but I owe her a proper visit to make up for my unprofessionalism at our last meeting and the one I'd cancelled.

'Oh, don't worry. Is she okay?'

'Yes, sorry, I shouldn't have said anything. She's fine. Has a chest infection, but the antibiotics are kicking in and she's on the mend.'

'That's good.'

We walk through to the lounge where Billy is playing on a baby gym in the middle of the room. Leanne sits down next to him on the floor, but doesn't look at him or touch him.

'How are things?' I ask and as I do my stomach sinks. I don't want to know. I don't care. I want to be home with Anya, not here.

Leanne sighs. There are tears in her eyes and I hand her a tissue from my bag.

'Did you have a little memorial for Emily after we last met?'

She looks at the photo of her daughter. 'Yeah. It was nice, actually. And I was doing better for a bit, but he,' she frowns at her son, 'hasn't been sleeping and I'm exhausted. The panic attacks have started again.'

'Have you been trying the breathing techniques we talked about?'

She shakes her head.

'How about the progressive muscle relaxation?'

Again she shakes her head and I suck in my cheeks. I have nothing else to offer and am frustrated.

'Right. They really do work, you know, if you give them a try.'

'I don't like focusing on my breathing,' she whispers. 'It makes me feel sick and dizzy.'

'Of course, that's not unusual, but if you stick with the deep breathing then your body calms and relieves the panic. I promise.'

Leanne picks at a crumb in the carpet in front of her, but remains silent.

'Has anything else happened, apart from lack of sleep?'

'Is that not enough?' She looks at me, challenging. 'I slept for an hour last night in twenty-minute chunks. You coming round here telling me I'm not trying hard enough doesn't help.'

'I'm sorry. I didn't mean to imply that you weren't trying. I know how hard sleep deprivation is.'

'Really? Do you know how losing a child feels? I can't relax. I can't love him in case he dies too.'

'No. I don't know what that is like.' But an unfamiliar emotion shifts inside. I feel as though on some level I do understand. Or maybe I've imagined losing Anya so many times I feel like the worst has already happened.

'Sometimes,' she takes a deep breath in, 'I can't look at him because it's too risky.' She wipes tears from her cheeks with the back of her hand. I look up at the ceiling to stop my own from falling.

'I'm sorry to ask another question,' I say, 'but remind me, have you ever spoken to a bereavement counsellor?'

Leanne glares at me and I remember asking this question before. That she'd been told to write a journal but couldn't.

'I know a good one if you'd like me to refer you? She works at the hospital, normally with mums who have stillborn babies, but she is very experienced and I'm sure she will be able to help.'

'Okay.'

Leanne glances at her son, maybe to check he's breathing, before picking again at crumbs on the carpet. Billy gurgles on the mat unaware his mother can't bear to love him. Or is he unaware? On some level I wonder if the separation between them will affect him at some point. As though her behaviour will determine how he interacts with others, maybe even his own children one day.

'Right,' I say, but Leanne doesn't look up. 'I'll go and give her a call then, if you're sure?'

'Yes. Thank you.' She doesn't move to see me out. Often the clients I support take a while to trust me and Leanne and I haven't had the best start. But I'm glad she's agreed to see the bereavement counsellor.

'I'll be in touch,' I say. 'In the meantime, do try those breathing exercises if you can.'

She flicks a crumb towards the sofa. I suspect she may stay there, next to her baby, crying for a while. Her tears will wash away some anxiety and sadness that haunts her exhausted body.

In the car I text Anya to let her know I'm on my way home and remind her to take her inhaler.

She replies with the eye roll emoji.

'What are these?' she asks, wide-eyed after I walk through the front door.

'Oh my God, what are you doing? When is it ever okay to go through someone else's stuff?'

Anya is on the floor next to the boxes from my mother's house. She's opened them and is reading the letters and looking through the photos I haven't even had a chance to glance at yet.

'Who the hell is this in the photo with Gran? That *is* Gran, isn't it?'

Anya thrusts a photo in my face. She's right. The lady on the left of the photo, laughing with a blob of ice cream on her nose, is my mother. A lightness shines from her in the photo, a freeness that I never saw in her myself. Her shoulders are looser, her brow not knitted and tight, as though it was only after I was born that she wore a heavy cloak that weighed her down from head to toe.

Next to her is a lady I don't recognise. She laughs too, a dab of ice cream on her finger, scraped from the cone she holds in her other hand and placed on my mother's nose. Her eyes sparkle, her smile is wide. Happiness radiates from their faces. They are close, comfortable with each other; that's obvious from simply looking at the photo. I turn it over. ***Me and Daphne***, it says on the back in my mother's handwriting. 1973. Four years before I was born. My mother never mentioned a Daphne. And I don't remember anyone by that name ever visiting, or even coming to her funeral.

'I don't know who that is.' I'm cross Anya has rifled through this stuff. 'Now put them back, these aren't yours to look at.'

'But they're so interesting.' She pouts in defiance. Then she coughs and tries to catch her breath.

'And what are you doing out of bed anyway?'

She rolls her eyes like the emoji.

'I needed to take my medicine and so I came downstairs to get some water. And I fancied a change of scenery. I'm bored.' Her phone beeps and she frowns. I'm guessing the antibiotics have kicked in.

'Who's that?'

'Jamie. He's sick too. Can't go to work again and they're refusing to pay him as he hasn't got a doctor's note.'

'Oh, sorry.'

'Not your fault.' She puts her phone down without appearing to reply to him.

'Here.' She hands me a letter. 'Look at this. It's to Gran.'

I'm not sure I want to read what is inside.

'Why aren't you opening it?' she asks, tipping her head to one side like a puzzled dog waiting for a command.

'Because I don't know if I want to find out more about my mother at the moment. If she didn't want to tell me about this while she was alive then I feel like I'm prying. You wouldn't understand.'

'Fuck, Mum, you're so weird sometimes.'

'Don't start, Anya.'

'Don't start what? I'm just saying, she's been gone for a while now; this might be a way of understanding her better. Help you grieve, give you some closure.'

'I don't want to understand her better,' I snap. 'And I have closure.'

Anya holds up her hands in front of her. 'Whoa there. Okay, okay, I'll shut up. Might go back to bed and watch TV on my laptop for a bit, that all right?'

'Fine.' My chest swells with an unfamiliar emotion.

Sighing, she picks up the letters, puts them back in the box and seals it closed. A waft of menthol greets me as she leaves the room and I'm catapulted back to my mother rubbing Vicks onto my chest before leaving me alone in bed to inhale the fumes through my mouth as my nose was too blocked.

The room is empty without Anya; the scent of mint and illness lingers in the air. But at least the colour is back in her cheeks. They are not as rosy as Snow White's rose-red cheekbones, but pink like they are about to blossom.

The photo of my mother and Daphne is on the coffee table in front of me and I pick it up again. In this picture my mother has a new soul instead of an old and weary one.

Maybe I have no choice; I have to read the letters, but not now. Now, I need a nap before another night of watching Anya sleep. My anxiety is like a sail caught in the wind propelling me forward. If the wind dissipates and the ship stops then Anya will be in danger. One more night, I tell myself. She's getting better; there'll be no need to keep vigil after tonight.

But I know – like an alcoholic downing one last shot, or a smoker inhaling the smoke from their final cigarette – I am lying to myself.

Addictions are hard to break.

34

CATHERINE
TUESDAY 22ND OCTOBER

Waves of panic jolt me awake every time I drift off. I'm uncomfortable and bent out of shape. Hot and sweaty. My heart beats erratically. My stomach lurches. The duvet doesn't fit right in the duvet cover and my pillow pops out of its case.

The boiler hums. Branches bash against the window. A scooter revs in the distance. I need a wee, but know that nothing will come out. Over and over again I toss and turn. Am I ill? Am I having a heart attack?

After what feels like a blink it's still dark, as though sunrise will never come and I'll forever be locked in this half-awake, half-asleep cycle. A foggy dream penetrates, a footstep outside the bedroom door, a black shoe, polished beneath a smart trouser leg with a crease down the middle. Sean coming home from work? My father at a funeral? Or the Grim Reaper coming to claim me as his own? Then a faint smell of burning. Isn't that the sign of a stroke?

I sniff, but the scent is gone. Sweat pools beneath my breasts and at the base of my spine. I waft the duvet up and down to cool myself, sticking my feet out of the side. The panic will pass,

I know, but I hate the physical response fear provokes. A fresh wave of nausea sweeps over me and I wiggle my toes to distract myself. I'm on fire. Alert. Ready to attack.

Or protect.

I haven't checked on Anya tonight. I promised her I wouldn't. Yesterday, she was almost back to her old self. The cough gone. The medicine working. I've told her over and over again she needs to take the complete course of antibiotics, even though she's feeling better.

Jamie's on the mend too so she told me, but he's struggling with money having taken so long off work. His parents can't afford to give him any more than they already have. Anya's tempted to give him some of hers, but we spoke about how that wouldn't help either of them in the long run. She's fortunate that between Sean and I she doesn't need a job while at university, like Jamie does.

Staring at the ceiling I give up on sleep. I don't want to know what time it is. My pillow is damp and I swap it with the one beneath and fluff them before leaning back. The rain has stopped, but a steady drip from the trees taps on the windowsill.

I. Must. Not. Go. In.

My bedroom door is open a crack and I stare at the darkness in the hallway separating our rooms like a curtain. Once again I wish for X-ray vision. I want to look through the walls and check she's breathing without having to leave my bed or risk waking her.

Anya wouldn't be happy if she found me in her room in the middle of the night again, and I don't want her to go back to university with things awkward between us. I promised her I wouldn't go in, but I ache to know she's alive.

The rest of the night passes in a blur of panic and light sleep, but I resist sneaking into Anya's room.

Fully awake and downstairs in the kitchen, I pour myself a large coffee to counteract the sleep loss. As I drink I think of Leanne. I should've been more empathetic yesterday. I'm amazed at how little sleep I can function on and have forgotten how debilitating a lack of rest can be. And the endless sleep deprivation that arrives with a newborn is soul destroying. I vow to give her a call later.

'Morning.'

Anya is dressed already. She's more excited about going back to university than I'd appreciated. My heart sinks.

'Morning, love. Coffee?'

'No thanks, I'll have tea I think. What time's Dad getting here?'

As she asks the doorbell rings. He wasn't due until nine. It's eight thirty.

'I'll get it.' She bounces out of the room. Since she left for university the tie that binds us together has worn down to a single thread. Her new friends know her better than I do. They know what makes her laugh, or cry. Her sense of humour has changed too. Her taste in food. Her favourite songs.

Everything about her is a mystery to me and seeing how happy she is to be going back, I know she'd rather be with them than me, which stings. Long gone are the days where my hand was the only one she held. My bed the one she curled up in. My lap the one she rested her head on. I blink away the tears before she walks back in with Sean.

'Hey, Catherine.' Sean's aftershave mingles with the smell of fresh pastries he's brought. He kisses me on the cheek and I catch Anya averting her eyes, finding the image of her parents together hard to swallow for some reason.

'Coffee?'

'Please.'

'You need to take your tablet.' I raise my eyebrows at her, anticipating the rolling of her eyes. She doesn't disappoint.

'I know. And I also know that I'm not allowed to drink alcohol until at least twenty-four hours after my last tablet. Plus my contraceptive pill won't be working while I am taking it either.'

Sean winces and I imagine him putting his fingers in his ears and screaming, 'lalalalaaa I can't hear you' at his daughter.

'You've drummed it into me enough times,' she continues. 'It might be wise to let me make my own mistakes or I'm never going to be able to function as an adult.' She accompanies this advice with a teasing chuckle.

Pregnancy isn't the best mistake to make at university, I think, but don't say.

'What time are you off?' Sean asks.

'As soon as possible.' Anya presses her hands together in prayer and I feel another stab to my heart.

'Let me finish my coffee at least. And you need to have some food with your tablet.'

Leaving Sean and Anya to have breakfast together I go upstairs and sit on the end of my bed. A storm brews inside me. Waves of anger and frustration are drowned by sorrow. I want to scream into my pillow and cry until I am dry. But I remain mute like a statue. My emotions sucked up and ignored.

'Mum?' Anya knocks on my bedroom door. I've no idea how long I've been in a trance, staring out of my window, looking at the trees in the distance. The branches dance in the morning sun. Each leaf moving to its own individual beat.

'Yes, love?'

'Can we go?'

'Of course. But I need a wee. There's no way I'm using the death toilet at your halls.'

'Oh it's not that bad.'

'It really is. No wonder you got ill.'

'Stop.' Her expression changes. 'Why do you keep having a go at me.' It's a statement not a question. One sentence is all it takes for me to annoy her these days. Might as well keep my mouth shut.

'Sorry. I'll meet you downstairs.'

She leaves and I grip the duvet.

The coffee has deposited a bitter taste on my tongue. I exhale slowly, but can't calm down. The last time I saw Fiona she'd told me that the second time Anya left would be better than the first, but this is worse.

'Come on!' Anya shouts from the bottom of the stairs and I steel myself. A dull pain gnaws in my gut; my grief burning and ready to consume me in flames. The pain radiates up to my neck and shoulders and I roll my head to relieve the tension.

'On my way.'

I catch my reflection in the bathroom mirror. Bags under my eyes look like I've not washed my make-up off. A fresh batch of grey hairs burst from my left temple. I tuck them behind my ears, but the grey remains, taunting me for being old and alone.

'Mum, what are you doing?'

'I'm coming.'

'I told Jamie I'd be home in time for lunch.'

As I reach the bottom of the stairs, Sean is hugging Anya, her face buried into his chest.

'Bye, sweetheart,' he says. She doesn't push him away, but sinks deeper into his embrace. 'See you at Christmas, right?'

'I promise,' she says and they release.

Opening the front door I head straight for the car in an

attempt to avoid another cheek kiss from Sean as he leaves with us.

Anya gets in beside me and rummages in her bag. 'Shit, my inhalers.'

I say nothing and wait as she dashes into the house for them. The gnawing in my stomach gains momentum. I rub under my ribs, which makes me feel nauseous. I close my eyes and breathe out as though blowing through a straw.

'Right,' she says and climbs back in. 'Let's go.'

Anya turns the radio on, stares out of the window, and taps her foot to the music as I drive.

We arrive at her halls and I shiver. I can't remember the journey here; my mind wandering into a world I don't want to inhabit, but have no choice.

The building looms above us, four floors, every window closed. I can smell the hangovers inside, the warm air filled with alcohol fumes, sweat and stale smoke with an undertone of vomit.

Anya leaps out of the car. By the time I've joined her, Jamie is running over from the gates to Anya. He picks her up and swings her around. She giggles. I look away as they kiss, and then a thought occurs to me. I look at Jamie, at the way his eyes light up as he stares at Anya.

No. No no no. I couldn't do that. Could I? No. If Anya found out she would never forgive me. No.

But if he agreed, then my anxiety would be alleviated.

No.

I shake the thought away and unload the boot.

'All right,' Jamie says.

'Hi, you feeling better now?'

'Yeah. Didn't have it as bad as Ans.'

'Thank goodness,' Anya says. 'Here, can you take this?' She hands him her rucksack. As he takes it he pulls her in for another hug, but she doesn't sink into him this time. Her hands press against his chest instead of wrapping around him. She's only been away a few days. But then, I forget the intensity of young love. In fact, any love. Again, I am hit full on in the chest as to how alone I am. Like a vice tightening around my heart, squeezing any capacity for love out, inch by inch.

'No need to come up, Mum,' Anya says. 'I know you think my bedroom is a death trap full of germs and filth. Don't want to prove you right.'

Of course I think this.

'If you're sure?'

'I am. Thanks for driving. I'll send Jamie down for my last bag.'

Wrapping my arms around my body I force myself to smile. I don't get a hug like Sean. She can walk away from me without a second glance. Not like she did on her first day at primary school. That morning, she'd clung to my legs, her eyes wide with fear, her lips set in a firm pout. Part of me had felt soothed by the fact she hadn't skipped in without so much as a wave at the threshold.

I'd been her comfort blanket. I'd had a purpose.

A few students pass in and out of the gated village while I wait for Jamie to return. I think of their parents and wonder if they feel like I do.

And then the idea rears its head again like a bite that's been scratched and is raised. This time I entertain the thought. Then Jamie runs over, keen to grab Anya's bag and get back inside with her.

'Jamie,' I say after handing him her belongings. 'How much do you love my daughter?'

His cheeks flush red and he dips his head. 'What?' He shuffles from one foot to the other, reminding me of a child being told off.

'How much do you like Anya?' My body fizzes with electricity as if I'm an MI5 agent on a secret mission.

'Yeah, I like her. She's cool.'

'Are you together most nights?'

'Um, this is a bit awkward.'

'Sorry, I'll get to the point.' My palms are clammy. I can't believe I'm doing this. 'Anya, she might have told you, but I worry about her. Especially at night. It's a long story.' I wave my hands, wafting the truth away. 'And, I know you're short of cash at the moment so...'

'So what? What are you saying? You want me to watch her at night?' He catches on quick. I'm impressed. 'And you'll pay me?'

I raise my eyebrows. Blood whooshes in my ears. This is perfect. I can't check she's breathing in the middle of the night, but I've found someone who can.

Again he shifts from one foot to the other, but this time in thought. He scratches the hair under his hat. Then he chuckles and shakes his head.

'It's not a hard decision.' I'm feeling a thrill at being back in control. 'We've all done crazy stuff when we're desperate for money, right?'

He makes me wait a few moments.

'Okay. Yeah okay. I'll do it. Just check she's breathing, right?'

'Yes, in the middle of the night. You don't go to bed until then anyway. Say around 3am? And text me to let me know she's okay. You can grab my number from Anya's phone. She must *never* find out.'

'Right. This is totally fucking weird, you know that don't you?'

'Yes. I do. But it's necessary. I can't explain why. Believe me, I've tried.'

He frowns.

'Text me your bank details too,' I add.

He nods before walking back through the gates.

In the car I grab hold of the steering wheel and rest my head on the top arc. Closing my eyes I laugh like a woman possessed.

What have I done?

35

ANYA

You didn't hang around after you dropped me off like I expected you to. I watched you and Jamie chatting out of my bedroom window, my hands balled into fists leaving little nail dents in my palms. What was he telling you? How much he loved me? How you needn't worry, that he'll look after me now I'm back? Because if that's what he was telling you then don't believe him, Mum, because it's bullshit.

There wasn't an opportunity to talk to you about Jamie when I was at home. Either you were at work or I was napping or you were staring at me from the other side of the sofa to check I really was okay when we were watching some crap you like on the TV.

That's not fair. I'm making excuses. I could've spoken to you, made time, if I'd really wanted to, but not gonna lie, I know you're gonna freak out even more because I've actually been ill and so telling you about me and Jamie and how messed up I think we are, when maybe there's nothing to worry about, wasn't a good idea. I nearly did though, I nearly asked you what you thought about our relationship but I couldn't.

I know you were crying this morning when I went to let

Dad in though. I think he knew too. But you held it together in the car and I was so fucking pleased you didn't pull me in for a hug as I walked away because I reckon then I'd have started crying too and you wouldn't have left without me telling you why.

On the stairs, that first night back, I was sure you'd seen the marks on my wrist. But you didn't say anything and so I didn't say anything. The bruising has gone down anyway and when I think back the injury wasn't really that bad and it wasn't all his fault. Jamie had been trying to stop me make a drunken fool out of myself and had held on a bit too tightly. I wouldn't have got home safely if it wasn't for him. I think I remember telling him he was hurting me, but I don't remember what he replied.

And the next day I was grateful he'd held me back and made me come home. Vodka isn't my friend. Vodka makes me a violent drunk. Vodka is like liquid fuel to any smouldering fire in my body. That night I'd done too many shots and this girl was grinding on Jamie and he wasn't doing anything to stop her and I lost it. Went fucking nuts at them both and the bouncers had ended up throwing *me* out.

Jamie had come outside to find me shouting at one of them to let me the fuck back in and without speaking he grabbed me by the wrist and pulled me away and took me home. And then I think we had sex, although I'm not sure, but the next day I felt as though we had and if we did then I think it was rough because I was sore.

I'd like to tell you that night is the only time he's manhandled me, but I'd be lying. He says I need to learn to pace myself and not drink so much on a night out, that my inhibitions disappear down the toilet with my vomit. And I'm trying, I really am. But he needs to learn to not pour me the next one or maybe I need to be strong enough to say no. But I can't help getting carried away because I love the freedom of being able to drink and smoke and do whatever I want whenever I want with whoever I want.

I've escaped you controlling me although I reckon you still track me and that's fine, I don't give a shit, but sometimes I have no idea how I've ended up letting someone else do the same.

36

CATHERINE

WEDNESDAY 30TH OCTOBER

The text comes through at 3.20am.

She's breathing.

I transfer the money into Jamie's account, and close my eyes. Every night for the last week Jamie has been true to his word and texted me around 3am to let me know Anya's alive. The reassuring vibration of my phone is enough to push the anxiety from my body and allow me to sleep.

There are no thoughts about what will happen if Anya finds out. After the incident in Bristol before she left, and the drunken phone call, she wouldn't forgive me. And I've given up questioning my motives. I'm simply going with them. I know all too well that a feeling is not a fact, but the feeling that Anya is in danger in the middle of the night is visceral. I'd have to ignore every single one of my motherly instincts to fight it.

Time plays with me and I blink once before my work alarm wakes me. My boss has asked me to come into the office first thing this morning and I'm nervous.

The toast I've made moves around my mouth as I chew, unable to swallow. When I do the bread lodges in my throat and I gulp hot coffee to move the lump along. Gone are the days where I'd have a cigarette and a black coffee for breakfast. Maybe I should revert back to the person I was until I fell pregnant with Anya.

Giving up on the toast I walk into the lounge and see the boxes on the floor. The letter Anya told me to read is on the coffee table and I pick it up and smooth the envelope before putting it into my handbag. I'm about to leave when I notice another photo in one of the boxes.

Taken in woodland, I look closer. The trees and shrubs in the picture remind me of the woods behind my mother's house. The stream looks the same too – the mound of mossy grass beside the water unmistakable. In the front of the photo are two pregnant women.

The lady on the right is my mother. She wears the same carefree smile as she does in the other photo Anya found. And next to her is Daphne. Sunlight streams through the branches above and lights up their faces, brightening their smiles.

I wonder if my father is the one who took the photo. And whether or not I am the baby inside my mother's bump.

She's wearing a floral dress, like a smock, and it sticks out over her feet, on which she wears sandals. Her hair is tied up, highlighting her strong cheekbones, which I didn't inherit. My thoughts go to their friendship and I wonder what happened. I have no memory of Daphne at all. The women must've fallen out over something huge.

Pulling myself away from my mother's hidden past I get in the car. The traffic on the way to the office is pretty clear and I find a parking space without any trouble. I glance at the tracking app. Anya has an early lecture on Thursdays and it's always a good day to check she is alive, even though Jamie's reassured me she is.

The blue circle around her photo hovers above the main campus. I cuddle the phone to my chest and smile.

As usual on the walk to work I pop into the local coffee shop and get a takeaway, before nipping into the small supermarket to pick up a sandwich and some crisps. A homeless person waits for me outside and I give him my change. Then I walk down the small road to the office, ducking out from under the scaffolding even though I claim to not be suspicious.

Bird poo litters the pavement alongside a single splodge of human vomit in a doorway. The office is off the main pub and club strip in the centre of town and I always have to step over at least one pile of stale sick, usually from students who've had one drink too many and haven't made it home in time to throw up in their own toilet.

An image of Anya throwing up on a street corner enters my mind, Jamie rubbing her back and handing her a cigarette when she's finished.

Fiona is outside the office door, waiting to be let in as I arrive.

'Hi,' she says, a look of concern etched on her face.

Worried that I'd said the wrong thing the last time we met I search my brain to think when that was and what we'd spoken about. 'Hello. Are you seeing people here today?' She sometimes works from the main office here instead of at her own.

She looks puzzled. 'Did Sarah not tell you?'

I slowly shake my head. 'Tell me what?' A tightening sensation traps my breath in my lungs. My stomach gurgles and I wish I'd finished my toast. A metallic taste fills my mouth and I sip my coffee, which burns my tongue.

'Sarah asked me to come along to your meeting.'

We stand on the threshold to the office in silence. Why do I feel like I've made a mistake? Pins and needles buzz in the ends of my fingers. Before I can stop them, tears bubble in my eyes. I don't understand.

Before I can dwell on what's happening, Sarah opens the office door with a wide smile and stands back to let us in.

'Hey, you're both here. Good timing. Coffee?'

'I've got one thanks.' I try to smile, but my lip quivers and I bite the inside of my cheek.

'Yes please,' Fiona says and closes the door, trapping my escape. The sounds from outside are muffled and the air is thick with damp and the remnants of dirty nappies and stale milk. Our office is a wonderful place for mums to bring their children and have some respite from their demons, but today, the building only invites them out of the shadows.

'Shall we use the counselling room?' Sarah appears light and breezy, but she tucks and untucks her hair from behind her ear and I know she's nervous too.

The counselling room has a large window overlooking an alleyway at the back of the building. The space is light and airy and I've always thought it the perfect room for people who come here for support.

The alleyway is quiet. Colourful graffiti adorns the surrounding buildings. I lose myself in the different colours, shapes and designs mingled with the random tags. Someone has drawn a house, two windows up and two down either side of a green door. The picture reminds me of the way children draw houses and I wonder how old that graffiti artist is.

'Catherine, are you okay?'

'Yes. I'm tired, that's all. Zoned out for a minute. Sorry.'

My cheeks flush red and I know a telltale rash will spread across my chest as it always does when I'm embarrassed.

'There's no easy way to say this,' Sarah starts. She's opposite me, a notebook open on her lap, pen poised. And it dawns on me that I'm in big trouble.

'Have I done something wrong?' I ask.

Sarah and Fiona exchange a glance that makes a lump form in my throat.

'One of the ladies you support,' she looks at her notebook, 'Leanne...'

'What about her?' Has she attempted suicide? Harmed the baby? Shit shit shit. She was really down the last time I saw her, but not suicidal. Or was she? Damn it I can't remember if I asked her if she'd had any intrusive thoughts. Or had I? I need to check my notebook, but then I remember not using it that day. I hadn't recorded anything about our session. My mouth is dry. I can't speak.

'She's made a complaint.'

The room spins. I feel sick.

'What?' I whisper. My brain races through our meetings. Everything I've said. Everything I've done. Tears prick my eyes. Fiona notices and hands me a tissue laced with pity I don't want.

'She mentioned a few things. She said you didn't listen to her and that you made her feel as though she's somehow to blame for what happened to her daughter, and for not being able to get better.'

'No.' My voice is louder than intended. 'That's not fair.'

'She also said you took a phone call from your daughter when you were with her?' Fiona takes over the inquisition and I want to cry at the thought of them discussing this, discussing me and my professionalism, without me there.

'Yes I did, but she said I could. Anya has been unwell and...'

'She says you talk about Anya a lot.'

The edges of my vision blur and the floor falls away. A seed of realisation that maybe I have been too personal with Leanne grows inside me. My boundaries were blurred because her case triggered me in ways I still don't fully understand.

'I know you've had anxieties around Anya going to university.'

That's confidential, I think, not brave enough to challenge Fiona. *I told you that in supervision, Fiona, and you should not have told anyone else.*

'Anya leaving has been very difficult. And with her being unwell recently, it threw me off kilter.'

'We understand how hard it is when a child leaves home. We really do.' They look at each other, nodding. 'And in hindsight we should've encouraged you to have a bit of time off, especially with losing your mum recently as well.'

They'd asked me if I'd wanted compassionate leave, but I'd told them I needed to work. Needed to block everything: the past, the present, the future, out.

'Work helps.' I wipe the tears that fall down my cheeks whether I want them to or not.

'Leanne doesn't want to take things further, but we do think you need to take a break.'

This is an order. They're making me go on sick leave. Except I am not unwell. Am I?

I look at my lap. The tissue shredded.

'I'm happy to have another session with you,' Fiona says. 'See if we can get to the bottom of this. Something is obviously deeply affecting you at the moment and Anya leaving home is forcing you to deal with it. You know better than anyone that there's no shame in asking for help.'

'But I don't know what I need help for!' I shout.

They look at each other again and I breathe deeply into my stomach.

A bead of sweat drips at the base of my spine. It's stuffy in here. I need air.

Outside the window a lad smoking a cigarette tags the wall opposite us with a can of spray paint. I haven't smoked for ten years, but at this moment that fag looks like the best thing I've seen in weeks. The smoke being blown from his mouth is like a slither of liquid ribbon swirling around him. His lips form the perfect 'o'. He takes another drag and I imagine the smoke in my throat, filling my lungs and calming me.

'Fine,' I say and move to stand. 'Let me know when you're free, Fiona.' I turn to Sarah. 'How long do you want me to have off?'

She looks taken aback at my directness and waits a moment to answer me. 'Shall we start with a month?'

'Perfect.' I go to leave, then a thought occurs to me. 'Do I need to apologise to Leanne?'

They shake their heads as though I've suggested they drink poison.

'No.' Sarah holds up her hands. 'She's asked you not to contact her again.'

Nausea ripples through my stomach and I swallow it down.

'Right.' I smooth my jumper. 'If that's all?'

We don't speak as we walk back to the door, the sound of our feet on the floorboards forming a beat none of us want to dance to. I'm too frightened to say anything in case I dig myself into an even deeper hole.

I pull the door open and leave with a quick wave of my hand and mumble of goodbye. Without hesitation I march into the shop opposite, buy a packet of cigarettes and chain-smoke all the way back to my car.

Then, even though it's only eleven o'clock, I drive to the bar I'd been to not long ago.

I order a bottle of wine with a tequila chaser.

And I drink the lot.

37

DAPHNE

The sun filtered through the gaps in the branches above me, dappled shadows danced on the piece of paper I held in my hand. Several hours had passed, but I still couldn't write the letter I knew I had to. I needed her to read it. I needed her to know the truth. I needed her to understand why.

And then I needed her to explain everything to my daughter.

The pen fell from my trembling fingers and I picked it up from between the long blades of grass. My hand brushed against the knitted blanket beside me. The fibres stung my skin like wires.

She was here. Next to me. My baby. But I didn't look at her or check her breathing. I didn't need to because she wriggled on the blanket and she cried and cried and cried.

The bond hadn't come. I'd spent hours kneeling beside my bed, praying and praying that it would. Asking for forgiveness. Begging to love her. Everything I'd tried had failed.

We'd bathed together and slept together and I'd breastfed her for hours and days on end, but a barrier between us remained like an invisible shield between my body and hers. She deserved better. I at least wanted that for her.

The guilt hung over me like a fog that wouldn't clear, blocking any chance I had of loving her. The fear of losing her had won.

The blank page on my lap taunted me, but I didn't know where to start. Sorry wasn't enough. Nothing would ever be enough.

Before I could write anything a sudden breeze took the paper from my lap. It fluttered down onto the stream and washed away before resting on a rock, the blank whiteness shone out in contrast to the dark water. Like Heather when they found her, her hair floating around her upturned head, swaying in the current as though there were still life in her somewhere escaping through each strand.

My fault. There was no one else to blame. I cannot wake up to that nightmare again.

And so I must sleep forever.

38

CATHERINE

THURSDAY 31ST OCTOBER

This isn't my bedroom. The wallpaper is a different shade of blue and as I reach for my phone my hand bashes against a bedside table that is too tall. My room smells of lavender, and this one smells musky. My breathing picks up a notch.

Groaning, I wriggle onto my back. The curtains are open. Splashes of sunlight tremble on the ceiling and clouds floating across the sky make the light appear to flash on and off. The lightshade above me is blue. Mine is grey. I pull the duvet over my head and hide.

'Morning,' someone says. My heart tries to make a bid for freedom.

The voice is deep, but not Sean's. My breath sticks in my throat. I daren't peek out from the duvet to see where the *morning* came from. Feeling my skin stick to the sheet, I realise I'm naked.

What the actual?

'I said, morning.' The bed dips to my right as he sits down. 'I brought you a coffee.' Would a murderer bring me coffee? I feel between my legs, but there's no sign of any intrusion.

And then, in the darkness of my brain where memories go to die, there's a glimmer of recognition, accompanied by a sickening flashback.

I knew I'd see you again.

'Are you going to come out from under there?'

My breath is hot and smells of stale cigarettes. If I stay under here any longer I'll pass out from my own toxic fumes.

Taking a deep breath I yank the duvet down a fraction and squint at the sunlight streaming in through the window, resting on the duvet like strips of ribbon.

'Hi,' he says. The man from the bar whose name I can't remember. The man in the suit. Tom? Ollie?

'Hi,' I croak. I blink the grittiness in my eyes away and pull the duvet up to my neck, feeling naked and exposed.

'Thought you might need this.'

'You thought right. My head's banging.'

'That'll be the tequila shots.'

Remorse twists my gut. I frown.

'You don't remember?'

'Not really.'

A look of sadness sweeps across his face.

All of a sudden I think of Anya and scramble for my phone. Panic fizzes through me like a drug. Had I woken up at 3am to check Jamie had texted? Or was I too drunk? A wave of adrenaline runs through me. My phone isn't here.

'Are you okay?' he asks, as I delve about in my bag, the duvet slipping from beneath my armpits.

'My phone, where's my phone?' A cold draft brushes against my exposed left breast, but I don't care. I face him. 'Where's my phone?'

'Calm down.' He picks it up from his side of the bed. 'Here. You wanted me to charge it when we got back.'

Grabbing the phone I open my messages.

Anya's okay.

Text received at half past three. I'd already replied with a brief 'thanks'. I hold the phone to my chest, squeeze my eyes closed and think.

'Do you recall anything?' he asks and I'm not sure how honest to be.

Scrunching up my face I shake my head.

'I remember leaving work and smoking far too many cigarettes on the way home.'

'Except,' he pauses, 'you didn't go home.'

'Evidently not.' I chuckle, but I'm not sure what's funny.

My bladder is full and my teeth are furry. I want to leave, but I can't even see my clothes.

'Did we...?' I raise my eyebrows and grimace, hoping he knows what I'm asking.

His cheeks redden. He looks down at the bed. 'No, we didn't.' He smooths the sheet around him. 'I slept on the couch.'

He might be lying but I know my body. It's been a long time since I've had sex, but I don't think I had sex last night.

'Oh. Thanks.'

'Your clothes are on the floor at the end of the bed.' He stands and hovers as though wanting to ask me a question.

I sip my coffee. 'Why am I here and not at my house?' I put the mug on the bedside table. I think I know the answer.

'You didn't want to go home to an empty house. You were in a bit of a state when I found you.'

Ashamed, I shake away the unwanted image of me begging him to let me come here.

'That would be your fault for making me do tequila shots.' My cheeks flush red. I haven't blacked out after drinking too much in years.

'Hey.' He holds his hands up in mock surrender. 'That

wasn't me. You'd drunk them before I got there. The barman was refusing to serve you.'

A snapshot of me crying against the bar rears its head and I cringe and cover my face with my hands. 'Oh God. Don't tell me any more.' Shame and anxiety run through my veins, feeding the muscles and organs in my body with guilt and horror.

'I need to go home.' I get off the bed, attempting to use the duvet as a cloak of invisibility.

He averts his gaze and rubs his forehead as though trying to get rid of some dirt.

'Absolutely. I can drive you to your car if you like?'

At that moment it fully dawns on me that I don't even know where I am. How could I have been so stupid?

The room darkens around me and I collapse back onto the bed. Head in hands I sob, not caring that he's watching. Even if I was going to see him again, which I'm not, this isn't the worst state he's seen me in. Last night was. Now I've started to cry I can't stop. My shoulders shudder. My breath bursts out of me in groan after groan.

'Catherine?' He shuffles and I can tell he's unsure of what to do. 'Do you need anything?'

'I'm sorry,' I splutter, holding out my hand to keep him away. A waft of body odour from my armpit makes me want to sink further into the blackness. 'Please, leave me to get dressed.'

'Are you sure?'

'Yes.' I wave to dismiss him. 'Please. I'll be out in a minute.'

He softly closes the door behind him and I take some deep breaths.

In his en suite I splash my face with cold water. For a second, I consider using his toothbrush, but instead squirt the paste onto my finger and rub it over my teeth and gums, using my nails to scrape off the tartar. My head pounds as I bend down and I put my mouth under the tap and gulp the fresh water.

Maybe some parents are thrilled to get their lives and independence back after their children leave home. Empty nest syndrome has broken me.

I get dressed and pick up my phone from the bedside table. A picture of Anya aged five on the beach stares back at me as the screen lights up. One of the happiest memories I have of her, running in and out of the waves.

We hadn't needed anyone else. Of course I'd been worried about the usual things, like most mothers. And the responsibility of doing everything alone had been overwhelming at times. Like when she'd cried out with a temperature in the middle of the night and I hadn't known if she was teething or had meningitis. Or when she'd fallen over in the park and there was no one to reassure me her arm was bruised and not broken.

Watching her in the night had always been an action I felt compelled to do, but not to the point of obsession. That had come later. And almost overnight. My joy at watching her sleeping had become a darker, more visceral need. *Check on her or she'll die*, the voice in my head told me night after night after night. *Don't. Fall. Asleep.*

'I'm really sorry, for everything,' I say as I walk out of the bedroom to find him at the top of the stairs. 'Thank you for letting me stay.' I'd been wrong about the wife I'd thought he was cheating on the first time we'd met.

'Don't worry.' He lets me pass and we walk down the stairs in silence. He has a nice house. Minimal, but clean. All sharp edges and white walls. And the musty smell I still can't place.

He picks up his car keys from the hallway table.

'No,' I say. 'I'll call an Uber, I don't want to be a burden any more than I already have.'

'It's not a problem.'

'You probably have to go to work or something.' Although, I notice for the first time this morning that he's not dressed in a suit. He wears grey jogging bottoms and a T-shirt.

'Actually, I took the day off. Thought you might need a friend.'

He's sweet but I don't need a friend. And he certainly doesn't need me in his life. I've already put him out and we've only met twice.

'That's kind, really kind, but I'm fine on my own.'

He looks at me with an expression that reminds me of the way I used to look at Anya when I knew she was lying.

'Really,' I say with force. 'Yes, my mother died a while back and then my daughter left for university, but I'll get there.'

He chews the inside of his left cheek. 'Okay, if you're sure. At least you know where I am if you change your mind. And I mean here, not the bar.' He smiles and a small dimple appears in his right cheek.

'Thank you.'

We share an awkward moment. I hover by the door, not knowing if I should hug him or shake his hand, before I let myself out. Then I wave before closing the door behind me.

The road he lives on is familiar and I decide to walk for a bit to clear my head. Trees line the pavements on either side, each trunk surrounded by cracked black concrete at the base where the roots have tried to reclaim the land.

These trees, planted by hand not by seed, will not communicate with each other like trees in woodland. They stand tall and proud, but each one fights for itself. In the summer I imagine their leaves are green and abundant. Their bark is thick and protective. But I know better than anyone how appearances can be deceptive. Like a Twitter feed or Instagram account; the perfect filtered selfies hide a multitude of truths.

The end of the road meets one of the main streets in the

suburbs on the other side of town from where I live. I've supported a mum near here before. As I delve into my bag for my phone to call the Uber I see the packet of cigarettes I bought yesterday and want to retch.

The house is silent. The dirty coffee cup from yesterday morning still on the end of the counter like a shadow of the past. Knowing I won't be leaving the house again today, I shower and change into my pyjamas, then make a cup of coffee and head into the lounge where my mother's boxes pepper the floor.

Finally, I'm ready to look inside them.

The box Anya had been so interested in is next to the photos of my mother and the mysterious Daphne. I settle down and pull a couple of the other boxes closer.

Then I open the tracking app on my phone and check on Anya again. Her blue circle hovers above the university and I imagine her in the lecture hall taking notes and laughing with her new friends.

The ones who know her better than I do.

I throw my phone into a cushion where it bounces onto the floor. Leaving it there I turn my attention to the boxes to find out what my mother had hidden for so long.

Inside the first are photos of me as a child, aged about four or five. Some are of me on the beach, although I don't remember ever being allowed to jump the waves. I'm wearing a pink frilly bikini and holding a bucket in one hand and a spade in the other.

As I look I'm reminded of birthdays and Christmases, but there are no photos of anyone other than me. Me blowing out my candles, the surrounding space devoid of friends. Me opening Christmas gifts beside the tree, smiling only at the person behind the camera. Some of the photos have my father in, but not many. He'd left before I can remember.

A sudden tidal wave of exhaustion buffets me and for a moment I give in, resting my head on a cushion and curling up under a blanket.

I was positive the contents of these boxes would give me the answers to the questions I still don't know to ask. But all I've found is a heap of nostalgia and uncomfortable memories and I'm drained. Then, as I am about to give up, I see a photo on the floor I must've dropped.

A baby, wrapped in a bright yellow knitted blanket, is nestled on a mossy mound next to what looks like a stream. On the back, in handwriting different to the writing on the other photos is one word. A name.

Heather.

39

CATHERINE

THURSDAY 31ST OCTOBER

'Dad? Do you know who this is?'

Showing the photo of Heather, I hold my breath in anticipation. This is the only thing I could think to do after seeing the photo of the baby, Heather. I need answers and my father is the only person I can think of who might be able to solve the riddle. He may be able to help me track down Heather and Daphne, whoever they are.

He takes the other photos of my mother and Daphne from my trembling hand and stares at them, one after the other, turning them over and over, again and again.

'Dad? Are you okay?'

My chest constricts as tears form in his eyes. He is looking at the photo of Heather. His thumb, the skin worn and wrinkled, strokes her face. Tears drop from his chin onto the photo. But he remains silent.

We sit by the window in his room. His chair is tall and he leans back and closes his eyes. I've lost him. There is no humming. His fingers don't move. But he has shut me out, shut the photos out, shut everything out. Sometimes he can be like this for a few minutes, but on other days he can remain mute and closed off from the world for hours.

Someone knocks at the door. One of his carers, Iona, pops her head round.

'Hi, everything okay?'

'Hi,' I say. 'I'm not sure. I showed him a photo, this one.' I point to his hands where he is grasping the photo tight to his body. 'Maybe I shouldn't have, I don't know. But he cried and then shut his eyes.'

Her face creases in sympathy. 'I wish I'd caught you on your way in.' She comes into the room, closing the door behind her. 'He isn't having the best time at the moment. Most days he is at least calm, but more often he becomes upset. He talks about someone being missing, about it being someone's fault and he can't forgive them. He's very confused.'

Iona sits on the end of my father's bed, and I feel uncomfortable with her being so familiar and encroaching on his personal space. Even *I* don't sit on the end of his bed.

'Do you think it's more hallucinations? Or ... is his mind playing tricks on him again, messing with his memory?'

'I'm not sure. To me...' She pauses and looks at my father. Her eyes are warm and I can see she cares for him. 'I think, maybe, that there's more to this.' She holds out her hands. 'Do you have any other photos?'

Several are in my bag, I'd thrown them in without looking, and I pick them up and hand them to her, but the photo of Heather is in his grasp and I don't attempt to extract it. We sit in silence as she leafs through them.

'Do you know who these people are?' She shows me the photo of my mother and Daphne.

'This is my mother, and I think that is me she is pregnant with.' I point to the lady on the right. 'And so I assume the

207

woman she is with is Daphne like it says on the back, an old friend of hers, but I'm positive I've never met her.'

'They look happy.'

'They really do.' The words catch in my throat. Again, sadness that I never saw my mother so happy washes over me.

'You definitely don't know this woman, Daphne?'

'No. Not at all. I mean some memories of my childhood are a bit hit and miss, there are gaps, but that's normal isn't it? We remember stuff from photos, like implanted memories, and then we must forget or misremember things as well. Maybe she was my mother's best friend before I was born, but then something happened between them. A fight maybe? Or an affair with my dad? I can't think of anything else.'

Iona scrunches up her face in thought.

'The past is often confusing. It's strange to discover our parents as people with secrets we don't know about, happens more than you'd think, especially after someone passes away. We often see it here. This generation,' she nods towards my father, 'hid a *lot* of stuff. Things that always come out at some point even though they've tried really hard to bury them. It's a shame their children, or in some cases grandchildren, have to pick up the pieces of their broken lives.'

'But what if those children and grandchildren never discover what happened?'

She sighs as though she too is living with a trauma that isn't hers. With no warning I have the urge to hug her. I want her to put her arms round me, to comfort me and tell me I'm not alone. Tears fill my eyes and I twist away from her.

Outside the window the wind swirls the last of the autumnal leaves around the grounds. Many of the trees are bare, sleeping and resting before springing back to life. The urge to hibernate along with them this year is overwhelming.

'Are you okay?' she asks.

I wipe away a stray tear. 'I'm fine. I don't know why I thought Dad would be able to help. He and my mother rarely spoke even when he was at the house to see me or drop me off after taking me out for the day. They split up before I was even born, maybe he didn't even know Daphne either.' But then I look at the way he's grasping the photo of Heather, his knuckles white. He knew her.

'I'll leave that photo here,' I say. 'It's obviously important to him. But if he mentions anything, anything about a Heather or Daphne, anything, you'll call me, right?'

'Of course.'

Outside in my car I look at where Anya is on my phone, and see that she's back at her halls of residence. Switching my phone off I lean back against the headrest and close my eyes. My whole body aches. Every limb weighed down.

Tears bubble beneath the surface as well as a strong urge to scream out loud, or punch a wall. Maybe I have the flu or some nasty virus, or Anya's chest infection. My body feels uncomfortable, like a badly fitting jacket. The arms are too long, the chest is too tight, and the buttons are refusing to do up. I rub the base of my neck; my shoulders are bruised and tender.

Sleep is the magic pill I need right now. But every night – even though I can close my eyes a little easier with the reassurance that Jamie is watching over Anya – fresh nightmares have come. A little girl with blonde curls, who I can't quite grasp, runs away from me. A cascade of water rushes over me so I can't breathe. And then there are the sweats, the palpitations, and worst of all the panic I feel when I wake up. Sleep doesn't restore me. My dreams are not sweet.

And I am sick of it.

Before paying Jamie, the only thing that eased the nightmares and insomnia was seeing Anya, or drinking myself into oblivion, but I can't do that every night. The hangovers are too painful. Jamie texting me works, but I can feel the familiar twitch of my addiction returning.

Even though every bone in my body is screaming at me to go home and sleep off the rest of this hangover, my mind is running the show. I need an Anya fix, a glance at her alive and breathing. The blue dot on the app isn't cutting it today; the slow descent into the grief of not seeing her taking hold once more as though I am a gambling addict buying a scratch card instead of attending a poker game with my credit card in my back pocket. I know Jamie isn't lying, I see the blue dot of Anya's location move and I know she is alive, but him protecting her isn't the same.

It needs to be me.

Without stopping to think I drive towards the motorway on autopilot. One quick look at her will do. I could call, or text, but that's not the same. My mind works overtime; Jamie could pretend to be her and text back, or he could be carrying her phone around with him and lying to get my money.

Of course that's what he's doing, I convince myself. How have I trusted him? He might not even be with her when he texts to say she's breathing. I know nothing about him. He could be making her ill so I worry more and pay him more. Oh my God, what have I done?

If a friend was telling me they were having these thoughts I'd tell them they were intrusive, and not real. But the trouble is, when they are your thoughts and your beliefs, rationalising them is harder.

Addiction *is* hard. And I have to accept that, until I discover why I feel this way, this compulsion to protect Anya at all costs is one I can't stop. I feel as though the guilt is already there, buried in my bones, waiting to yell at me, *I told you so.*

Before I know what I'm doing or can question myself, I'm on the motorway heading towards my daughter.

I lean over and pull the packet of cigarettes from my bag and as I drive I smoke one after the other until the packet is empty, opening the window a fraction and exhaling through the crack.

She'll thank me one day, I think.

And she'll understand.

40

CATHERINE

THURSDAY 31ST OCTOBER

Parked opposite Anya's halls, I rub my arms to generate some heat. There isn't enough petrol for me to leave the engine on. My legs jiggle and I ignore the pressure of my full bladder.

Anya might not leave her bedroom this evening. She may have planned to drink at home or watch a film for Halloween, but I'm calmer being close to her. I want to reach through her window and stroke her hair; let her know I'm protecting her.

We haven't properly spoken since I dropped her back after she was unwell. I've no idea if she completed the course of antibiotics. I'd texted to ask, but she responded saying she was fine and to stop worrying.

Students mill around the gates smoking and I wish Anya was one of them. They huddle wearing cropped coats that I'm not sure serve any purpose, their midriffs exposed to the air. Like me at that age, these teenagers don't notice the cold.

A small part of me wishes I could go back. I'd do everything differently.

Having grown up with my mother as my only role model I thought mistrusting people was normal. That not letting them in was a necessary tool to protect myself from the pain they had the potential to cause. Every time a colleague got dumped and spent days in mourning, my resolve to stay locked away, untouched by anyone, was strengthened. I may not have experienced the highs of life, but I also didn't suffer the lows.

Looking back I can see it was bullshit. In truth, I don't know how to love or be loved. I mean, what kind of love is this, sitting outside your daughter's university house waiting to stalk her if she goes out? I'm fucked-up.

As I reach for my keys, planning to drive home to sleep off my shame and hangover, she appears.

But something's wrong.

Anya lights up a cigarette next to the group already there. One of them puts their arm around her and every single part of me wants to hold her tight, promise to make everything better, and vow to kill whoever has upset her. But I don't. Instead, I grip the steering wheel and watch as if I'm at a drive-through.

The uncomfortable sense of dread inside me intensifies and I shift in the car seat.

I can't hear what they're saying as they pull her into a group hug. She takes another drag of her cigarette and wipes the tears from her cheeks, thick black smudges of mascara darken beneath her eyes. She coughs in between drags and I snarl. This is wrong. Her crying. Her coughing. Her smoking. But I can't leave my car, or hug her, or bring her home. My ears hum. My fingers tingle and my vision is blurry.

One of them flails their arms around, clearly giving Anya a stern lecture, while another rubs her back and offers another cigarette, rolling it far too thick, the filter falling onto the floor. Anya's sobs merge into laughter as their words work their magic. There's no way I'll know what has upset her. Whether she's struggling with an assignment or arguing with a friend.

All of a sudden the girls look at the gate, before gathering around Anya in a move I can only describe as fish shoaling together to protect each other from a predator.

Jamie appears. He reaches out to Anya, but she turns away from him, wiping the fresh tears falling from her eyes. And only then do I realise that what I thought was mascara, is bruising.

What has he done to my baby?

Anger surges through me. I grip the steering wheel and pull myself upright. I'm torn. If I get out of the car I risk Anya hating me even more for spying on her *again*. But I can't sit here knowing she's in pain and do nothing. Not while Jamie is next to her. The little shit.

My fingers hover over the door handle, my mind twisted, but then Anya and her friends walk away from the student village. One of them shouts words I can't hear to Jamie, her finger pointing at him, eyebrows furrowed.

I wait for Jamie to go back inside and then get out of the car and follow Anya and the girls, my arm brushing the walls of the buildings we pass in case I need to melt into the bricks unseen if Anya turns round. I wish I had a dark cap and hoody. Although more than anything, I wish had a coat.

One of the girls pulls a small bottle of vodka from her bag and they take it in turns to swig. They laugh, singing songs I don't know and stumbling through the dark, cold streets towards the centre of town. They're not aware I'm following them, lost in their own carefree world. A world I never fully inhabited, at any age.

Before long we cross over the river that runs through the centre of town. A pathway below runs beside the water, diving underneath hidden tunnels, with no railings in places. The water looks murky and brown, parts highlighted by street lights; I imagine shopping trolleys laying to rest on the bottom, covered in rust, plastic rubbish and debris.

The girls disappear inside a pub over the bridge. A bouncer

on the door checks the ID of one of them, the shortest of the group, but not Anya. She waltzes straight past him with the confidence of having been here many times, but I don't recognise the location from when I have tracked her on the app.

Then I look at my phone and see I have no signal. No location found. The pub looks like the kind of building you'd only enter if you were a regular, no welcoming fairy lights or signs outside inviting you to come and sample two-for-one drinks. One of the windows is boarded up and I wonder if a fist or a chair had smashed the glass behind the wooden sheet.

The clouds are swollen, blackened and full of water. I will them not to dump a load of rain on me. An icy wind makes me pull my cardigan tighter and I walk back towards the trees that line the riverbank, cowering underneath them, hoping their bare branches will offer me some form of protection should it rain.

My mind whirs. Had Jamie punched her? Or was the bruise an innocent drunken injury? But then why were they so mad at him? He must've hurt her, but that could've have been anything from dumping Anya to flirting with someone else. The bruise might've been mascara after all. The frustration at not being able to walk into the pub, pull her out and take her home is unbearable.

Without warning, Jamie appears at the top of the steps leading down to the river and walks over to the pub. Holding my breath I sink back towards the metal railings and further under the tree. He doesn't see me. He sways as though drunk, his legs unsteady, his arms hanging beside him.

He's come for Anya. I should tell the bouncer. He needs to know Jamie's dangerous, but I can't get to him before Jamie does. Helpless, I watch him let Jamie through the large wooden doors. They close behind him creating a block between Anya and me. A barrier I can't penetrate.

Leaves scurry around my feet. Wind shakes the branches of the tree. A distant siren screams.

I have to protect her.

The bouncer raises his eyebrows when I approach him, not the usual clientele of the pub, he's probably thinking. My wrinkles and grey hair giving my age away and my lack of make-up revealing that coming to the pub tonight wasn't my original plan.

'Hi.' I flash him my best smile. 'This is going to sound weird, but I need you to listen. Please.'

He folds his arms. I wonder if he's considering alerting the police to a mad woman on the loose. Or maybe he's not interested. Merely paid to watch the pretty girls go in and out and break up the drunken fights over them.

'My daughter, Anya, she's in there.' I point to the big wooden pub doors. 'And the guy you let in a few minutes ago is her boyfriend, or ex-boyfriend, I'm not sure. Anyway, he attacked her earlier, or at least I think he did.'

The bouncer's frown deepens. He holds up his hands to stop me talking. 'You're telling me you think the guy I just let in is a danger to your daughter, right?'

'Yes.' I'm so relieved he believes me. 'But she mustn't know I'm here or that I've been talking to you. She thinks I'm a bit overprotective.' A nervous laugh escapes me.

He laughs too, but as though I've told a joke.

'I know why you're laughing. Me standing here having followed my daughter to the pub without her knowing gives the impression that I definitely am overprotective, but this is serious.'

He rolls his eyes and shakes his head. A ball of frustration forms in my gut.

'Look,' I say, my voice loud and steady, 'I mean it; she's in danger. I know she is. You have to trust me. Mother's instinct. I need you to help.' Short of grabbing on to his shirt, which wouldn't be a good idea, and shaking him to get him to understand, there isn't a lot else I can do. For a second I think about bursting through the doors of the pub and to hell with the consequences, but then he speaks.

'Fine. I'll keep an eye on them when they come out. She'll be safe in there, it's packed tonight cos it's Halloween. Will that do?'

No that won't fucking do, I want to scream, but I can't, so I guess it'll have to.

Walking away, I nestle myself over the road in amongst the trees again and wait for Anya and her friends to emerge. He watches me and shakes his head. My teeth chatter. I hop on the spot and stamp my feet into the ground to force some blood down there and warm them up.

The rational side of my brain tells me to go back to the car and drive home; that I've done all I can by alerting the bouncer. He wouldn't want a young woman to be attacked on his watch. She's safe. For now.

But the other, cavewoman, part of my brain, tells me Jamie won't care about the bouncers. He'll attack her anyway. How long has he been texting me in the middle of the night, taking my money and lying to me for? He fooled me. Or did I fool myself?

Maybe there was a part of me that knew he couldn't be trusted, but I refused to listen because more than anything I wanted to keep Anya safe. I'm so stupid.

A fox ventures out of the shadows further down the road, its fur darker than the bright orange of storybook illustrations. She stops. Her eyes glow in the street lamps. She looks up at me and we find ourselves in a standoff.

Is she questioning what I'm doing? Even though the fox does worse? She leaves her cubs to forage for food. There's a moment of stillness as we stand apart, locked in a shared stare. Both of us following our instincts and doing the best for our children.

The spell is broken as the door to the pub opens and a group of people burst out. The fox runs away and I know it's too late for me to do the same. I scan their faces. And then I see Anya.

Her friends have their arms around her, pulling her away, more tears in her eyes. She wobbles and I fear she's downed shots non-stop since being inside. I retch at the memory of last night's tequila and swallow the image of me sobbing at the bar down.

'Everything okay?' I hear the bouncer ask and with horror I realise I hadn't told him what Anya looks like. He doesn't know this is the person he's meant to watch out for. How dumb can I be?

I take a step forward, towards Anya, and then stop.

Jamie falls out of the doors and the bouncer puts his hand out to stop him. 'Anya, wait. Please.'

'Whoa there, mate. I think she wants to be left alone.'

But Jamie pushes the bouncer's hand away. 'Gerroff me. I'm not your mate.' He looks to Anya who stands not far from him, surrounded by her protective crew. 'Don't listen to them, Anya. It's not true. Please.'

Anya is perfectly playing the part of a vulnerable young woman. The camera zooming in on her tortured face as the screen fades and the drum beats. The nearby street light highlights her tears as though placed there by a professional to make the scene more intense.

'Leave me alone, Jamie!' she screams, her words slurred. 'I saw the texts. I know what you've been doing with my mum.'

Oh shit. Shitshitshit.

'It's not how it looks,' he shouts over the bouncer's arm, which rests across his chest, barring him from moving forward.

'I don't care!' Anya shouts at Jamie.

He moves towards her, but the bouncer uses both hands to stop him.

'Leave her alone, mate,' he says and Jamie pushes him away and turns to go back into the pub shouting, 'Fuck this,' as he does.

He faces Anya one more time.

'You need to be having a go at your mum, not me. *She's* the one that started this!' he shouts before slamming the door behind him. The bouncer faces Anya, and with a feeling of dread I know before the words are out of his mouth what he's going to say.

For a brief moment I consider climbing the tree to hide amongst the bare branches. Everything blurs as I watch him tell Anya that I was there earlier, and that I'd spoken to him about her and about Jamie. There's confusion in her eyes as she listens. Why did I think he'd be loyal to me? Or maybe he thinks he's doing her a favour, by telling her I was right about Jamie and that she should've listened.

Then my stomach drops. He faces me, holds out his hand, and points.

Anya's eyes narrow and her mouth purses as she looks at me huddled beneath the tree.

And like a mouse in a trap, I'm caught and unable to move.

41

CATHERINE
THURSDAY 31ST OCTOBER

R un, run, run, the voice in my head tells me, but I am stuck to the pavement like spat-out chewing gum. I can't come back from this. Anya won't see that everything I have done is to protect her and keep her safe. She'll only hate me even more.

Holding my breath I hear Anya mutter to her friends who walk away, glancing over their shoulders to look at me, the psycho mum. With her arms folded, Anya marches over the road and I'm thrown back to my childhood where I'd hide under the kitchen table to avoid being told off by my mother. My knees pulled up to my chest, my arms wrapped around them.

Anya comes close and points at me. 'I don't want to know why the fuck you're here, or what the fuck you're doing,' she spits and I can smell the alcohol on her breath. 'But I need you to leave me the fuck alone. You need help.'

'Anya, please,' I say, an echo of Jamie's words.

'No.' She holds up her hand. 'Stop. I saw the texts Jamie sent to you. And I know you've been paying him to watch over me. As if I'm not fucking capable of even looking after myself. Do you know how that makes me feel? I mean, what the hell were you thinking? Getting my boyfriend to be your own personal spy, that's fucked-up. And how many times have you come up here to watch me? You're twisted.'

'Love, I can explain.' I realise I sound like Sean when I'd caught him cheating. Is there always an excuse for shitty behaviour? But I don't know where to start or how to explain my paranoia, my anxiety, and the insistent instinct telling my gut she's in danger.

'I don't want to know. Seriously, you need help, Mum. And you need to go and get that help far, far away from me.'

I bite the inside of my cheek. I want to cry. She's my daughter. Why doesn't she want to be the one to help me? Then I remember how I felt about my mother at eighteen and how I blamed her actions for making me feel that way.

'Fuck off,' Anya says, crying. 'Please, go home. Get some help.' She stumbles away and down the steps to the river and I don't understand why she's heading home down a dark pathway next to a river instead of along the lit roads. She hates water.

Maybe she's so desperate to get away from me that she has become disorientated. Or the booze is fooling her into thinking she's safer down there, removing any sign of fear. But I can't let her walk home that way by herself. I don't care that she wants me to leave her alone; I am not leaving her alone down there.

The bouncer is watching us from over the road and until now the pub doors have stayed closed with Jamie safely locked inside drowning his sorrows. But they open and Jamie emerges. He looks over at me and starts to cross the road, the bouncer following not far behind, calling at him to stop.

Without hesitating I race to escape Jamie and follow Anya down the pathway by the river. The water is murky and brown; moonlight mingles with the lights from the street above and makes it look like quicksand. A body of liquid that could suck you under and never spit you out. Anya walks not far ahead of me. She is fast, her long legs taking her further away inch by inch.

She doesn't look back, but I can see her wipe tears from her cheeks. My heart sinks. This isn't what was meant to happen. She wasn't meant to find out. Or hate me. I've ruined everything. At the top of the steps behind me, I can hear Jamie and the bouncer in a heated argument. I hope the bouncer can hold him back, unless they decide that I am the dangerous one. I carry on in pursuit of Anya.

'Anya,' I call out, not caring anymore. The need to protect her drives me forward. I need to explain. And I need to keep her away from Jamie. 'Anya, wait. Please.'

Her shoulders slump as she stops and stands facing away from me. Her head drops. Hopeful, I race towards her, thinking she wants to listen after all; the loyalty towards her mum overtaking her anger and frustration.

'Anya?'

Fraction by fraction she twists round to face me. The pathway peppered with sticks and twigs from the fierce wind blowing from the trees. She kicks a twig away and stares at the ground. The tears fall freely down our faces.

But there's no softness as she looks at me. The anger still burns. Her chest rises and falls as she breathes and tries to contain her rage. She clenches her fists either side of her and I stand opposite and wait for the explosion.

'What the fuck do I need to do to get you to leave me alone?' she shouts. 'I can't deal with this now.'

'I'm sorry,' I whisper, too afraid to move or say anything else. I want to hold her, to comfort her like I'd done when she'd hurt herself as a child or woken crying from a nightmare. To kiss her pain away or scare off the monsters lurking under her bed.

'I'm sure you *are* sorry. Like I'm sure Jamie is sorry, but that doesn't excuse what you both did.'

'I want to keep you safe,' I explain, but she rolls her eyes and huffs.

'No you don't. What you want is to not feel guilty if something does happen to me.' She steps towards the edge of the pathway. 'Don't pretend this is about protecting me. This is about protecting you. It always has been. Every time you made me hold your hand to cross a road, even though my friends had been doing it by themselves for years. Every time you wouldn't let me go to a party or a sleepover. Every single bit of your fucking overprotectiveness. None of those actions were for my safety, they were to prevent you having to live with the consequences of something happening to me.'

'No, Anya, that's not true. It was for *you*. Always.'

'Wake up. Gran was the same; I could see it. The way she spoke to you, the way she treated you. You've suffocated me for years like she suffocated you.' Again, Anya steps nearer the edge, nearer the river.

'No.' I don't know what else to say. Anya has always had the freedom I never did. She'd been allowed out, she'd gone to sleepovers and on school trips abroad.

'I thought coming to university would finally allow me to break free from you. You can't protect me forever.'

'But...'

'No buts. I can't fucking do this anymore. Do you want me to throw myself into the river to get rid of you? Because I will.' She takes another step closer and I worry I've driven her to insanity.

'Anya, don't be ridiculous.' My heart is pounding.

'Mum, go. Please.'

Her hair blows around her face and long dark-brown strands stick to her tears. Her freckles have fully melted away and left behind smooth pale skin. I want to reach out and hold her close. I want her to curl up in my lap like she used to when we'd watch a film together. I want to brush her hair after bathing her before she would instruct me how to style it. I want her to tuck her feet into the top of my pyjamas as we co-sleep.

Her life has gone by too fast. A snapshot. A split second as the shutter flickers and the photo is captured.

'Anya, don't do this. Let me walk you home.' Instinctively, I take a step towards her, but she recoils and steps back.

'No!' she shouts. She takes another step. She's too close to the edge, full of anger, full of alcohol, devoid of sense.

'Okay, okay.' I hold my hands up in surrender. 'But you've been drinking. You need to go home.'

Anya sways. She puts her hands to her head and pulls at her hair. Then she moves backwards again.

'Anya, careful. You're near the—'

'Stop telling me to be careful. You can't protect me anymore. I don't need you.'

Her words cut me like a knife and I bat them away.

She's still too close to the edge. If I move to her she'll step backwards. Into the dark brown water. Be swallowed whole.

'Fine,' I say. 'I'll leave you alone. Please call a friend, someone to come and walk you home, please.'

She shakes her head and closes her eyes. And then I watch in horror as she spins around. Her foot catches on a fallen pile of twigs and leaves. Her leg gives way. Her knee bends underneath her.

'Anya!' I shout. 'Anya, no!'

She lands on her knees and steadies herself inches from the edge of the pathway. Then, dusting off fallen leaves from her trousers, she turns to look at me and holds up her hands to keep me back.

'Please, please leave me alone, Mum.' Her voice is soft now, defeated.

Every part of me wants to stay with her until she leaves the path. Instead I stand still, my heart thudding, as she walks away from me, swaying gently as if the wind is rocking her. I can't bear to leave her like this.

'I'm sorry,' I call.

My unexpected words cause her to jump and she wobbles again. But this time she can't steady herself. And I can't catch her before she falls.

She is silent as she tumbles. Her arms swing, her hair floats in the air around her, her mouth the shape of a perfect 'o', but the splash her body makes as she enters the river is as though a thousand waves have crashed over me at once.

Screaming her name I race to the edge of the pathway and look down.

But she is gone.

42

ANYA

Your face is filled with horror, watching me fall backwards. Drawn to the filthy water like a magnet, but I'm not scared by this strange force I don't understand and can't control sucking me in deeper and dragging me down.

This is what you feared, right? Losing me forever. But don't you see? You caused this; I am falling because of you. You haven't protected me or saved me.

You've made everything worse, so much worse, and we will both suffer, but you'll suffer more than me though because as I hit the water I can feel my fear leaving my body and then a familiar sensation fills the space the fear has left, an emotion I can't quite grasp, but calms me and calls me home, as though this was always meant to happen.

You could've stopped this, Mum, if only you'd listened.

But it's too late.

43

DAPHNE

My darling, I wrote, thank you.

Thank you, I continued, my handwriting shaky, thank you in advance for everything I know you will do for me and for my daughter. I'm sorry it has come to this, but I see no other way. I cannot protect her. I only cause her harm even though I have tried and tried to keep her safe.

You'll do a better job than me. I know Catherine isn't the baby you lost, and that no one can replace her. And I know she cannot replace Heather either.

I thought our grief would unite us, but instead, it's only torn us apart. You blame me, like he did, for Heather's death. And you're both right. Her death was my fault. I fell asleep, and she died. The guilt over what happened suffocates me so I can't breathe anymore.

I stopped writing. My hand released the pen before I put it to my mouth to stifle a sob. Writing this letter was harder than what I knew had to come next.

A smell of smoke wafted over the garden fence. Someone was having a late lunchtime BBQ. I imagined the father stood over burning coals, sipping from a bottle of beer and turning the burgers over and over, wrapping bananas and chocolate in tin foil, while reminding the small children who ran and laughed around him to be careful. The mother inside the house, buttering the rolls and preparing a salad.

My garden was empty. There was no husband. I was no longer a wife. And my daughter napped in front of Bagpuss on the television. She'd already slept for an hour, but I wouldn't wake her until I was ready. Besides, she needed her sleep ahead of what was to come.

The summer sun vanished behind a cloud and a chill spread over me. The trees at the end of the garden rustled as though throwing my plan to and fro and I urged them to keep quiet a while longer. They didn't scream to wake me up and save my daughter, so they could repent now and stay silent.

The pen rested on my lap and I read through the words on my letter. There was no editing that could hide the horror behind what I was writing to say.

Or what I was about to do.

44

CATHERINE
THURSDAY 31ST OCTOBER

'Help!' I scream into the darkness. 'Help her, please.'

The river doesn't spit her out. The murky water carries on flowing and minding its own business as though untroubled by the intrusion. To the right, for a second, I think I see a flash of her hair, a hand reaching up, but then the ripple vanishes.

'Please!' I shout into the night again. 'Help her.' I can't dive in, even though I know I must. But I don't want to be the one to pull my dead daughter out of the river. I don't want to have to explain that I'm the reason she's in there.

'Fuck.' Jamie appears behind me. He runs his hands through his hair. 'Call an ambulance.'

My phone's in my bag and I fumble with the zip, my hands frozen and cold. *Please let there be a signal.* Jamie starts to undress, taking his shoes off and his coat. But before he is done we hear a splash and we turn to see the bouncer, fully clothed, jump in and under the water, pulling Anya up within seconds. The river isn't as deep as he is tall and he holds her in front of him and shouts up to us.

'Help me,' his deep voice bellows through the darkness. 'It's fucking freezing in here. And fucking filthy.' He spits water from his mouth off to the side of Anya's head.

Anya's arms are wrapped around his neck and her hands are gripped together. That means she's not unconscious, I think, and sob. But she is pale. How long was she under for, seconds? A minute?

The swishing of the swaying trees and the roaring of the river grate like nails on a chalkboard. Everything is blurry. I am on a fairground ride I want to get off. I close my eyes.

She'll be okay.

When I open them again, the bouncer and Jamie have somehow managed to get Anya back on the pathway. Relief floods through me. She lies against Jamie, who has covered her with his coat and is rubbing her arms to generate some warmth. She is awake, but sleepy, her eyes closing every now and again.

Her upper body shakes and jolts her into full consciousness. Her lips are blue. Her teeth chatter. Water drips off her clothes onto the pathway below, staining the tarmac as if she is melting into the ground beneath her.

Guilt wraps around me like a blanket. She'd be at home and safe if I hadn't come here tonight. At every opportunity, if I'd left when my gut or someone had told me to, she'd be safe. Like a punch in the stomach I realise that since coming out of the river she hasn't even called out for me, for her mum. She doesn't want my comfort. Instead her fingers reach for Jamie's hand and he takes hers and squeezes tight.

The branches rustle above us. The sound sends bristles along my arms and makes the hairs stand on edge. The world spins around me. Every muscle is drained of power, my brain unable to think. I want to sleep. Forever.

A waft of smoke passes by, a taste of sourness on my tongue, my senses doing everything they can to wake me from this nightmare, to make me present. But I rub my temples and force the noises from my brain. Firmly embedded, they only become louder.

I could've killed her.

A cloud moves to reveal the moon, lighting up the pathway next to the river with a haunting silver glow. I want to dive into the murky water and drown everything out. Blue lights and sirens fill the night air and an ambulance arrives.

The hustle and bustle make me feel once again like I am watching a scene from a film, removed from the action and nestled in a safe place. Standing at a distance, I watch the paramedic wrap Anya in a blanket and give her some water. A cuff is wrapped around her arm and a monitor clipped to her finger.

You'll need some more tests, I hear them tell her. They ask if there is anyone she would like to call and she shakes her head. She doesn't look at me. Not once. The paramedics' words and their concern pass by in a blur. They think I'm an innocent bystander. They have no idea I'm her mother. Or that I caused this. I am an uninvited guest.

But more than that, I am the reason this has happened to her. Not Jamie. Not a bacterial chest infection. Me.

I'm the danger I was afraid of.

So when the police arrive soon after to question everyone about what happened, I slip away unnoticed into the shadows under a bridge. Anya will tell them she lost her footing and fell. There's no doubt in my mind that she won't mention her mother, because I know she doesn't want anything to do with me ever again. And she's right. In order to keep her safe I must leave her alone.

My heart beats louder the further away from my daughter I walk, as though it is trying to remain connected to hers, wanting to find her heartbeat like a distant signal. I open up the tracking app on my phone and see the blue dot around her photo moving along the main road to the local hospital. I wonder if Jamie is in the ambulance with her, if they've resolved their argument, if young love wins out again.

The wind buffets me and the world comes back to life. A siren blares in the distance. Branches on the trees whisper even though they are devoid of leaves. A fox screams. The river roars. I cover my ears with my hands and try to shut everything out. I can't think straight. Has Anya called Sean? Should I?

No. I won't call him. She will. And as soon as she tells him what I've done he'll be in touch to let me know how much I've messed up. But I don't need his judgement or criticism.

Anya is right. What I need, is help.

45

CATHERINE

THURSDAY 31ST OCTOBER

The halls of residence is dark. No one arrives or leaves. The light outside the little shop flickers; the bulb is about to die. I count the flickers until I reach one hundred, then check my phone again.

The battery is on three per cent. Anya's blue dot hovers above the hospital as it has for the last few hours. Jamie hasn't returned here. I know because I've been watching. I can't leave. My mind has two main thoughts. The first is that I am a danger to Anya and need to stay away. The second is that without me, the real danger will come and claim her.

Either way I know I mustn't fall asleep.

With trembling hands I look at my phone. The second thought niggles at me, taking hold. She isn't safe there. Hospitals can't always save people. I need to go there and check she is okay for myself, whether she wants me there or not. She doesn't need to know. But I have to go. If I leave her alone, if I don't watch out for her and make sure they are doing everything they can to make her better, then she'll die.

I'm her mother. Only I can save her.

Recoiling at the smell as I enter the hospital I don't question why I am here. Everything is bland and sterile. Not only have germs been wiped out, but also all colour. This place has no soul.

At the bottom of the stairs and lifts next to reception I pause to catch my breath before a stale smell insults me as I inhale. Behind me a porter pushes a large yellow bin and I cover my nose and mouth with my hand. The label on the bin tells me it is waste, filled with blood or urine from inpatients. Tainted with infection. The doors to the lifts open and I dive in and inhale the clean inner air deeply.

The receptionist had told me a few minutes earlier that they'd taken Anya from A&E to a ward on the fifth floor, information I'm not sure she should've given out, but I was grateful she'd seen my distress, trusted I was who I said I was, and answered my questions. I'm hopeful the nurses on the ward will do the same.

The mirror in the lift reveals the true extent of my distress. I look like I've been dragged through a hedge backwards, then forwards and then up and down again and again. My hair sticks out, the part on the crown looking like it's been backcombed. Desperate to look presentable I lick my palms and smooth each stray strand down.

Then I wipe the dirty smudges from under my bloodshot eyes and pinch my cheeks. My lips have a tinge of white and blue around them; I still haven't warmed up from being outside without a coat for so long. My stomach grumbles. My mouth is dry. But there is no food at the bottom of my bag. No water. I couldn't eat anyway. Each wave of panic causes bile to rise at the back of my throat.

The lift pings and the doors open. Outside in a small square space devoid of colour a group of people wait even though it is the middle of the night. Their faces are etched with either concern or fear. Their brows furrowed. Their hands clench and unclench. Their eyes are red from crying or from lack of sleep.

One woman takes a tissue out of her handbag and dabs at her cheeks before blowing her nose. She has no one with her for comfort and I wonder who she's been visiting. She is about my age. Maybe it's her mother who is unwell.

A fresh pang of guilt is strong. My mother had been in this hospital before she died, but I had not come to visit as often as I should've. And I wasn't with her when her time had come. Although, I think that was probably what she'd wanted anyway, her privacy, as always, overriding anything else.

'Can I help you?' a soft voice to my right asks from behind the nurses' station.

'Yes,' I say and then I pause. How do I ask for Anya without her finding out I am here or raising the nurse's suspicion that I shouldn't be here at all? 'Anya Williams, I think she was brought in here earlier? Or at least to one of the wards on this floor.'

If the nurse is concerned or confused she doesn't give anything away. Her face remains smiling, her eyes warm and welcoming. She looks down at a screen in front of her and frowns.

'And you are?' she asks, looking up at me, a fresh smile having removed the frown.

Coughing to clear my throat and compose my voice I take a deep breath.

'I'm her mum.' Emotion washes over me and I can't stop myself from crying.

The nurse comes out from behind the desk and puts her arm around my shoulder.

'Come with me.' She leads me to the empty visitor's lounge across the hallway. Faded posters hang from a noticeboard at one end reminding people to get their flu jab. Another asking if you think you might have an STD. The nurse hands me a tissue and sits down next to me on one of the faded red chairs.

'I'm sorry,' I sob and she rubs my back.

'It's fine, really. You're not the first person crying in here today. All part of the job. This is what we do when visitors aren't with patients.'

'You're clearly in the right role,' I say and try a small laugh. She's not really doing anything special, but already I feel calmer and safer with her. Her hair smells of coconuts.

'It's normal to be upset when one of your children has had an accident. The shock often comes after the event when everything catches up with us. Let it out. We've got time; your daughter isn't going anywhere.'

She's given me the permission I've needed to release the emotions trapped inside me, but I'm too frightened to let everything out because I don't know what I'll uncover in the process. This year has changed me, the catalyst of Anya leaving throwing up things I don't want to deal with and those I don't even understand. Put everything in a box, close the lid, lock it shut. Throw away the key into the deepest darkest ocean. Suck. It. Up.

Sniffing, I wipe my eyes.

'Such a silly accident. And so sudden. One minute she was there and the next–' I sob again and she hands me another tissue. 'I'm sorry, I can't stop crying.'

The nurse's face oozes sympathy, eyes soft and warm, a hint of a smile, but also an expression I can't quite read.

'Like I said,' she stands, 'this is a perfectly normal reaction to a traumatic event. I'll go and make you a cup of tea, give you some time before I take you to see her. I need to check on a patient.'

Standing I shake my head.

'No, thank you, but no. I think I'd just like to see my daughter.'

The nurse's face crumples and for a second I am terrified she is going to tell me Anya is dead. The nurse looks at the floor before looking back to me. Or has Anya already told her not to let me in?

'Is she here? Anya. Is she okay? Tell me she's okay.' Panic spreads through me like a wild fire. 'Doesn't she want to see me?'

Why isn't the nurse speaking? I take a step towards her, my arms outstretched for the second time tonight, ready to grab on to someone and shake them for the information I need.

She steps backwards and holds up her hands to stop me. 'Mrs Williams,' she starts.

'Miss,' I say even though it isn't important. 'What is it? Where is she?' I'm hyperventilating. The edges of my vision blur and a ringing fills my ears.

'Miss Williams, take a breath. You've gone very pale.'

Closing my eyes I clench my jaw. Why won't she tell me? Oh my God. I killed her, didn't I? I killed Anya. The paramedics were wrong; she wasn't okay. I once heard that when someone you love dies, even if they are on the other side of the world, you feel it at that exact moment, and you know. A part of you dies with them. Why don't I feel it? Why can't I sense she is gone? I crouch on the floor, my hands pulling at my hair. Messy sobs escape my mouth.

'Miss Williams.' The nurse's voice is fuzzy and I don't understand the muffled sounds. She places her hand on the back of my head, gently as though cradling a baby, and pushes it down between my knees.

'Breathe,' she instructs. 'In and out, deep breaths.' She rubs my back with her free hand. 'You're having a panic attack.'

I try and try, but can't fill my lungs.

Black and white spots dart in front of my eyes as if fireworks are going off around me. I blink them away. My pulse beats faster. Sitting here on the floor I want to shut everything out. I don't want to know about Anya. With my head between my knees, everything is okay. Anya is still alive. At the moment I haven't been told otherwise.

Time passes where I struggle to control my panic. The nurse sits beside me, her hand on my back, her thumb gently stroking me through my cardigan. The movement is rhythmic and soothing, like being rocked.

My eyes close, but I force them open. A voice inside my head is telling me I mustn't fall asleep.

Noises from the corridor of the hospital filter into the room. Footsteps race by. Muted conversations. An alarm in the distance.

'Are you feeling better?' the nurse asks and I look up and face her.

'I think so.'

'Have you had a panic attack before?'

I nod.

'They can be very frightening. And quite draining.'

'Is my daughter here?' I ask, my voice a whisper. She doesn't need to tell me about panic attacks. I support women who have them.

The nurse's face changes and again I can't read her expression. She looks concerned, but also suspicious. An expression like the one my mother used to wear when I was a teenager and she hadn't believed I'd been at the library after school. Something would pass over her eyes as she scoured my face for any sign that I was not telling the truth.

'Come and sit back up here, slowly,' the nurse says and points to the seats behind us. My knees are stiff as I stand and my lower back aches. 'I won't be a minute. Please try not to worry.'

Watching the door close behind her I brace myself for the worst, already knowing where I'll go and what I'll do if the nurse tells me the words I never want to hear. My palms are sweaty. My hands shake as they rest on my lap, my fingers working at the skin around my nails and picking it off in chunks. I bite my lip until I taste blood on my tongue. But I don't feel any physical pain. I'm floating above my body, watching the nightmare unfold further.

My cheeks are flushed and tears fall down my face. I make no effort to stop them.

I can't do this. I can't hear this. I want to shut out the world. Fall asleep and never wake up.

Suddenly the urge to flee is overwhelming as though every bone in my body has been injected with adrenaline and I need to run until it is burnt off.

I race to the door. I can hear the nurse calling after me from her station, but I don't stop. I will not turn back. She'll see the guilt in my eyes. She'll know this was my fault. She'll hate me as much as I hate myself.

The lift takes too long and so I reach for the door to the stairs and flee down them two at a time, falling and tripping and getting back up again. The nurse is a monster, one that wants to tear my heart from my body, chasing me. The creature has no face, only long arms like branches, fingers like twigs, reaching out, clawing its way towards me. I run and run, not catching my breath, not stopping.

Rushing, I bash into someone coming up the stairs the other way, but I don't stop to apologise. I ignore their disgruntled calls.

Outside the cold air slaps me, forcing its way into my lungs and chilling me from the inside out. I cough and splutter before finding my car in the car park. On autopilot I start the engine, not knowing or caring where I am about to drive. I let my instincts take over.

Cars beep as I refuse to give way.

Like a robot I drive into the darkness. Numbness spreads over me as though I am freezing bit by bit. My toes. My fingers. My heart.

The moon travels across the sky, the only indicator I'm aware of that time is passing and then without knowing how, I find myself outside my mother's house.

Not stopping to question why, I use my spare key, still on my key ring, and step inside. The door to my right opens into the lounge, empty. No dust. No china dogs. No rats. Sighing, no tears left to cry, I head up the creaky bare wooden stairs to my old bedroom.

Imagining I can shut everything out, I close the door behind me. Then I curl up on the floor in the slit of moonlight shining through the bay window.

And there, like I used to as a little girl, alone and scared, even though I try to fight it, I sleep.

46

CATHERINE

FRIDAY 1ST NOVEMBER

My mother and I rarely went to church when I was a child. But lying here, on the floor of my childhood bedroom, half asleep and half awake, my mind plays tricks on me and I remember a day when we did, the memory – hidden in the floorboards for decades, waiting for the right time to reappear – awakened simply by me being here.

I remember my mother had instructed I dress in my smartest clothes. My corduroy trousers and a blouse had been all I could find in my wardrobe. Smart clothes were rarely needed and I didn't own any.

It was a cold Sunday morning and frost was welded to the windscreen of the car. Twiddling my thumbs, I sat in the passenger seat as my mother scraped at the white crystals with the edge of an open cassette case. The effort made her huff and she groaned in anger. She hated being late.

My shoulders rose towards my ears in anticipation of her frustration. The atmosphere in the car would change when she got in. Cold air would follow her, cloaking us in silence.

A small patch on the windscreen where she had cleared the

ice appeared and she sat next to me, her glare suggesting that the frozen windscreen was my fault.

We drove to the church and passed several of our neighbours walking there, having left early enough to do so. They were wrapped up in dark coats, hats and gloves. Mr and Mrs Smith walked arm in arm, each supporting the other.

Next to me my mother alternated between sighing and sniffing. She would put her hand to her chest that made me think she was checking her heart was still beating, and then, when she discovered the dull thud inside her, she'd pat it as if to say, *There there, well done for keeping going.*

We pulled up into the church car park and after she'd turned the engine off we sat in silence for a bit.

'Are we going in?' I asked, closing my eyes and waiting for her answer.

With a swift movement, but no words, my mother undid her seat belt and got out of the car.

'That's a yes then,' I muttered and did the same. She walked five steps ahead of me up the path, not turning around to check that I was following. The pathway wound around the back of the church. A high bank to the left, with gravestones peppered at various angles along the top, gave the impression of us being buried in a long tunnel-like open grave alongside the people already laid to rest there.

The pathway was dark and I was glad to feel the sun on my face as we emerged near the entrance to the church. The vicar was at the door, greeting people as they entered and holding out hymnbooks. As my mother approached I thought I saw him do a double take, eyes wide in surprise, and then narrowed in sympathy.

My mother looked at me. 'Wait here,' she instructed.

As always, I did as I was told, hopping from one foot to the other to stay warm. The thin socks I'd put on were unable to block the cold from the ground beneath me and I was scared that death would cover me entirely in ice while I waited. My mother and the vicar mumbled to each other. There was a gentle touch on her arm before a look of understanding passed between them. Then a strange glance at me.

After several minutes my mother beckoned me over and we walked into the church and took a seat in a pew near the back.

Brightly coloured flowers lined the end of each pew and two huge displays stood at the front and I wondered if we'd come to a wedding for people I didn't know. The flowers were yellow and red with small bead-like petals, nestled amongst larger flowers with pink streaks down the middle of them and huge orange buds of pollen.

A mixture of smells filled the air: my mother's perfume, the scent of the pungent flowers, and a waft of dampness. A lady two pews ahead of us sneezed and wiped her nose with a white hankie before immediately sneezing again.

Next to me my mother wrung her own hankie in her hands. Twisting the material into a long, thin rope and winding it through her fingers. Her legs jiggled and I looked down to see what was causing the vibration underfoot. She looked straight ahead. Her eyes darted from left to right and I realised she was looking at the hymn numbers displayed on a wooden board at the front of the church.

She reached for the hymnbook that she'd rested on the small wooden shelf in front of us and turned to the numbered hymns one after the other. 'Morning Has Broken'. 'Give Me Joy'. And then, as she opened up the book to discover the last one, she sobbed. She put the hankie, crumpled and creased, to cover her mouth. 'Shine Jesus Shine'. We'd been made to sing that at school and it was always several pitches too high for me.

Not knowing how to comfort my mother or for what reason the sob had been allowed to escape, I shuffled in my seat and pretended I hadn't noticed. Those hymns were hymns of celebration. Uplifting. I wasn't sure why the thought of singing them made her sad.

She closed the hymnbook and put it back to rest on the shelf in front, above the crocheted prayer cushions.

'Are you okay?' I said, my mouth letting the words out without my permission.

'Fine,' my mother replied. 'The pollen from the flowers is irritating my eyes and my throat, that's all.' Proving this point the lady two rows in front sneezed again.

'Why are we here?' I asked, a small fire of bravery burning inside me.

'To pay our respects.'

'To who?'

My mother sighed and stared at me. I could not read her expression. She looked like she was toying with the idea of telling me a piece of important information. There was a small ball of mascara in the inner corner of each of her eyes and her lipstick was bleeding into the cracks that ran along her top lip. And then it struck me. Make-up. I couldn't remember the last time I'd seen her wear any. And I certainly wasn't allowed to. This was important to her.

She took a deep breath in and looked down at her hands scrunching the hankie inside them.

'Your grandmother,' she said and then turned to face the front of the church again, signalling that I was to ask no more questions.

My grandmother had always been what felt like a figment of my imagination. There was an image of her in my mind, built up from snippets of information my mother had imparted as well as one single photo that rested on the dresser in the dining room. She'd died before I was born, so I am told. I didn't even know where she was buried.

'Oh,' I said and looked forward to see the vicar take his place on the small step at the end of the aisle.

'Good morning, everyone,' he said, his hands clasped a hymnbook close to his chest. 'Firstly, may I draw your attention to the beautiful flowers. They were for a wedding yesterday and the bride and groom kindly said we could keep them here for today's memorial service before collecting them later.'

So my mother was telling the truth about this being a memorial.

'We'll start by singing our first hymn. Number 367. "Morning Has Broken".'

The organ fired up, a sound that, from the few times I had been in church with school, always made me think the person behind the keyboard had drunk far too much alcohol. Either that or the organ itself was drunk.

Without saying a word everyone got to their feet. Some placed their handbags behind them on the pews and shuffled around on their feet in preparation. Some raised their chests and looked upwards. Others looked down, studying the words to the hymn in great detail. Smiling to myself, I could tell the ones who were mouthing the words instead of singing them out loud.

But my mother sang. Her voice was beautiful. She hit every note, even the stupidly high ones. My own voice was muted beside her because I didn't want to drown her out with my off-key attempts.

For a second, I was lost in the moment listening to the gentle voice I had no idea my mother possessed. I was shocked she could sing so tenderly. That there was a part of her that wasn't rock hard and impenetrable.

The hymn ended and my mother placed her hand on my arm and pulled me to sit back down.

The spell was broken.

After that first hymn I couldn't concentrate. The vicar

spoke, but I only caught some of the words, *taken from us too soon, forgiveness, God loves you all, he understands.* Then a list of names I assume were the people we were here to remember. Roger. Heather. Daphne. George. Kevin.

My shoulders slumped with the shame that I didn't even know my grandmother's name. I'd sensed my mother tense at one name, but was still unsettled from her singing. Had she ever sung to me as a child? A lullaby to soothe me to sleep? I didn't think so. Her voice was fresh to me as if I'd never heard it before. If she'd sung to me as a baby I'd remember, wouldn't I?

'Catherine,' my mother whispered to me. 'We need to leave.'

'But we haven't sung the last hymn yet,' I said, desperate to hear her voice again.

'There isn't time. Move.' She pushed me and I wriggled my way to the end of the pew and released us. She took hold of my arm and marched me to the back of the church and out of the doors as the organ started to play the final hymn. 'Shine Jesus Shine'. A blob of mascara trailed down her cheek. She wiped it away with the hankie, released her grip from my arm, and marched ahead of me back to the car.

The frosted windscreen was clear. The engine on before I'd even reached the car, and then without having time to strap my seat belt in properly, she'd pulled off as though the church was a tidal wave we needed to be clear of before the water crashed over the car and washed us away.

Heather. Daphne. I think now. Those were two of the names the vicar had read out that day. They were the names my mother had tensed at when she'd heard them. Overwhelmed with new questions I look at my phone and see Anya's blue dot is still above the hospital. No one had called me to update me, or tell me she'd died. But that meant nothing; they might not even have my number. My eyelids close, betraying me, sleep calling me again.

If you fall asleep, she'll die, a voice tells me, but my body is shutting down and I have no control over anything anymore.

Sleep claims me fully.

47

CATHERINE
FRIDAY 1ST NOVEMBER

Flecks of fluff pepper the floor around me. My whole body aches, but I don't move.

Slowly emerging from sleep, I lie on my back on the floor beside my old bedroom window and watch the shadows dance in the sunlight on the ceiling above me. Inside I am empty as though every emotion has been sucked out of my body. My chest is hollow, my heart broken and shrivelled. How long have I slept for?

My phone has run out of battery and I pull a charger from my bag and plug it in.

I lie back and imagine the shadows above me are ripples of water, dappled in sunlight. Not the murky water of the river, but clear blue water from the ocean or from a stream.

They say people can live without love. But no one has ever lived without water.

A life without Anya, for me, would mean there is no need for water. No need to be hydrated and replenished. Sean had once told me, no malice intended as he claimed to have adored me at the time, that you can't make someone love you. He'd tell me that if nature hadn't intended for two people to have a bond then an attraction couldn't be forced.

He is living proof that if love fizzles out and is no longer there, then the emotion can't be coerced into returning. Like a spell, when the magic wears off, it can't be tempted to return. The heart moves on. The emotions transfer elsewhere.

All of the time I spent craving love from my mother was a waste. The only love I'd ever needed was the love I'd found in Anya.

A faint knocking in the distance disturbs my thoughts, but I close my eyes to drown the sound out. It can't be Dave and his clearance men. They finished last week and the house isn't on the market yet.

But the knocking comes again. Louder this time. More insistent.

Probably a cold-caller. They can sod off. The new owners will need to get one of those stickers that says they'll ring the police if the cold-caller insists on ringing the doorbell anyway.

Then I hear a shrill voice through the letterbox. 'Hello, dear. Are you okay?'

My body protests as I sit up, my back creaks and a shooting pain penetrates my right hip.

'Catherine, are you in there?'

I recognise the voice, but at first I can't place where from. Flattening my hair and wiping the dust from my eyes I get up and head down the stairs. Through the frosted glass I can see an outline of someone. They are holding their hands up to block out the sunlight and are peering in before knocking again.

I open the door and am surprised to see Mrs Smith from next door standing there shaking. She holds on to a cane with one hand and leans against the wall with the other, panting as though she has run a race.

'Oh you're in here.' She smiles. 'I saw you arrive. Please

don't think I was prying, but you looked very upset and I was surprised,' she stops to catch her breath, 'to see you. I had thought the house was sold already.'

'Mrs Smith, are you okay? Do you need to sit down?' As soon as I say this I realise she can't sit down here because there is no furniture and I'm convinced she wouldn't get up again if she sat on the floor.

'I'm fine, dear,' she says in between short, sharp breaths. 'It's you I'm worried about. You remind me of her.' She wobbles in front of me and I reach out to help her steady herself. 'Maybe I do need to sit down. And you look like you need a cup of tea. Come on.'

An instruction not an invitation.

After running upstairs to get my phone, I follow Mrs Smith next door and settle her into a chair in the lounge – which overlooks my mother's driveway – and make us a cup of tea. The normality and familiarity about the process enables me to blank out everything else, I'm simply making a neighbour a hot drink.

Her milk smells a bit off but doesn't curdle when I put it in the tea. My phone buzzes in my pocket and I look to see Sean's name. Rejecting the call I stir the tea. The dark brown liquid swirls and reminds me of the muddy river that had swallowed Anya whole. I throw the spoon across the kitchen and pour my cup of tea down the sink, and then turn on the tap to wash the offensive liquid away.

'Everything okay, dear?' Mrs Smith calls from the lounge.

'All good,' I say as I go in and hand her the remaining cup of tea. 'Sorry, I dropped a spoon in the sink.'

'Do sit down.' She gestures at a chair opposite her. The room is the antithesis of my mother's lounge before Dave and his team had cleared everything out. This space is clean and devoid of any junk. Framed photos are spread out on the cabinet at the far end. Young smiling faces beaming at the camera. Grandchildren, maybe. Fresh flowers, lilies, their strong scent makes my nose itch, and a jar full of what looks like tiny pieces of sea glass have been carefully placed in between them.

She catches me looking.

'My grandchildren,' she explains and her face lights up, the reaction a grandmother should have. My mother had sighed when I'd told her I was pregnant with Anya. There'd been no tears of happiness. She'd looked jealous. I'd wanted to slap her.

'They're beautiful. You must be very proud.'

'Oh I am. They are a joy. Noisy buggers, but I love them anyway. And how is your daughter?' Mrs Smith asks, sipping from her tea with shaky hands.

Anya's face flashes before my eyes. Her hair draped across her cheek as she sleeps. Her freckles that darken in the sun. Her body as she vanished beneath the water.

'I...' I start, but I can't bring myself to say the words. I swallow and start again. 'She had an accident. Fell into a river and was taken to hospital, but we had an argument and I don't know if she's okay.' My T-shirt rips a little where I fiddle with a small hole at the front and I pick at the frayed edges, tears dropping onto the material before being absorbed.

'Oh I am so sorry, dear. That sounds very worrying. I fell out with my son once, dreadful time it was.'

We sit in silence a while. Each of us locked in or own painful memories. But I'm grateful for her giving me space to breathe before she speaks again.

'It's a shame your mother has passed away. She'd have known how to support you after what she went through.'

Mrs Smith clearly hadn't known my mother well. She would not have known how to support me. She'd always viewed death as a necessary evil. A process you don't cry over, like spilt milk. It happens. You move on.

'What do you mean, what she went through?' I ask. 'Do you mean when my dad left? Or when her mother died?'

She shakes her head and a look of confusion washes over her wrinkled face. 'No, dear, I mean with your cousin.'

'But I don't have a cousin.' My mother was an only child and my dad too. I'd envied a girl at school who came in every Monday with tales of the fun sleepovers she'd had with her cousins at the weekend. It was worse than hearing about siblings, which always came with a hint of rivalry and unhappiness. Cousins were free from such angst. I'd envied her for being surrounded by extended family when my weekends were filled with long hours spent alone.

Mrs Smith looks sad. She sips her tea and coughs as it goes down the wrong way. There is a box of tissues on the coffee table and I hand her one. She blots the spittle from her chin. Then she looks at me, her eyes watery.

'You did have a cousin, dear.' Her voice is soft and I know she is about to deliver bad news. 'But she drowned.'

'Oh my God.' The hole in my T-shirt grows larger as I pick at the edges. 'Are you sure?'

'Yes. Your mother told me the story once. Tragic. She was devastated.'

'But I didn't even know I had an aunt.'

Mrs Smith looks puzzled.

My phone buzzes again in my pocket and I know I can no longer ignore Sean or Anya's fate. For some reason with daylight comes the return of my thoughts being rational. Holding my hand up by way of apology Mrs Smith looks at me as if she no longer wants to be the one to give me bad news.

'Sean,' I answer the phone.

'Bloody hell, Catherine, what the fuck are you playing at? I've been calling you for hours now. Where the hell are you?'

'I'm sorry.' My voice wobbles. My fingers tingle from

gripping the phone too tight. 'I'm at my mother's house. I came to the hospital, but I couldn't stay. I didn't want to know she'd died. I couldn't hear it.'

'For goodness' sake, Catherine. Listen to me. She isn't dead. Anya discharged herself. Before I could get there. She's with Jamie at her halls. I haven't been able to see her, but we've spoken. What the hell happened?'

'She what?' My heart beats as though it's trying to break free from my body. 'She's alive?'

'Yes she's alive, you idiot. She wasn't in the water long enough to do any real damage she says the doctors told her. She was in shock and a bit cold. They only wanted to keep her in for observation and have given her some medication in case she's got a parasite from swallowing the dirty water.'

'I'm going to see her.' I pick up my handbag.

'No, you aren't.' His voice is stern. 'She doesn't want to see you. She told the nurses at the hospital you were insane and dangerous and I can see why.'

So that's why the nurse was being so cagey. I should be grateful she'd not called the mental health team – I was insane at the hospital.

'But...'

'No buts, Cate.' Cate. He hasn't called me that since we were together. I close my eyes.

'Fine.' I give in. 'But *please* call me after you've seen her and tell me how she is. Please.'

'Of course I will. Give her some space, yeah?'

'Do I have a choice?'

He chuckles, but it isn't funny. At least not to me.

We hang up and I let the tears fall, not caring that Mrs Smith is sat watching me like I'm a character in a soap opera, the drama unfolding in person instead of on the small television in the corner of her lounge.

After a few minutes she asks, 'Are you okay, dear?'

'Yes, thank you. I am, but I need to go. I'm so sorry for being rude. Thank you for letting me come in and talk to you.'

'Oh I'm always here, if you ever need a chat.'

She smiles at me and huffs and puffs as she attempts to get up from her chair.

'Stay there, please. I can see myself out.'

Relaxing back she looks relieved. 'I'm sorry to be the one to tell you about Heather,' she says.

Time stands still.

'Heather?' I ask.

'Yes, Heather. Your cousin. The one who drowned.'

Heather. My cousin. The one who drowned. Everything is slowly starting to make sense and yet make no sense at the same time. As though I am locked in a room and every clue I solve only throws up five new ones to puzzle over before I can escape.

As I walk to my car I'm compelled to look at the tracking app on my phone. Anya's photo is surrounded by a small blue circle, hovering above her halls of residence on the map. I know I should feel relieved and calm.

But I am more on edge than ever.

48

ANYA

I miss you, Mum, but I can't tell you because if I did then you'd think we were back on good terms and trust me, we are not. But I'm scared. Ever since I came out of the water I'm having fucking awful flashbacks where I can't breathe and I reach out for you, but you stand at the side of the river, arms folded, face blank and you don't grab my hands and save me.

And Jamie won't leave me the fuck alone, even though I have told him again and again and again that we have fucking broken up. You know that bruise around my eye? Well, he didn't punch me or anything, nothing as sinister as that, but he is rough with me when I am drunk and he tries to control where I am and who I am talking to, it's why I ended things with him, and that black eye was the final straw.

I was talking to this bloke, Harry, from my course, he's gay and so don't know what Jamie's problem was, but he kept telling me to leave with him and not talk to Harry anymore, but Harry and I were having such a laugh and I didn't want to go and then Jamie pulled at my arm and I yanked free but fell over onto a bar stool behind me and whacked my face. Hurt like fuck. I was so embarrassed.

I thought of you when I was sat on the floor holding my throbbing eye. You'd have got an ice pack from the fridge, made me some comfort food, told me everything was going to be okay, rubbed arnica into the battered flesh and helped me cover the bruising with make-up. But then I left the bar and went back to my halls and dumped Jamie on the way.

He thought I was being drunk and stupid and didn't believe me at first and then, when I told him to go fuck himself for the millionth time he told me about you, paying him to watch me breathing at night and I fucking swear right then and there I was so angry I nearly got an Uber to drive me home to confront you, but I'd lost my purse and my head really hurt and so I told Jamie I didn't believe him and went home to sleep and forget about everything for a bit.

And then when I woke up I wanted to call you and ask you to come visit so we could talk about Jamie and the texts and, not gonna lie, I needed a hug from you, but then the girls came in and wanted to take me out for brunch to cheer me up, and get me away from Jamie who was literally pining at my bedroom door and so I didn't call you after all.

The night I fell in the river, the night I found you hiding in the trees, I was going to call you and ask if I could come home for a bit, leave a week before my lectures were due to finish and start the Christmas holidays early. I'd got so caught up with partying and being this grown up, independent person, I'd forgotten about you a bit. Forgotten to miss you and ring you and love you and I'm sorry because that was wrong of me, but I was so caught up in my new life that I let go of my old one before I was ready.

I told Dad I wanted to go to him for Christmas, but that's a lie. I'd like to come and see you soon, I think, because I'm worried about you and there is so much we need to talk about and I'm sorry we didn't talk about this before I left and that I didn't get how hard being alone would be for you once I'd gone.

Maybe I'll call you later and we can talk or maybe we can meet for lunch, Wagamama, like we used to, and we can laugh about getting you on Tinder and about dick pics.

Maybe everything really will be okay.

49

CATHERINE

THURSDAY 7TH NOVEMBER

Letters and papers are spread over the sofa and the floor of my lounge and I rip open another box and dive in. The notebook I'd found all that time ago at my mother's house had offered no more clues as to why she had never told me about Heather. Or indeed who Heather was and if she was really my cousin.

Since coming home and throwing everything out of the boxes Dave had found I'd started to doubt Mrs Smith's recount. She is old and easily confused. There are other neighbours on the street she could've been talking about.

But the name Heather is too much of a coincidence for me to ignore.

The rest of the notebook contains more pages, this time filled with letters of apology. As well as scribbles and pieces of words that are illegible. And the last few pages are simply black, the pencil having concealed anything that may have been written underneath the deep repetitive strokes.

I find more letters from someone called Daphne, who I assume is the same Daphne as the one in the photos with my mother, but every one starts with, Dear Friend, or My Love, or

Sister Dearest and so I have no idea who they were meant for. Besides, I don't think they'd ever been sent. There are no postmarks or stamps on the envelopes. No creases where the words on the paper have been pored over and read again and again. They all say the same thing; that she is sorry for the hurt she has caused. And that it will be over soon.

To me they make no sense. All I can conclude, piecing the bits of the jigsaw from Mrs Smith and the letters together, is that the person writing them feels responsible for Heather's death.

I stare at the one painting from my mother's house that I've dragged into the lounge. The rest are in Anya's room, Dave kindly dropping them off in his van after they finished up. The colours swirl before me, dark greens and browns mix together like overhandled playdough, highlighted by yellows and bright greens. The trees look alive and I imagine a swoosh as a gust of wind blows through them.

These paintings are so detailed they could be photographs. Intricate observations only a lens can pick up. The artist has sat for hours absorbing every individual colour and shape. A flash of white at the bottom, a butterfly flying towards the stream in the distance.

I find myself worrying at the hole in my T-shirt as I look at the water of the stream; its smooth surface rolling over the rocks painted below. The image should provoke a sense of calm, but instead I feel agitated. I want to swat the butterfly and run away.

My phone rings and I jump, bringing me back into the room.

'Sean? Is everything okay?'

'Yes. Anya's fine. I've been to seen her and she's really okay I promise. The antibiotics are doing their thing. And she's warm, nice pink cheeks.'

'What about her inhalers? Has she been taking them?' I clutch my top in a bundle at the base of my neck.

'They were on her bedside table.' I can imagine him rolling his eyes at me like Anya would in response to this question. 'You need to relax, Cate.'

'I can't relax. This is so hard for me. I don't know who I am anymore and I can't stop worrying about her.' The words tumble out. I have forgotten who I am talking to.

'Anya is worried about you too.' His tone changes. 'She told me what happened on the night she fell in the river. About you following her.'

'Sean, I can't even–'

'Look, you don't need to explain yourself to me, but this had bad consequences. Anya could've drowned. And as for how it's made her feel about you.'

His words feel like a knife has sliced my heart in two.

'I know. I know. She hates me.'

'She doesn't hate you,' he sighs deeply down the phone, 'but she is mad at you and I don't know how long that'll last. She's even talking about her coming here for Christmas this year.'

The chain on my necklace snaps as I tug on it too hard. The silver thread dangles over my fingers and the pendant, an imprint of Anya's fingerprint as a baby, falls to the floor. Anya has never spent Christmas Day with anyone but me.

'Sean, I can't be by myself for Christmas,' I whisper, forcing the tears away. 'I can't.'

'Let's not worry about it now. She'll probably change her mind; she simply needs some time to calm down.'

I bend over and pick up the pendant, running my finger over Anya's fingerprint. The grooves so tiny they can barely be felt. The chain of the necklace like the thread that joins a mother and daughter, Anya and me, snapped beyond repair.

'Is she going back to lectures?'

'Yes, on Monday.'

'And Jamie, was he there?'

'No. She says they've split up. They did a while ago apparently. Her flatmates are helping to look after her.'

'Oh okay, I thought seeing as he helped save her.'

'No. She's definitely done with him. But that's another story we won't get into now. Don't worry.'

Those two words. Telling me not to worry doesn't stop me worrying. Anxiety is more complex than that. I *know* I need to stop worrying. But I *can't*. The fear I feel is like a seed that has been nurtured inside of me and has grown into a giant oak, each acorn a new fear dispersing and forming new baby trees under the canopy.

'Would she see me, do you think, if I went up there?' I don't know why I ask; I know the answer.

'Cate, please listen to me when I say you need to give her space.'

I want to punch the wall. 'Fine, but if anything changes or she calls, can you let me know?'

'Of course.' There is a moment of silence. Then I hear his new baby crying out in the background. 'Look after yourself, Cate, okay?'

'I will.'

Closing my eyes I hang up. The mess around me makes my skin itch. Fiona's voice rings in my ears. I hear her words, that bathing in woodland is good for the soul, so I grab my keys and head out to the woods.

Walking into the woodland is like diving underwater. The canopy shelters me and the further into the wood I delve the more the light dims and human noises dissipate. The mix of trees and plants wrap around me and I leave my life and worries behind.

Taking a moment to breathe in deeply, tension leaves my shoulders and neck. I walk to the clearing. The space has a fresh feel today and I nestle into the grass beneath a large oak tree. My eyes close as I listen to the wood. Leaves rustle together and birds call to one another. The noises echo around me and I drift into a different state. For a second I imagine myself alone, settled deep in the underwater wooded world forever.

The sound of the stream in the distance makes me squeeze my eyes shut. The noise grates and I don't want it to penetrate the blanket of calm that is wrapped around me.

A cloud throws the clearing into sudden darkness. Exhaustion catches up with me and I feel myself falling into another slumber, my body demanding it catches up on every bit of sleep I've lost in recent months. I have no say in the matter. The edges of the world blur and my limbs are weighted.

I smile. No one needs me. No one wants me. I can stay here ignoring the real world and in this state of limbo for as long as I need.

Without warning I drift into an unsettled dream. I am running through dense woodland screaming for help. Anya is a baby, wrapped in my arms and I fall, throwing her onto a woodland floor carpeted with multi-coloured leaves. The leaves swallow her whole. I thrust out my hands to grab her and bring her close, but I can't reach. Her fingers slip through the leaves into an endless pit below.

Jerking, I wake breathless and sweating. My arms and fingers tingle. I sit up straight and pull my coat around me.

As I fully wake, the sound of the trickling water in the distance weaves its way through the trees to me. And I feel full of grief. But not for my mother. For Heather, I think.

Then I have a thought.

Daphne's letters and journals have struck a powerful chord with me. They are more than familiar. They are as real to me as though I'd written them myself.

For the first time I begin to think that maybe I did know Daphne, even if I can't remember her or Heather. And I slowly begin to wonder if the fear I feel every minute of every hour of every day isn't mine.

It's Daphne's.

50

DAPHNE

'We're going to see your aunt,' I said, working hard to keep the tremor from my voice. 'You like her house. She always has cakes.'

'Can I see the baby?' she asked me and I shook my head.

'No, the baby is gone. We talked about this, remember?'

My darling girl nodded. Her eyes sparkled at me, full of innocence and trust. Swallowing the doubt I reassured myself that she was too young to remember me and not yet old enough to understand the pain she might feel. Children adapt. They accepted their change in circumstances and moved on better than any adult did. Adults got stuck in the past and in the guilt that enshrouded it.

Either way, her emotions were not going to be my concern anymore.

'Can I take teddy?'

'You must,' I said and watched as she ran up the stairs to fetch him. She'd slept with teddy since birth. He'd never been washed and smelled of breast milk and childhood tears. He had patches of dark brown all over from where he'd been dropped in puddles and soaked up the rainwater. He would comfort her as she cuddled him to sleep, instead of her curling into me.

The numb feeling that had spread over my body remained as I packed the rest of her bag. Her favourite snack, a KitKat, four fingers, only allowed as a treat on Saturdays. Her best dungarees to change into tomorrow, blue with a rainbow on the front chest pocket, and her multi-coloured jumper to go underneath them. Her hairbrush, a hairband and the two pink spotty clips she loved. Her red toothbrush, with the bristles worn down and no longer standing to attention. The green flannel she washed the chocolate off her face with, freshly laundered yesterday.

'Got him,' she said as she jumped off the last two steps of the stairs.

'Good girl.' We stood and smiled at each other for the last time. She hadn't noticed how clean and tidy the house was. How there was no food in the fridge or dust on the shelves. Everything was in order.

As I opened the front door, echoes of Heather's laughter rang in the hallway.

'Not long, my love,' I whispered and closed the door behind me.

The guilt that drowned me lurched as though having one last hurrah.

But there was no need to worry. I know what I did and what I must do.

The guilt had already won.

51

CATHERINE
FRIDAY 8TH NOVEMBER

'Anya! Oh my God, what are you doing here?'

She's here, my beautiful daughter, on the doorstep and in front of me in the flesh. I go to embrace her, but I hesitate and hold back, not sure if she will accept my arms around her.

'Hey, Mum.' She has her phone in her hand; her knuckles are white from holding on tight. A rucksack is on her back, but the material sags as though empty and my heart sinks as I realise maybe she isn't here for the night, only the day, or even a few hours. But that doesn't matter. However long she is here for, at least she's here.

'Come in, come in,' I say. And then I groan. The lounge is littered with the photos, journals and letters. The kitchen sink is full of dirty mugs, dregs of coffee staining their bottoms. She's going to think I'm even more messed up when she sees the state of the house. Turning into my mother by hoarding and never cleaning.

Her body spray wafts through the door after her and I inhale deeply. She's here. I can touch her. The house feels alive again, her energy swirling through the hallway, filling each space, pushing the shadows of loneliness deep down into the cracks in the floorboards.

'Ignore the mess, please. I couldn't sleep last night and so I was looking through stuff from my mother's house and I kind of haven't had time to tidy up. Or eat.' My head spins and my heart flutters.

'Mum,' she looks at me with her eyebrows raised as we walk into the lounge, 'I live in student accommodation. Seriously, this is nothing.'

'Okay.' I hold up my hands and laugh. 'But I don't want to know.' Grimacing, I wipe some dust from the remote control and move it to the arm of the sofa before sitting down into the space Anya used to use, which I'd taken to snuggling to feel closer to her.

'Jump in my grave, why don't you.'

'I can move.'

'I'm joking, Mum.'

Sat opposite my daughter a nervousness fizzes through me as though I'm on a first date. I need to watch what I say. What I do. More than anything I want to throw my arms around her and hold her tight to me, breathe in the smell of her, feel her warmth, but instead I sit on my hands to stop myself.

'How did you get here?' I pick at a bit of fluff from the cushion beside me.

'Jamie drove me.' She looks down at her hands. 'We're still friends. He was a bit much as a boyfriend, but he gets that now.'

'You don't have to explain yourself to me,' I say although I want to ask about the bruise around her eye, a yellow tinge still visible. Then I'm aware of the irony as I imagine that the only reason she is here is so that I can explain myself to her.

'Is he in the car outside? Does he want to come in?'

'No, it's fine. He's gone into town for a bit and he'll be back when I text him. He can wait in the car.'

My cheeks redden. She's embarrassed by me and I don't blame her.

'I'm so sorry, Anya. For everything.' I wipe the tears away with the heel of my hands.

I never knew silence could be so loud. How the absence of sound enhances other noises, those of day-to-day life that hum under the radar. A ticking clock in the kitchen. Anya's steady breathing in and out, in and out. The inner squelching as I swallow the bitter saliva in my mouth.

'I know you're sorry, Mum.' Her voice is steady. She has rehearsed this. 'I do know. But what happened, you being there that night, I want to understand what's going on with you.'

How do I explain to her when I don't fully understand myself? Mother's instinct has always been a quality I've prided myself on having. And I've always known that I'm one of the lucky ones. So many others claiming they don't have any instincts, and that it's not fair to ask a new mum to rely on an abstract concept they have no idea how to access.

But me, from day one I knew which cry was which, as if Anya could communicate with me telepathically. I trusted everything my gut told me from the minute she was born. Maybe that stemmed from having to do motherhood alone. With no one but me to calm my fears or question my thoughts my instincts were all I had. And so when they went into overdrive and I became convinced Anya was in danger, I couldn't ignore them.

'Anya, from the day you were born,' I pause to catch my breath, 'looking after you and keeping you safe and happy has been my only priority.' I wipe tears away from my eyes with my fingers. 'And now, I guess I don't know how to let that go. That need to protect you went into overdrive.'

'I understand that, Mum. And you were amazing and I've always felt safe with you as my mum. But don't you see? It's that

exact obsession with my safety that made me fall in the river.'
She laughs. But she is right. It was a self-fulfilling prophecy. If I
hadn't been so consumed with keeping her safe then she never
would've been put in danger.

'I know. I'm finding it very hard to explain, especially to
someone who is still so young, and isn't yet a mother.'

'That's not fair.' She folds her arms and looks down at the
floor. 'I'd quite like you to be safe but I don't sit outside your
house at three in the morning to check you're alive.'

'No, I know. I'm sorry. But you know what else isn't fair? No
one has ever tried to understand any of this from my point of
view. You all think I'm crazy and annoying and overprotective
and–'

'We also think you're grieving,' she interrupts me. And I can
see a flash of guilt that tells me she's spoken about this to other
people. Most probably Sean. And Jamie, maybe. Behind my
back.

'Grieving for who? My mother? No. This isn't about her.'

The walls around me close in and I feel trapped in my own
house. My mother doesn't need to be brought into this. She had
no instincts other than those that made her lock me away and
reduce my life to nothing but isolation.

'I haven't even seen you cry for Gran,' Anya's voice is raised,
'not once. And since she died, it's like all your love, all your
focus has been on me and it's suffocating.' Her hands go to her
throat as though I am strangling her.

Closing my eyes to stop the tears I think back. The anxiety
around Anya had escalated since my mother passed away, but
that's because it coincided with Anya leaving for university.
Isn't it?

'Crying isn't the only way you can grieve for someone, you
know,' I snap. 'And Gran and I had a very different relationship
to you and I. But I'm sorry you feel suffocated. That's awful. I

hate that I've made you feel that way. You leaving has been hard to adjust to.'

'You've gone too far. You've been stalking your own daughter.'

'Don't say that. That's not what I was doing.'

'That's exactly what you were doing.'

Wanting to hide, I pull a cushion up to my chest and hug it like she used to when she was young and had been naughty. When did she become the parent and I the child?

'It wasn't like that,' I explain. 'There was this anxiety in me that wouldn't stop gnawing away until I saw you were okay.' Do I tell her about Daphne? Heather?

'I know you paid Jamie to check on me,' her voice is barely a whisper. 'How could you do that?'

I want to put my hands over my ears and shut her out. Spoken like this, these words, the truth, coming from her mouth, I'm so ashamed of myself.

'You do need help. You know that, right?'

'So you keep saying. Is that why you've come today? To tell me I need professional support?'

Her eyes are watery. 'Partly. I'm worried about you. And I'm worried that if you carry on like this we'll definitely end up like you and Gran. I don't want that.'

'Me neither.' We pause and stare at each other. 'I love you so much, Anya.'

She shuffles over to me on the sofa, reaches her arms out and draws me close. But this time it's my head that rests on her chest and listens to the reassuring beat of her heart. She's the one who strokes my hair and whispers in my ear that everything is going to be okay. I'm the one who sobs, my tears staining her top. Hers is the breath I can feel on the top of my head. Mine are the arms that hold on tighter around her back and never want to let go. Time stops for a moment.

'I love you too, Mum.'

We pull apart like limpets from a rock, wiping tears from our faces, unsure what to say next. She needs me to back off, but my instincts need me to hold on to her even tighter.

'Did you read that letter I found?' She changes the subject and looks around the lounge at the mess. The spell between us is broken.

'I've been reading all of this, and looking at the photos and it's so confusing.' I sniff and wipe my nose with the cuff of my jumper sleeve. 'Is it *that* one?' I vaguely remember putting it under the candles in the centre of the coffee table. I'd been so preoccupied with everything I'd forgotten it was there.

'Yes.' She takes it from the table. 'You need to read this.'

She gets up and hands me the letter. 'I'm going to make a cup of coffee, do you want anything?'

'Tea, please,' I say and then add, 'can I have a sugar, or two?'

She grins and leaves the room. Sugar is good for shock we'd always agree when she ever fell over as a child. A chocolate button or two helped heal a grazed knee. A whole bag needed when a bone was fractured.

This letter is more crumpled than the others, as though it has been read over and over again. Dark fingerprints smudge the edges and other stains, drops of coffee or tea, darken the paper. I open the envelope and begin to read.

But the words can't be true.

They make no sense.

Anya reappears with two steaming mugs in her hand. She sees the look on my face and her eyebrows raise. 'Told you that you needed to read it.'

'Why didn't you force me to read it before now, Anya?' I shout. I'm angry. This letter changes everything. 'Why?'

I look at her and she recognises the emotion behind my furrowed brow.

'Anya, you should have made me sit down and read this straight away.'

'I thought you had.' Her voice is high-pitched in defence. 'I did tell you to. I'd forgotten all about it.'

'But you didn't tell me why I needed to read it. I had no idea it was so important.'

She sits down next to me. 'I'm sorry,' she says. And looks it. Her puppy dog eyes staring at me, begging for the forgiveness I always gave.

The sugary tea burns my tongue, but I continue to sip it anyway, needing the sweet hit to calm me down.

Finally, like the pieces of a jigsaw puzzle I've been unable to solve, all of the pieces are fitting together.

'How do you fancy coming to see Grandpa with me?'

'Now?'

'Yes, now. Do you have time? I think it's important.'

She nods. 'I'll text Jamie and let him know.'

The letter sits on my lap and I smooth the envelope.

More than anything I hope my father is having a good day today. I need him to answer some difficult questions.

52

CATHERINE

FRIDAY 8TH NOVEMBER

'He's in the garden,' the care worker tells us and points to a fire escape opposite the reception desk. 'You can go out this way, don't tell anyone, but the alarm is never switched on.' She winks at us and I'm sure I should be questioning the health and safety of this, but I smile at her and leave it for now.

The air is calm today. Thick clouds cover the sky like a blanket; keeping a small amount of winter heat locked in, but it is still cold. The trees at the edge of the garden at the home are bare and exposed. Their leaves on the ground, decaying and injecting the soil with their nutrients, feeding the tree that produced them, giving life back so next year's shoots can spurt and thrive.

My father is in a wheelchair at the end of the garden under several blankets, next to the fence that blocks his access to the woodland beyond. He is alone. I can see his fingers move to the rhythm of the music in his head and for a moment I don't want to disturb him.

'It's bloody freezing,' Anya says and I roll my eyes.

'Of course it is when you refuse to wear a coat. Here.' I hand her my scarf and she wraps it around her neck and stuffs the ends into her jumper.

We walk arm in arm down towards him, her using my body to warm up, me glad to have her close, knowing I'd freeze so she'd be comfortable. His wheelchair is by a wooden bench, the golden plaque drilled onto it reading, *For Nicholas, who has gone fishing*, and we sit down without saying anything. We wait for Dad to finish the symphony in his head. His hands still and rest on his lap. His eyes open.

'Catherine,' he says as he sees me, and smiles. 'How wonderful. And you've brought Heather too.'

Anya opens her mouth to correct him, but I squeeze her hand tight and will her to remain silent. She takes the hint and smiles back at him. His watery eyes sparkle at her.

'Hi, Dad.' I reach out to put my hand on the thick coat covering his arm. He moves his other arm and places his hand on top of mine.

'Aren't you beautiful.' He looks up at Anya and then the trees opposite us. 'I remember when your laughter rang through the house. You were always happy. You rarely cried, even as a baby.'

I don't want him to stop. He's never been so animated.

'More than anything you loved playing hide and seek in the woods, oh it was your favourite game. Always calling me to count to twenty and then come and find you before you'd bound off and disappear. But your giggling gave you away every time.' He laughs, lost in his own memories.

He pauses and closes his eyes to recall more clearly, I face Anya, who looks confused.

'Who is Heather?' she mouths at me and I realise that maybe in my haste to get here I should've slowed down in the car and explained my theory to her, but it's too late for that now.

My father removes his hand from mine, closes his eyes and

begins humming again. Not a symphony this time, but a more modern song. At first I can't place the tune, and then I remember. Warmth spreads across my chest as I recall sitting on his knee as he sang. 'Isn't She Lovely' by Stevie Wonder. The lyrics come back to me now, another buried memory resurfacing, and for a second I am back there, lost in the memory with him.

Then without warning, Dad's expression changes. Where sunshine rested stormy clouds form. His eyes no longer glisten. Instead they darken.

'But, you died.' He looks down at his hands, rubs his forehead in confusion. I'm scared he will become agitated and distressed.

'One day,' he says slow and measured, 'you went in to the woods. I couldn't go with you, I had to work and to this day I regret my decision. Maybe if I had been there, things would've been different. I could have kept you safe.'

He takes a deep breath in, but instead of breathing out peacefully the air comes in coughs and splutters. He pulls a tissue from his coat pocket and covers his mouth. Not sure what to do I get up and rub his back, but he bats me away.

'I'm fine.' He dabs his wet mouth. 'A bit of saliva went down the wrong way.'

He closes his eyes and hums again. The tissue scrunched in his hand.

'I think Heather was my cousin,' I whisper to Anya. 'And I think the letter you found was written from my Aunt Daphne, to my mother.'

Her eyes are wide, but she remains quiet. The theory worms its way around her head as it had done mine.

For a while I've been wondering who Heather was. No one in my classes at school had had that name, and there were no children on my street whose mothers I remember calling

'Heather' at teatime. Yet, every time I hear her name, or read it in one of the notebooks from my mother's house, it strikes a chord in me. As though I'd known a Heather, or been told about someone with that name in the past.

'Dad?' I lightly touch his arm again and rouse him from his trance. 'Who did take Heather into the woods to play that day?'

He looks at me as though he is seeing me properly for the first time in years.

'Catherine?' he asks. 'Is that you?'

'Yes, Dad. It's me.' We smile and squeeze hands together before I probe him again. 'Who was with Heather, the day she died?'

He shrinks in the wheelchair and I notice how his shoulders hunch over in an attempt to get himself into the foetal position.

His hand shakes in mine.

Then he looks at me again, tears once more in his eyes.

'Your mother,' he whispers between gritted teeth. 'She couldn't keep up, you slowed her down.'

He must see the confusion in my eyes. The shock.

'My mother?' Not my aunt. Or is he confused again?

Tears slip off his chin onto the blanket below.

'Your mother was so exhausted she fell asleep by the stream. Heather wanted to catch some fish. She drowned. My poor baby girl drowned while your mother slept.' He stifles a sob.

Heather. My mother. I still don't understand.

'It wasn't your fault. You weren't even born,' he says. 'And then when you *were* I was in no position to have you myself, the drinking, it had gotten too bad; you wouldn't have been safe with me. Oh I'm so sorry.'

His hands are white where they grip mine so tight. 'Where is she?' he calls out. 'Heather, where are you?' He starts to shake and look around him. 'Take me away from these trees,' he says. 'Heather, where are you?'

He is confused.

'I think we should go, Mum,' Anya says into my ear. 'We're making him too upset.'

'It's okay, Dad.' I place a hand on his arm, but he shoos it away.

'Anya, go and get someone.'

I can't bear to see him like this.

His care worker comes quickly and understands when we tell her we need to leave, that we're sorry to have upset him. We walk to the car in silence, wind nipping at our bare flesh, pinching us awake.

'Are you okay?' Anya asks me as she gets into the car beside me. 'I had no idea you had a cousin.'

'Neither did I,' I say. 'But I'm not sure Heather was my cousin; he said it was my mother that went into the woods, who fell asleep, not my aunt. But then, maybe my mother was looking after Heather for the day.'

'Did you know you had an aunt?'

'No. That's why this is so confusing. And there's no one I can ask.'

'Why don't we go home and have a proper look through Gran's things? In fact, I don't know why you haven't looked already, you really are weird.'

'It's not that simple, Anya. Grief does strange stuff to you, I didn't want to look.'

'Okay. I get it, I think.'

I rest my head on the steering wheel and exhale loudly, forming my mouth into an 'o' shape as though blowing out smoke from a cigarette. For a second I consider asking Anya if she has any, and then change my mind.

'It's going to be okay, Mum.' Anya's hand is on my back, rubbing up and down. 'I'll call Jamie, tell him to go back to uni without me and come back tomorrow. I've got no lectures before you nag me about that, besides, this is more important.'

'Thank you,' I mouth at her and start the engine.

She's right. There has to be another letter.

One that I hope will reveal the truth.

53

CATHERINE

FRIDAY 8TH NOVEMBER

'I give up,' I say, flopping onto the sofa. My head throbs and I press hard onto my temples to rub the pain away.

'I really thought we'd find something, not gonna lie.' Anya looks defeated. 'I'm sorry.'

'Not your fault.' I'm frustrated, but I mean it. 'This is just like my fucking mother, burying the truth. Ignoring any difficult emotions.'

'Mum.' Anya looks shocked.

'I mean it; she was such a closed book. She made me miserable.'

'Why didn't you say anything?'

'To who? I didn't have anyone who would listen. You don't understand, Anya. When I was younger I didn't know any different. I thought every house was the same behind closed doors. By the time I found out they weren't I was a teenager, and used to my own company. It's not like she hit me. There wasn't abuse.'

'Kinda was, Mum. There is such a thing as emotional abuse you know.'

I sigh and shake my head. I can't begin to unpick each

individual strand of the truth and weave them back together in the right order. Who knows why I stayed with my mother for so long. Loyalty runs deep. Or maybe I'm pathetic.

Anya stretches towards the ceiling. 'Coffee?' she asks and I look out the window. Darkness has spread over the garden like a cloak and the moon hovers behind the trees, starting its slow ascent into the sky.

'I'd prefer wine,' I say, but Anya frowns.

'You've been drinking a lot recently; I've seen the empty bottles. Are they from this week?'

'No.'

She folds her arms.

'No. I forgot to put the recycling out for the last few weeks. No point until the bin is full.'

'Fine, but I'm having a coffee.'

'There's an open bottle in the fridge,' I call after her. 'Thank you.'

The lounge resembles a crime scene and I start to gather the pieces of paper and photos up. There is a reason I'm not a detective. I couldn't even win at Cluedo when Anya and I used to play when she was younger. She would guess the murderer and the weapon before I'd even discounted Mr Plum.

She appears in the doorway with a glass of wine in one hand and a coffee in the other.

'That's enough wine for one mouthful, Anya.' I smirk. I know searching for comfort in the bottom of a wine bottle isn't ideal, but I'd fallen asleep faster drunk than I ever had when sober with my heart pounding and my brain working overtime.

'Who are the paintings in my room by?'

I hadn't heard her go upstairs. The paintings from my mother's house had been taking up too much space in the hallway and so I'd moved them into Anya's room as it was the only place they would fit. Sometimes I went in there and sat on her bed, sniffed her pillow and stared at them. They had an air of menace, the shadows between the trees as powerful as the flashes of light.

'I think my mother painted them.' I shrug. 'They were in the loft at her house, I couldn't bear to throw them away.'

'I can see why, they're beautiful.'

'I know. I had no idea she could paint like that. I never saw her ever do anything creative.'

'Do you think they're of the woodland behind her house?'

'Yes. I do. The one with the big oak, it looks so familiar. If I did have a cousin, and she did die in the woods, then it would make sense that Gran hid them away and stopped painting.'

The death of a child is a tragedy I imagine you never recover from, especially if it was under your watch. And while I am angry with my mother for keeping secrets from me, I'm beginning to understand why. I think of Leanne, and how the guilt consuming her stopped her from loving her new baby.

'Let's go and have a look at them.' We climb up the stairs to Anya's bedroom. She turns on the main light and I squint.

'Now I know why you kept those fairy lights on all the time, this light is harsh.'

'I know, right?' she says as though she's finally been validated.

We sit on the bed in silence and stare at the paintings lined up against the wall.

'It's like actually being in the woodland,' Anya says. 'Don't you think? They could be photographs.'

The detail on the tree trunks, on each bundle of moss and each leaf of the ivy that wraps around them, is intricate. Sweeping shades of green I've never seen before. Mingled with swathes of blues and yellows.

'And you never knew she painted?'

'Never. Honestly.'

But these are definitely hers; her signature in red paint is at the bottom of every frame. The curl of the g with a flick at the bottom is unmistakable. None of the g's in any of the letters we have found and read have the same form. None of them are written by her, I am convinced. I stroke the painting beside me, tracing the lines of the branches to their very tips. Following the trail of leaves as they fall from the canopy onto the grassy mounds below.

A hint of a stream between the trunks, a flash of water, deep blues and greys. Is this the river Heather drowned in? Are these the woods that took her? A place full of beauty, a treasure trove of hiding places for a small child to disappear into forever.

'Wait.' Anya gets up. 'Look, there's a darker patch there in the top corner. It's not part of the painting.'

A shaded rectangle at the top right, an object stuck to the back, is highlighted by the glow from the fairy lights.

'Is there something there?' I am on my feet too. Moving from one to the other as though I need the toilet, or am waiting for exam results. Anya pulls the painting forwards, away from the wall and stretches her head around to look at the back.

'Fuck, Mum. It's a letter. In an envelope the same as the others.' She reaches a hand around and I gulp my wine. Some of the liquid dribbles down my chin and I wipe it away, my hand shaking.

'Can you reach?'

'Yes.' She pulls the letter free with a tug.

Then hands the envelope to me.

Grace, it says on the label. My mother's name.

'Are you going to open it?' she asks.

'What if it doesn't give me any answers? None of the others really have.'

But as I speak the words I know this letter is different.

54

DAPHNE

My hand shook as I wrote my name at the bottom of the letter, before I placed it in the envelope and sealed it closed. No going back. There were no tears left. No emotion. Numbness washed over me like an incoming tide. There was no darkness or light. No ups or downs. No love or hate.

Earlier, I'd walked to the bottom of the garden to smell the flowers, but they'd brought me no joy. Their colours were muted. Their scent was stunted. I pulled the heads off the roses, whether they were alive or not, until they lay before me like someone was creating a romantic moment, petals leading a pathway to the bedroom. But this time there would be no passionate lovemaking at the top of the stairs at the end of the red petal trail.

For a second, I stood frozen and turned the envelope in my hand one last time before putting it in my pocket. Then, without further hesitation, I headed out of the back gate towards the woods. Heading to the large oak tree in the clearing. The place where I would right what was wrong. To be with Heather again, both of us suffering the same fate, except this time when I fall asleep, I will die, not her.

I walked into the woodland and the darkness of the canopy

swallowed me whole. I heard no birds today. The air was still as though the woodland had been waiting for me. A minute's silence before the death occurs. Showing respect for me, confirming what I already knew, that I had no choice.

Catherine, my darling daughter, was happy with Grace. This knowledge brought me peace. After losing her own baby, Grace had struggled, but Catherine would help her. Grace deserved her love more than I did. Watching me, her sister, give birth around the same time that Grace had been due had broken her more than the late miscarriage had. There was a daily reminder of what should have been. Each milestone measured, the first tooth, the first step, her first birthday, everything she was missing played out for her through her niece in a cruel twist of fate.

The pathway to the clearing where the giant oak grew was covered in leaves and twigs. The ground was damp beneath my feet. A chilly wind whipped around me spurring me on, and for a second the hairs on the back of my neck prickled as though I was being watched. Holding my breath I stopped, but there was no one there. There was only the memory of Heather running ahead, calling for me to run after her, to find her, walking beside me deep into the woodland.

'I'm coming, baby!' I called.

And then, a few minutes later, I was there. I sat beneath the tree, the sounds of the stream tinkled in the distance and I closed my eyes and shut out the image of her hair, floating beneath the water.

I pulled the letter from the envelope, ripping open the seal. I needed to check I'd said everything. As I did, one last emotion called to me, but I squashed it down and read, mouthing the words from memory, hoping Grace, and Catherine, would understand.

. . .

Dearest Grace,

My beautiful sister, I am sorry. When your baby left your womb so forcefully, and before she was ready, I knew you'd need a miracle to recover. All hope had left you along with her. The colour drained from your skin, and no amount of transfusions would bring it back. I know your soul split in two. I know a piece of your heart turned black and stopped beating that day.

And I know, even though you never voiced those words, how much you'd wished it were me who'd lost my baby. And you're right. I am the one who deserved to never be a mother again. Not you. You'd waited for so long to carry a life inside you and I'd had two chances and already thrown one away. You have so much love to give and so I need to do this for you. For you both.

Ever since I woke by the stream to find Heather missing I knew I wouldn't be able to live with the guilt if my worst fears were to come true. I knew I could never love another child of my own for fear of losing them too. If I could be so careless as to let my daughter die then I didn't deserve another. But you do.

You deserve Catherine's love. She can heal you. Call her your daughter; let her call you mother. Love her as though she were your own. You don't need to feel pain now, she has many firsts to come and you can experience every one.

More than anything I am sorry I am not telling you this in person, but I know you'd convince me to stay. You'd say she needs me, but she doesn't. You're both better off without me. Besides it's too late now, I have taken the pills. I have drunk the vodka.

I am at peace with my decision. This is my fate and I am not scared. Heather is waiting.

Look after each other as I know you will. Fill the gaps that have been created within you and make each other whole. I love you more than life, more than anything.

My darling sister, my love, thank you.

Goodbye.

Daphne.

My hands wouldn't work and I could not get the letter back into the envelope. But it didn't matter. My last words could rest here on my lap until they found me and gave them to you.

I grasped the paper in my hands and leant back against the tree. It was cold and dark and I looked up to the sky behind the bare branches. A light twinkled in the distance and I closed my eyes.

I'm coming, Heather. Hold on.

55

CATHERINE

Silently, I hand the letter to Anya and let her read my mother's words while I sip my wine. The fairy lights reveal the clearing my mum ended her life in on the painting before us. The soft blades of green grass she sat down on stand out, each orb of dew filled with a tiny rainbow as though perfectly planted there for maximum effect. I wonder if she painted the tree knowing she would fall asleep under the bare branches forever, or whether she painted this before Daphne and Heather even died.

'Fuck.' Anya looks up from the letter, snapping me from my thoughts. I don't berate her for swearing. She's voiced the one word I'd like to say over and over again.

'I know.'

'I mean shit, Mum. This is a lot to take in.'

'I know,' I repeat a little louder this time. But I need to remember this affects her too. Her gran was not her gran. Possibly not as shocking as finding out in your forties that your mother wasn't your mother, but still.

'Are you okay?' she asks and I don't know how to answer.

'Yes and no. I mean I always knew my mother, I mean

my aunt, oh God I don't know what I mean. Grace. The woman who brought me up, I always knew she didn't love me like a mother should, but then I thought every mother/daughter relationship was flawed. I feel so stupid that I didn't question it sooner. But when you're a child you don't know any different and then when you're a teenager everyone hates their mother and so disliking her didn't appear so strange. Then I thought we'd simply drifted apart.'

A sensation shudders through me. I want to cry for Grace. Who, unbeknown to me, had suffered a late miscarriage. And then was left by her husband, before losing a sister to suicide. A woman who had to take in her niece and raise her alone. A woman who had never met anyone else.

'Where's the photo?' I ask and rush downstairs.

Anya follows me shouting, 'What photo?'

'There was a photo of the two of them together, pregnant. Grace and Daphne. It was here on the table.' One of the only photos I have of my mum, my real mum.

'Do you mean this one?' Anya pulls a photo out from under the coffee table.

'Yes. That's the one.'

We look at the photo together. At the two women stood side by side. And I see everything so clearly now. The woman who I'd thought was an old family friend my mother had lost contact with. Her eyes don't shine like my mother's. Her smile doesn't reach them. And her arm doesn't cradle her bump like Grace's does. The clues were all there; the freckles of Daphne's face that Anya has inherited. The slight turn of Daphne's left foot, like mine.

'How did I not know?' I look to Anya for answers I know she can't give. 'How did I not know my mum had killed herself? That Grace wasn't my mother?'

'You can't blame yourself, Mum. She left you when you were a young child, you wouldn't have known.'

'Can you imagine how excited they must have been to find out they were pregnant at the same time?' I say, but as soon as I do I know that it wouldn't have been like that. Grace was mourning a niece and Daphne was mourning a daughter; that grief was always going to overshadow their pregnancies.

'I need to get out.' My lounge is too small. There is no air. I can't breathe.

'But it's dark, and raining.'

'I don't care.' I go to the hallway to pull on my coat. 'I have to go to the woods. To the tree. I have to.'

'I'll come with you.'

I nod. I don't want to be alone.

Under the trees the rain lessens as the thick canopy shelters us like a roof. The woods have come alive in the storm. Even though the light has faded there are noises of animals scuffling around in the undergrowth and rustles from owls and birds in the branches above. The animals are not hiding from the weather, they are coming out to play in the rain. Sounds I don't recognise peppered with the taps of the raindrops hitting leaves, while the wind, angry and turbulent, roars in the distance.

'Mum, can't we do this tomorrow?' Anya shouts behind me, this time she remembered a coat, but I carry on.

I run into the clearing, my breathing loud and strong as though I am being chased.

I had never liked being chased. Even as a little girl when my father and I had played 'catch' I'd been terrified. So much so that I'd often wondered if I'd supressed a memory about an awful thing happening to me. Every time my father ran after me up the stairs, or a stranger walked too close to me along the street I felt fearful and a scream would form in my throat.

It is happening now. I'm afraid.

The combination of the thick clouds and the leaves on the trees make the woodland too dark for shadows. I use the torch on my phone to guide the way, but stumble over roots and ivy. The rain smacks against the leaves and thuds on the ground. I jump as Anya pulls on the back of my coat.

'Slow down,' she begs and I pause for a moment to catch my breath. Water drips off the end of her nose, the tiny coat she is wearing that stops short of her hips doing nothing to keep her dry.

'You seriously need a proper coat,' I say and we giggle. The rain drowns the sound of our laughter out and reminds me of what we are doing and where we need to go. 'Come on, I think it's round here.'

The edges of the clearing are sheltered from the worst of the rain. The large oak tree at the far end shadows the grass and hides any sign of life or colour. For a second I can see her there, my mother. Nestled asleep at the base of the tree trunk, the small curve of a smile playing on her lips.

'She thought she was doing the right thing,' I say to Anya who wraps her arms around me as I sob. 'I wish I could tell her that thought was a lie.'

We embrace for a few minutes before I take her hand and lead her out of the other side of the clearing.

We reach the stream. The trickle of the water over the rocks roars like the sea crashing on headland. I bend down and dip my fingers into the water. I wince as the coldness pours over my skin.

Above us branches hang over the stream and grasp onto ones reaching out from the other side, as though they are holding on to each other to keep us sheltered.

'Can we go home now, Mum?' Anya asks and I nod. We traipse through the wet woodland, the mulch of leaves sticking to our shoes. My shoulders slump and a wave of exhaustion washes over me.

Inside the car I turn the heater up to full blast as we drive past my mother's house next to the woods, the windows black and lifeless, and on to home. We take it in turns to shower and warm up before I curl into bed; a cup of tea Anya made steaming on the bedside table.

She peers through the door, a towel wrapped around her wet hair.

'Night,' she says. 'You have a meeting at work on Monday, right?'

I groan. 'Yup.' I'd forgotten about my meeting with Fiona, scheduled for nine in the morning. The anxiety for what that meeting might hold will hover over me all weekend, but at least with Anya here it will be the only thing I have to worry about.

'Sweet dreams.' She yawns and goes to leave before popping her head back in. 'I don't mind if you want to come and check on me in the middle of the night tonight.' She smiles and her eyes twinkle. 'Or maybe I'll come and check on you.'

'Thanks, love,' I reply and smile back. But I know I won't need to check on her tonight, even though she is only across the hall.

The fear inside me has shifted.

And I think I understand why.

56

CATHERINE

The drive to the office gives me time to think about what I am going to say. I am only meeting Fiona today to discuss my possible return to work. I'm not ready for the world to know the truth about my twisted family tree.

A familiar ache appears at the base of my neck and I rub it away as I stop at another red traffic light – the fifth – the universe is inviting me to pause. A woman and young girl walk across the road as I wait. Before, I'd have assumed them to be mother and daughter, their hands entwined, their hair red, but now I question everything.

I read once that thirty per cent of father's names on birth certificates were incorrect. Was the same true of mothers' names? I have never looked at my original birth certificate. I have never felt the need to check the name in the box marked 'mother'. But I know where it is and when I get home I will look, even though I know what I will find.

A loud beep from behind jolts me and I look up to see a green light. I hold my hand up in the rear-view mirror to apologise and accelerate too hard. The car's tyres screech and I grab onto the steering wheel. The next set of traffic lights is green and I sail into the car park and find a space on the first floor, my time for contemplation up.

Grabbing my usual coffee from the coffee shop I make my way down the graffitied streets of Bristol to the office. There will be no one else there today. No groups or counselling. Only Fiona and me.

Before I get a chance to knock on the door she answers as if she'd been hiding behind and watching for me through the frosted glass.

'Hi, Catherine.' She holds the door open for me. 'Come in. Coffee?'

I hold up the disposable mug in my hand and shake my head. 'Got one, thanks.'

'Do you mind if I make myself one?'

'Not at all.'

'Go on through.' She points to the counselling room and I go in and take a seat. The graffiti on the wall opposite has gained some new tags since the last time I was here. Layer after layer, adding to its uniqueness and vibrancy. I wonder how many tags and sketches are hidden underneath the new artwork and marvel at how easy it is to conceal something so colourful and powerful.

'Right,' Fiona says, closing the door behind her, trapping in the faint damp musty smell with us, lifted only by the aroma of her coffee. 'So, how are you?'

Without meaning to I burst into tears. And I tell her everything. I have the suicide letter in my bag and I hand it to her along with the photo of Daphne and Grace. She reads, sipping every moment or two from her coffee cup.

When she is finished she folds the letter back up and hands it to me. 'That's a lot to take in.' Her voice is soft and reassuring.

'Yes,' I say, 'but also a bit confusing. You mentioned

inherited trauma a while ago and I want to know if you think that's what's been happening to me?'

She takes a deep breath.

'It's not that simple, Catherine, but yes, on some level I don't doubt that the fact your real mum lost a child when she was pregnant with you has affected you. There is a scientific theory called epigenetics, it's complicated, but evidence shows that if a traumatic event happens to your mother when you are inside her womb, or indeed your grandmother, that trauma can get handed down, especially if it isn't resolved.'

I take some time to digest this.

'But the anxiety around Anya, that only really started recently.'

Fiona stares at the door, lost in thought. 'Sometimes,' she says, her face alight, excited that a theory she's only read about before is living and breathing right in front of her, 'the inherited trauma reveals itself when the person who has inherited it reaches the same age as the person who suffered it, does that make sense?'

'I think so.' My temples throb and I rub my forehead.

'Like I said, it's a lot to take in. I've only recently started learning about it myself, but it's fascinating. Who knew that as well as inheriting blue eyes and blonde hair you can also inherit trauma?'

'Seems cruel.'

'I know, it can be, especially when you don't understand that the trauma isn't yours.' She pauses. 'The good news is that once you understand where your anxiety stems from you can help challenge it and overcome it.'

'That would be good.'

'You're also going to want to look into the suicide, sometimes when people reach the same age as the person was when they took their own life they have an overwhelming urge to do the same.' She raises her eyebrows at me and I wave my hands at her, batting away the suggestion that I'm suicidal.

'God no. I've felt nothing like that.'

'You know if you do...'

'Of course.'

She looks thoughtful again. 'You look tired.'

'Oh yes, that I most definitely am. This weekend has been the first since I can remember that I've slept well. And I've a lot of catching up to do.'

'You don't need to come back to work yet, the others have got your cases covered. Take some time.'

'I will, that's what I was going to say anyway. I mean, it's weird, the paranoia around Anya has completely lifted. Looking back I'm appalled at how I behaved. No wonder Leanne complained, I was totally unprofessional.'

'With good reason.' Fiona leans forward.

'Doesn't excuse my behaviour though.' Slumping, I pick at the empty takeaway coffee cup. Drips of coffee fall onto my trousers and I brush them away. Fiona doesn't speak. She allows me to sit with my feelings and work through them, a technique she has used with me before.

Outside, a youth in a hoody sprays the wall opposite the window. He covers the large surface of the graffiti with black paint. A blank canvas. A new start.

'What do I need to do?' I ask.

'Nothing for now.' Fiona puts her hands together and intertwines her fingers. 'But when you're ready we can look into everything a bit deeper and help you work on what belongs to you, and what you can let go of.'

'Okay.'

'Get some rest. Spend some time grieving for those you've lost. Or find out more about them if you want to. It might help you to understand.'

My phone buzzes in my bag. For a second my stomach lurches thinking it might be Anya before I remember she is at home, waiting for Jamie to come and get her and take her back to university, and safety. We'd said our goodbyes this morning. She'll come home again for Christmas, she said, and I was already looking forward to it.

'Answer it,' Fiona says. 'It's fine.'

I pull the phone from my bag. It's Dave the removal man.

'Hey,' he says. 'Am calling to let you know I forgot to clear out the shed at the end of the garden, remembered this morning and headed round. Sorry, love. Also, the estate agent has been and the sign is finally up.'

'Great, thank you. You know where to send the invoice to, right?'

'I do. But one last thing. We found a small box too, in the shed. Only thing in there apart from a few rusty gardening tools.'

'I'm on my way.'

'All okay?' Fiona asks, eyebrows raised and look of concern etched on her face.

'Yes. Fine. But I need to go if that's okay?'

'Of course. Same time next week?'

'Definitely.'

Dave is standing under the 'For sale' sign, a cigarette in place of the vape in his mouth, smoke flowing from his nostrils like a grey waterfall.

'Hey,' Dave says. 'Man, you look knackered.'

'Thanks. I am.'

'Here's the stuff.' He hands me a shoebox. He blows out a

long stream of smoke again and this time I catch myself trying to inhale some of the silver stream.

'Thank you. You guys have been amazing. I never expected it to take months.'

'Wasn't your fault we couldn't evict the bloody rats. Anyway, hope you get a quick sale.'

I mutter thanks and wave him off in his van. Then I stare at the house. For a minute I think about going in for one last walk around. One last lay down on my bedroom floor. But I stop myself. There's nothing in there I need to say goodbye to. The ghosts of my mother haunt me wherever I am, closing the front door to my childhood home will not lock her in. I'll have to face her somewhere else until the dust settles and I come to terms with the past she hid from me.

I put the shoebox on the passenger seat of the car and go to head home, but curiosity gets the better of me and I switch the engine off before driving away and put the box on my lap. I wipe a faint layer of dust from the top and take off the lid.

Inside are the answers to any remaining questions I have. Newspaper clippings. One of Heather's death. One of my mother's.

Five-Year-Old Drowns While Mother Falls Asleep By Stream

The first headline tells me everything I need to know. The truth in black and white with no emotion behind it unfolds as I read. My mum, heavily pregnant with me, fell asleep while in the woodland with Heather. When she woke up, Heather was gone. A local dog walker found her face down in the stream. She was alive, but it was too late to save her and she died later that night in hospital, while my mother was sleeping beside her.

Below it the other clipping, this one torn from the newspaper unlike the other one with smooth, cut edges.

Mother Takes Her Own Life In Woodland Where Daughter Drowned

I put them in the box and hold back the tears. I can't read the articles now. And besides I know the outcome. I know what drove her to take her own life. The suicide letter telling me far more than a newspaper article ever would. The rest of the shoebox contains Heather's birth certificate, and the death certificate for her and Grace's daughter. Stillborn at thirty-six weeks. Placental abruption. Too much tragedy and trauma in one box. Hidden away from everything else, her painting things, all of it.

Putting the lid back I place the box on the passenger seat and head home to my empty house.

Then when I am there I follow Fiona's advice and go straight to bed.

Sleep claims me within seconds, my phone switched off next to me on the bedside table.

57

CATHERINE
FRIDAY 29TH NOVEMBER

The truth is a bizarre concept when you've lived with a lie for as long as you can remember. It's like a brooch, beautiful and shiny that stabs you and draws blood as it's pinned on.

All mothers make mistakes. We let our babies roll off the bed, or scramble to pat their backs when they choke on a piece of bread a fraction too big, or force them to run outside and get some fresh air only for them to fall and break a bone.

These accidents don't make us bad parents. We haven't pushed them off the bed, or fed them an entire grape, or broken their arm with a cricket bat. We mess up. We turn our backs exhausted from being on alert every second of every day.

We're the ones the blame lies with. No one thinks to blame my dad for Heather's death, a man who left my mum alone from 7am until 7pm every day for work, and sometimes after work, the pub. And I know it's not fair to be cross with him, he was working so we could eat and have a home, but my mum was exhausted, why else would she have fallen asleep by the stream? They hid it well, Grace and Dad, that they were the ones who'd been married, instead of him and Daphne. I have no idea what happened to Grace's real husband.

Guilt is inevitable when someone dies, even when that death isn't preventable, but I can't imagine the overwhelming guilt my mum felt. I wish I'd been old enough to see her crumbling before me, to hold her close and tell her that she wasn't to blame. I'm sure my aunt did that, I'd like to think my dad might've, but I'm not sure he did, dealing with his own guilt didn't allow him the space to relieve my mum of hers.

He passed away last night and I am numb. I held his hand as it happened, Heather, the care worker, having called me earlier in the evening to say he was calling for me. He squeezed my hand once, but never opened his eyes.

The music that had lit up his soul flew away with him. I felt the rhythm leave his body. A great whoosh up into the ceiling above me as he took his last breath. When I kissed his forehead he was empty inside, the strangest feeling. And if energy never dies then his lives on somewhere outside of him, as does the energy of my aunt, my mum, Heather. The four of them reunited. Hopefully, finally, at peace.

Anya is on her way home, only for the weekend, but here to offer support as best she can. She says we can go to Wagamama for lunch, she'll drive so I can toast Dad with a drink. This time we'll order two sets of prawns so there's an equal amount. And maybe I'll let her convince me to try dating again. I could start with the man in the suit. Really ought to find out his name. But first, there is somewhere I need to be.

Alongside the pathway to Grace's grave I read the different gravestones as I've done many times before. They lean at different angles out of the ground, appearing to defy gravity by remaining standing. Some have been here since the eighteenth century and halfway up a stone cherub stands above a young boy's grave. Its left hand is always filled with fresh flowers and yet I've never met the person who puts them there.

Today pink and yellow freesias sway in the breeze, their stalks grasped by the stone hand. The cherub's free hand rises to the sky as if showing passers-by where the dead boy buried below him has gone. The gravestone says that this boy was seven when he'd passed away and flown up into the clouds where the hand pointed. Seven is far too young.

Heather had been five.

A distant rumble of traffic floats over the graves and reminds me that people are carrying on with their lives. Travelling to and from work or school. I ignore them. The sun moves behind a cloud and what little warmth it offered vanishes.

As I reach the grave I pull the zip on my coat right up to my chin, catching my skin. I wince and rub at the pain. A magpie sits on the grass nearby, watching me and I spit and salute, the superstitions handed down from my mother never far away. I have brought no flowers with me today, not thinking to stop at a supermarket or garage as I drove here. The gravestone looks bare and unloved.

I can't call her Aunt Grace. She's my mother. I might never understand why she never told me the truth, or why she couldn't love me how I needed her to, but I do forgive her. I sigh and shove my hands in my pockets. My breath forms clouds in front of me.

Instead of heading back along the path I came I start walking towards a part of the graveyard I haven't been to before. There's a hunch in my gut that what I'm looking for might be there, and it doesn't take me long to find them.

Strong emotions consume me; I'd never imagined them to be buried together, so close to my mother. Their gravestone looks dirty and unloved; the gold lettering is worn down and the words are barely there. If my mother had ever come here it was without my knowledge. But I doubt she did visit. Then I remember the church, the memorial, the rushing out as the hymns were being sung.

Here lies Daphne Mary Williams. Loving mother to Heather Ann Williams, who fell asleep, aged five.

I bite back tears. Bunches of carnations and roses on nearby graves, bright pinks and oranges and reds, only serve to highlight this one's neglect. Tomorrow I'll return with fresh flowers.

Voices behind me break the spell and I watch as a young woman and her daughter walk up the pathway to stand at a fresh mound of earth, a simple wooden cross marking one end. They wrap their arms around each other and the young woman dabs tears from her eyes. I take my cue to leave.

'Goodbye,' I say. 'Rest in peace.'

As I walk back to my car the sun appears, and for the first time in ages I feel hope for the future. Not with the man in the suit, not necessarily with any man. Knowing Anya is safe and happy at university is helping me to move forward now that I really believe my anxiety wasn't based on any real danger to her. I don't wake up at three in a cold sweat anymore.

I get into my car and close the door, shutting out the wind. Then I pull my phone from my pocket and unlock the screen.

One final part of the process is next and I don't hesitate.

Pressing down on the tracking app until the square wobbles, I click on the cross at the top right-hand corner of the box.

And press delete.

58

ANYA

TUESDAY 10TH DECEMBER

You used to duck my head under the bathwater, Mum, and I hated you for forcing me under, but now I lie here, beneath my hot bathwater for as long as I can, fire burning in my lungs. I gasp as I emerge and hug my knees to my chest.

You'd say the water is too hot, but I don't care, I like water to sting my skin as it touches me so I know I can feel pain and am alive. You gave me the lavender bubble bath that has produced the bubbles around me, and is dripping down my back, but I am the opposite of relaxed.

I downloaded an app on my phone, one you'd recommended when we talked about my fear of water, one that played soothing sounds to help you sleep, not that you needed help sleeping anymore.

You showed me how I could choose from the rhythmic dripping of raindrops in a rainforest, or the constant whirr of an aeroplane engine. The sounds worked at first. I'd listen at bedtime and they'd help me drift into a peaceful sleep, but then one night I tried the babbling brook noise and everything changed. Sleep came fast and rough. Nightmares tore me from slumber and threw me into an underwater world where no one could hear me scream.

Then, instead of asking you because I didn't want you to know what I was feeling and what you'd suggested hadn't worked, I asked Jamie to help and he suggested I try to lessen my fear of water by bathing daily and putting my head underneath, kinda like some weird exposure therapy, the repeated action numbing my anxiety. But it isn't working. The panic of not being able to breathe hasn't gone away.

And I can't tell you about this as I know you'll freak out, of course you will, because you're still working through everything, and shit I'm freaked out by it too, but I'm convinced I've experienced this before, not in the bath, and different to when I fell in the river, but the same, sort of. I hadn't been drowning in the river, just cold, so cold, but this feels as if I know exactly how drowning feels.

Like the fear has somehow, without me knowing, been handed down.

THE END

ACKNOWLEDGEMENTS

Eight years ago I left my job as a primary school teacher and studied an MA in Creative Writing at Bath Spa University. The years since have been full of acceptances and rejections, and without my amazing tribe of family, friends and fellow writers picking me up and pushing me on, this book (which is actually my third novel) would never have been written. I cannot express how blessed I am to have such a team of incredible people in my corner, believing in my writing and me, making me determined to persist.

In no particular order (how can you even begin to order awesome?) I want to give my heartfelt thanks to the following people: my family – every single one of them. Thank you to my inspirational mum, my brother and sister-in-law, Cheryl, who smiled and nodded and said, 'Of course you should do the MA – you'll nail it!' and never doubted my decision once. I know Dad would've agreed. That unwavering belief from the offset was a game changer.

Thanks to my fellow MA students – from those who were in the same groups as me, to the ones who were early readers of this novel. Thank you, Christine Stephenson, Morag Shuib,

Eleanor Barker-White, Margaret Grant, Rachel Egerton-Buckler and Ali Bacon. Huge thanks to my tutors Samantha Harvey, Lucy English and Fay Weldon. Fay's wise words, 'Well, if you give up then you clearly don't want to ever be published,' after I'd had a petulant tantrum due to a rejection, will stay with me forever. She is the one who first taught me to persist.

It was on the MA I got to meet one of my biggest champions, Emily Koch, without whom I almost certainly would've thrown in the writing towel a long time ago. Thank you for the unwavering belief, the constant encouragement, the endless words of wisdom, the honesty, the phone calls, and the hours sat opposite me as I wrote. I'm forever grateful.

Thank you also to Kate Simants, Gytha Lodge and Emylia Hall for reading and providing invaluable feedback on my work, for sorting out my synopsis and for giving me endless advice and support. Thank you also to everyone who has ever interacted with me and encouraged me on Twitter. #BookTwitter is the best!

Thank you to my latest team of phenomenal writers – my CBC Writing Gang. Your feedback was invaluable and undoubtedly made this book better. Without you all I would not be published and one day I know I will be featured in the acknowledgements of your debut novels. Thank you also to my tutor Charlotte Mendelson. Her constant cries of, 'But what's at stake?' continue to reverberate around my head every time I write.

Huge thanks go to my amazing publishers, Bloodhound Books. Thank you, Betsy Reavley, Fred Freeman, Tara Lyons and Hannah Deuce. Thank you to my wonderful editor, Morgen Bailey, for teaching me so much during the process and for making it as smooth as possible. Thank you also to my fab proofreader.

Thank you also to my brilliant friends and future readers.

To my Book Group girls who are the most supportive group of women I have ever met. And to Bronwen for giving me the inspiration for the novel when she said, 'Did you know that as well as inheriting blue eyes and blonde hair you can also inherit trauma?' Mind. Blown.

Huge thanks, for saving my sanity on far too many occasions and for reigniting my passion for writing with an idea for a blog, go to Rae. She reads all of my novels and gives me brutally honest feedback. She is the kind of friend everyone wishes they had and is grateful for every minute of every day.

And finally, the biggest thanks have to go to my gorgeous husband and amazing children. Thank you for always believing in me. For never allowing me to give up. For sharing my passion for writing as though it were your own. For giving me every reason I could ever need to persist. I love you all.

A NOTE FROM THE PUBLISHER

Thank you for reading this book. If you enjoyed it please do consider leaving a review on Amazon to help others find it too.

We hate typos. All of our books have been rigorously edited and proofread, but sometimes mistakes do slip through. If you have spotted a typo, please do let us know and we can get it amended within hours.

info@bloodhoundbooks.com

Printed in Great Britain
by Amazon